SCRIPTED UNSCRIPTED

KRISTINA MIRANDA

SCRIPTED
unscripted

a novel

TURNER PUBLISHING COMPANY

Turner Publishing Company
Nashville, Tennessee
www.turnerpublishing.com

Scripted Unscripted

This is a work of fiction. All the characters and events portrayed in this book are
either products of the author's imagination or are used fictitiously.

Cover design: Maddie Cothren
Book design: Meg Reid

Library of Congress Cataloging-in-Publication Data

Names: Miranda, Kristina, author.
Title: Scripted unscripted / by Kristina Miranda.
Description: [Nashville] : Turner Publishing Company, [2019]
Summary:
 Hoping to become an animal wrangler like her father, sixteen-year-old
 Ellie faces a life-changing decision when she is forced to the other side
 of the camera and everyone but the star seems to love her. |
Identifiers: LCCN 2018049258 (print) | LCCN 2018053757 (ebook)
ISBN: 9781684423071 (ebook) | ISBN 9781684423057 (pbk.) |
ISBN 9781684423064 (hardcover)
Subjects: | CYAC: Television programs--Production and direction--Fiction.
 Actors and actresses--Fiction. | Working dogs--Fiction. | Dogs--Fiction. |
 Fathers and daughters--Fiction.
Classification: LCC PZ7.M673517 (ebook) | LCC PZ7.M673517 Scr 2019
(print) | DDC [Fic]--dc23
LC record available at https://lccn.loc.gov/2018049258

9781684423057 Paperback
9781684423064 Hardcover
9781684423071 eBook

Printed in the United States of America
19 20 21 22 10 9 8 7 6 5 4 3 2 1

For my son Alejandro, who always tries to do the right thing.
You are one of the good guys.

one

HE'S PEEING, AND it's all my fault.

It doesn't matter that I've been in Kate's dressing room trailer for only *five* minutes, or that I've been patiently waiting for her to decide what outfit her Chihuahua, Hairy Winston *the Third*, should wear on the airplane. Apparently—as the dog trainer's daughter—I should have prevented this.

"Stop him!" Kate glares at me, as if I'm the one lifting my leg on her Louis Vuitton luggage.

I pick Hairy up off the floor and hold him away from my body with both hands. "Where's his leash?"

"Just go! I'll bring it."

"Wait! Take his baggage." Kate's manager, a.k.a. her mother Isa, lobs a giant tote bag over my shoulder, forcing me to cradle Hairy against my chest so I can slip my arm through the handles.

Warm pee seeps through my shirt as I push the door open and walk down the steps. I set Hairy on the ground near a light post so he can finish the job, but it seems he already has. He jumps against my legs, begging me to carry him.

"All done, little guy?" I scoop him into my arms and glare at Kate's trailer. I feel like going back and reminding them that (1) Hairy is not a part of the show and (2) I'm an animal trainer, not a personal pet sitter. But of course I can't, not if I want Dad to keep his job—or if I ever want to become a real animal wrangler myself someday. Kate's momzilla would have me blacklisted from every production in Hollywood—forever.

I carry Hairy through the rows of trailers until I reach mine and Dad's. As Hairy whimpers at my feet, I wash my hands and arms in the sink. I'm so done with this. There has to be a way to ditch my reputation as *dog sitter for the stars* around the studio. It was okay when I was a kid, but at sixteen? It's time to move on. I reach for a paper towel to dry my hands and accidently drip water on one of Dad's cast-off, unsold scripts that he leaves everywhere.

"Ellie! We're going to be late!" Rachel's voice booms from her megaphone outside, and Hairy barks. I know it's hard to be a production assistant on a show like this, which is basically total chaos, but seriously, she needs to relax.

"Coming!" I blot the script with a dry paper towel, throw on a clean shirt, grab Hairy and his baggage, and head out the door. We hop on the back of the golf cart, and Rachel steps on the gas, whipping us over to Kate's extra-large Stargazer Deluxe.

Of course a PA would never shout at the talent with a

megaphone, so Rachel turns and looks at me, her foot on the brake, as if to ask if I'd go knock on the door. Her eyes go to Hairy and all his accoutrements on my lap. She sighs and puts the cart in park.

"Wait. Here they come." I tighten my hold on Hairy as the door swings open and Kate saunters down the stairs, followed by Isa. They look like twins born in different decades, both ultra-blonde and beautiful, in a made-up sort of way. The kind of beauty you could wash off. Kate twists her long hair into one piece and wraps it over her shoulder, then climbs in front with Rachel, leaving Ice Queen Isa no choice but to slide into the back with me.

"Got my coffee?" Kate lifts her sunglasses revealing her trademark eyes—inhumanly blue, like a husky's—and bats her false lashes at Rachel.

"It's eleven thirty. I thought you would've had it by now."

"It's morning, Rachel. I need caffeine." Kate lowers her glasses.

Rachel gets on her radio and begs anyone who will listen to get a mocha soy latte to the front of our office building before the cars show up. "Make it two," Isa chimes in.

"Did you bring the leash?" I ask Kate as we fly through the lot.

"You're asking me *now*? See if there's one in his bag."

I don't dare dig in it while holding on to Hairy on a golf cart going at breakneck speed. As soon as we stop, I search the tote. I could open a dog clothing boutique with the contents, but there's no leash. "We need to go back. It's not in here."

"There isn't time," Rachel says. "Why aren't you prepared?"

Of course. My fault again. Doesn't anyone realize that dog sitting is not part of my job description? Am I supposed to check Kate's packing list before we go on location too? I don't bother explaining. Movie stars are always right, even if they're barely older than I am. I get off the golf cart and adjust both dog and tote.

"He prefers to be carried anyway," Kate says. "My coffee?" She smiles at Rachel.

Rachel's hand shakes as she gets back on her walkie-talkie, begging for lattes. I can deal with not having a leash. Ten minutes and ten commotions later, we finally get into the limo—lattes in hand. Hairy is desperate to get to Kate. "He wants you," I tell her, about to let him loose.

"No—don't let him go. He sheds." Kate brushes at her jeans and takes a sip of coffee. "Mom, will you see if you can find an outfit that fits Hairy in that bag?"

Isa rolls her eyes. "I'm not the pet sitter," she says with a pointed look in my direction. The corner of her lip twitches, reminding me of a miniature pinscher we once taught to growl on cue. "And I told you to call me Isa on the lot."

Ouch. It's not like anyone—anywhere—doesn't know she's her mother.

I catch Kate's face as her cheeks turn red, but she quickly resumes her annoyed pout when she notices me looking. Isa grabs Hairy's giant duffel from the seat next to her and holds up various articles of clothing for Kate's approval.

"Try the black T-shirt," Kate says.

Isa tosses it at me, and it lands on Hairy's head. It's so tiny I can already tell it won't fit. I put one of Hairy's front legs through a sleeve, but there's not enough give in the fabric to get his other leg through without hurting him. "It's too small," I say.

"I want a new one, *Isa*," Kate says, ignoring me.

Isa zips up the bag and shoves it to the floor. "I have no idea where that shirt even came from."

"Not the *shirt*—a new *dog*. Just look at him. He's huge. The breeder promised he would be a teacup!"

I practically choke. I feel like putting Hairy down and choking her. Who cares how big he is?

"Your picture with Hairy will be out in four magazines next month." Isa leans back against the seat and closes her eyes. "Buying a replacement would not help your image."

"But I told you I wanted a dog I could carry in my purse."

I almost remark that most of her handbags are big enough to carry a Bernese mountain dog, but I hold the thought and hope Kate's mom does the right thing—for once. I only had a mom for about an hour, on the day I was born. All I have are pictures and memories from Dad. But sometimes even that feels like more than what Kate has.

After a long pause, Isa answers. "I have an idea. You can give him to one of those ill children next month at that charity event. That wish thing. We'll see if there's a kid who wants a dog. It will be great for publicity."

"Hmm…give up my own dog for a sick child?" She shrugs. "Why not?"

I squeeze my eyes shut and take a deep breath. If I let Kate have it, we could lose this job. Even though Dad's always been a favorite with the director, *Born in Beverly Hills* was created for Kate—a spin-off from the last show she was in—and is already highly anticipated. No Kate, no pilot.

I keep quiet and stroke Hairy's head until we arrive at the executive airport. While Kate and Isa go inside the building, I stand on the tarmac in the hot LA sun, holding Hairy and his luggage. I look up at the jet we'll be boarding and see Kate's costar—and on-again-off-again real-life boyfriend—Logan Canfield, staring at me from one of the tiny windows.

Embarrassed, I turn away and quickly run my fingers through my long hair, which I'm sure is a tangled, sweaty brown mess by now. Logan hasn't been in any animal scenes, so we still haven't met, but it feels like we have. That's the thing with celebrities—it seems like you know them, but usually when you meet them in person, they're nothing like you imagined.

When we walk toward the jet, almost forty minutes later, my arms are killing me. It's not that Hairy's heavy, it's that I haven't been able to put him down since we got here. I follow Kate and her entourage across the tarmac toward the stairs. Kate is several yards ahead of me, and Hairy starts to tremble. He wriggles in my arms, and it's all I can do to hang on. A helicopter takes off nearby, and Hairy panics. The tote bag on my shoulder slips down to my elbow and jerks my arm. At the same time, Hairy twists forcefully in my other arm and tumbles to the ground. Next thing I know, he's running across the pavement.

I drop the bag and go after him, hoping he'll stop when he reaches Kate, but he doesn't. He runs in circles, nearly getting run over by a baggage cart.

Kate screams, but it's not Hairy's name she's screaming—it's mine, along with a few curse words. I chase Hairy around and around, but he's too frightened to come to anyone. I glance back at the jet and see Logan laughing his blond-hair-swinging head off.

I ignore him and lunge for Hairy again. It's become a game. I know how dogs think. You should never chase them when they get like this. I go back to the bag and take out his food. Then I get on my knees and try to get him to approach me while Kate screams at me to get up and do something. Next thing I know, Logan comes walking down the metal stairs, and Hairy prances over to greet him. He picks him up as I race over, but Kate gets there first.

Logan is still laughing. "Here's your dog, Kate. You're lucky he didn't get flattened."

Kate takes him from Logan's arms and glares at me. "My poor baby," she coos in Hairy's ear.

I want to gag. Like she really cares.

Logan winks at me and then holds his arm out to escort Kate up the ramp. I sigh, loudly, and follow them up. If it weren't for Dad, I'd turn around and leave. I don't need this. Any of it.

When I step inside the jet, I see Jimmy and instantly calm down. For one of the top directors in Hollywood, he's pretty down-to-earth. I don't know what Dad and I would do without him. He waves me over and pats the seat next to him. "I'll be right back," I tell Kate, leaving Hairy with her. I can feel Logan's eyes on me as I walk past him and sit down next to Jimmy. *Yes, Logan, I may be a nobody to you, but I'm somebody to Jimmy Gainer.*

"Ellie!" Jimmy gives me a one-armed hug. "Didn't feel like riding with your dad to location?"

Even though I would have had to get up at three in the

morning to ride with Dad in our travel camper, it would have been better than this.

"Kate wanted a dog nanny today." I shrug and give him half a smile. He looks like he wants to burst out laughing, but when he glances at my face he holds it in.

Logan walks down the aisle toward us, grinning. "Mr. Gainer," he says, "I've got an idea for that scene we were reading through yesterday."

"He calls me 'Mr. Gainer,' Ellie. Am I that old?" Jimmy's rubs his salt-and-pepper goatee, like maybe it's the culprit, and looks up at Logan. "Good, Mr. Canfield. Good. Have a seat. Have you met Ellie?"

"No, is she part of the service crew?"

And why would that matter? I'm getting tired of celebrities. *Really* tired.

He looks me over like I'm the daily special at the commissary. "Will you be playing Kate's sidekick?"

I give him a blank look.

"Hey, I didn't think so, because I know Kate's BFF has to be...um...not so attractive," he says.

Jimmy laughs, but I have no clue what Logan is rambling on about. I stare at him quizzically.

"Easy. I knew you couldn't be—you're way too pretty. But I thought 'Emily' was the only part being recast." He turns to Jimmy. "Help me out here, Mr. G. Is she going to be some rival of Kate's? Got a little love triangle brewing?" He raises his eyebrows at me, and I want to laugh.

"This is Ellie. Ellie Quinn. She's not an actress." Jimmy doesn't elaborate.

"I'm Coco's trainer. Well, my dad is anyway."

"Coco?"

"The dog. Kate's dog on the show. The beautiful white standard poodle?" I give him a fake smile.

"Oh, Coco." Logan stands abruptly. "I'll talk to you about that scene later, Mr. G. Nice meeting you, Ellie."

I watch Logan go back to Kate and wonder what that was all about. I can't help the little extra beat my heart takes. Logan Canfield said I was pretty. I take a deep breath and shake my head in an attempt to regain some common sense.

From the window, I see a girl with long brown hair, similar to mine, running across the tarmac toward the portable staircase. Let me guess. I look at Jimmy.

"The BFF," he says.

I nod my head. To star with Kate, you have to be her opposite. And this girl is the opposite of tall, willowy, and blonde. "Good luck," I say under my breath.

"Ellie..." Jimmy looks around nervously and then knocks on the burled wood trim of his armrest. I forgot how superstitious he is, how he goes ballistic if anyone wishes someone luck on the set.

"I mean, hope she breaks a leg!" I smile at him, but he shakes his head. I get up and make a beeline for Hairy. Sure, a lot could go wrong, but if it does, it won't have anything to do with me.

two

IT SEEMS LIKE we've been in the air for only a few minutes before the jet starts making its descent in the desert just outside the San Fernando Valley. Hairy whimpers as the plane dips, so I pull him tighter to my chest and rub his head, trying to soothe him. On the edge of the desert I see endless fields of some nondescript crop and think of Grandpa Pete's lettuce farm in Salinas, where Dad grew up. Boring would be a kind description. Brain-cell-killing would be more accurate. Thank goodness he escaped, or I might have been born there.

When the plane lands, we all walk to a pair of SUVs waiting to take us to the remote location. I hope they can get this filmed in one or two days, like they promised. I climb into the second truck with the other non-acting crew. Hairy has long since given up his struggles and is napping in my arms.

As we drive farther into the desert, I plan the lecture I'm going to give Dad about agreeing for me to take care of a star's personal pet again without my permission. But when I see him standing outside our camper, all smiles, I choke it back. His strong arms encircle Hairy and me, hugging me as if he didn't see me just last night. Like he hasn't seen me in years.

"Hey there, Hairy boy." He scratches Hairy's head. "Was he any trouble?"

"Don't ask." I give Dad a quick kiss on the cheek and go straight inside.

Dad follows me. "I didn't think you'd mind."

"I know, Dad." I set Hairy on the floor. "Where's Coco?"

"She's in the makeup trailer getting her hair done." Dad chuckles. He holds up a small aquarium. "Look at the lizards I brought."

"For what?" I open the fridge and grab a bottle of water for Hairy.

"One is going to crawl across Kate's head and make her scream. I brought four. How many takes you think we'll need?"

"Zero, unless they brought a stunt double for Kate. I can't see her allowing a lizard on her head. Ever." I pour some water into a plastic bowl and place it on the floor.

"They're harmless." Dad sets the aquarium on the table. "And you shouldn't underestimate Kate. She's not that bad, you know." Leave it to Dad to expect the best out of everyone—even Kate.

"You'll see." I sit down and watch Hairy lap up the whole bowl of water. "How's Grandpa doing?"

"Better. Aunt Jess said he's home from the hospital but can't do much." Dad sits on the opposite side of the table and reaches across to touch my arm. "I was serious the other day, Ellie. If this pilot fails, I'm letting Bill buy our half of Animal Stars Inc." He sighs. "Your grandfather needs us."

My stomach twists, and my heart feels like it's pushing up into my throat. We can't move to Salinas. We just can't. Dad will wither like the lettuce leaves when the irrigation machines break. *He'll* break. And so will I.

"And Jess has always said that you being tutored on TV sets is unfair to you. You're in high school now. You should be going to football games and homecoming dances. Things normal kids do."

Going to Salinas public school, living with Aunt Jess, my cousins, and—worst of all—Grandpa Pete, would *not* be normal. I push a vision from my mind of my cousin Brett, a.k.a. Brat, double-dipping in the salsa with dirty fingers. Cousin Annie, a.k.a. Annoying, fighting with Brat over the chips. Aunt Jess screaming at them from another room. The hard glint in Grandpa Pete's eyes.

"Ellie, are you listening to me?"

"Maybe *Born in Beverly Hills* will be a big success," I say, not believing a word of it. I give him a weak smile and take a deep breath. "And Grandpa has plenty of help on the farm."

Dad frowns. "I know this is hard."

Hard? Giving up Animal Stars Inc. would be giving up our lives. Our animals. Basically everything I love in this world.

Hairy finishes drinking and paws at my legs, begging me to pick him up. I reach down and scratch behind his ears. "What about that new show idea you had the other day? We could start working on the script."

"I pitched it to Jimmy, and he hates it."

"He's not the only producer in Hollywood."

"No, but he's right about this one." Dad's shoulders slump, and he gets that faraway look in his eye—the look that tells me he's thinking about Mom and how he hasn't been able to write anything decent since she died. He's never spelled it out in so many words, because how could he in front of the person who is alive precisely because she isn't?

Hairy makes a pitiful attempt to jump on my lap, so I pick him up. "I better take him out. I'm sure Kate never potty-trained him." I get up from the table, grab a leash, and slip it around his neck. No way he's getting away from me in the desert. He'd be the perfect snack for some bird of prey.

Outside, the cameramen are working out their shots. I look around for a place to walk Hairy. He'll have to go on some weeds, if I can find any. Bringing him here has to be the worst idea Kate's ever had.

But then she comes up with a worse one.

"What do you mean I don't have a stand-in?" Kate looks around the set as if she doesn't believe it.

I know it's tedious to stand on your own marks so the cameramen can check the lighting and things like that, but really, is it life or death? Kate takes one look at me and whines, "Can't *she* do it?"

I don't know if it's because of what she's planning to do to Hairy, or because she made me hold her dog for half a day with no leash, or maybe I've just reached my limit on hearing about *mocha soy lattes*, but I fly into orbit. "Are you kidding me? I'm an animal trainer, not your personal assistant, not your dog sitter, and *not* your stand-in."

Everyone in the vicinity is staring at me.

Our trailer door creaks open, and Dad comes out. "Ellie…"

I pass him the dog leash and storm off to do my real job, which is handling Coco. I can hear Kate having a fit as I search for the makeup trailer. I don't look back. I can't look back. It's not Kate I'm worried about—I could take her on any day. It's Dad. And Jimmy. I've just broken rule number one in showbiz, and it's not *the show must go on*. It's really *respect the hierarchy. Remember the pecking order.* Wishing an actor good luck by mistake is nothing compared to telling one off. If you want to survive in this business, you have to do what they say.

My hands are shaking, and the whole world looks blurry. I find the makeup trailer and go inside—only it's not the makeup trailer. Would it hurt to put up better signage when the trailers all look alike? The lights are off, but there's enough sun coming through the closed blinds to see some upholstered benches, a table, and a couple of beds.

"Is it my turn?" a voice asks from the shadows.

I jump and swallow a scream. When you work with animals, you need to keep a cool head. "I'm sorry. I thought this was makeup." I grab the door handle.

"Wait!"

I turn toward the voice and see a boy, maybe sixteen or seventeen, walking toward me from the back of the trailer. A boy I've never seen before. His dark-brown eyes are completely dilated. And huge. "I don't know what I'm supposed to do," he says with a faint Spanish accent.

"What do you mean? Are you cleaning the trailers?" As soon as the words come out of my mouth, I'm embarrassed.

I shouldn't have assumed that, even though he is dressed in coveralls and has dirt smudged on his cheek. I start over. "I'm Ellie. An animal handler." I take a deep breath and smile at him.

He gives me a nervous smile in return. "My name's Camilo, but I go by Cam. I'm here to rescue Kate—in the show. I'm the son of her gardener, who she calls when her car breaks down in the desert." He pulls out a script and shows it to me. "I have no idea what I'm doing."

"Is this your first acting job?"

"Put it this way, I've never even been in a school play." He shakes his head. "I've never even *gone* to a school play."

I've never even gone to a real *school*. To me, that's a good thing. My eyes have adjusted to the darkness now, and I get a good look at his face—his dark-brown, wavy hair and the dimples that form every time his nervous smile appears. I wonder where Jimmy found this guy. A modeling agency? I try not to stare. He's *that* cute. "Did you read for Jimmy? I'm sure you did fine at your audition, or he wouldn't have hired you."

"My sister's a teacher at his kid's school." He looks down and then into my eyes. A boy shouldn't be allowed to have eyelashes like that. "I was helping her set up this fair they were having, and the next thing I know, Jimmy pulls me aside and says he has a part for me."

"Happens all the time." I laugh. I'm not really kidding, either. I've seen people get all kinds of weird breaks in this business. "You were lucky!"

"Lucky? I can't act! I'm going to make a fool out of myself. I almost turned it down, but how could I? My sister was so proud. And my family...they...they need it."

I nod. I can relate to that. "Did you practice?"

"Only in my head. I live with a house full of people. But I memorized it."

"Well, listen, I've got to go. I handle Kate's dog in the show, and she's in the next scene."

He takes a deep breath. "Okay."

I smile and open the door. "Don't worry. It won't be that bad." I'm lying. Kate will eat this kid for breakfast. I feel an urge to protect him from her, but I really should protect myself first. I'm probably hanging from a thread around here—if it hasn't already snapped. But instead of leaving, I close the door. "Okay, Cam. One time."

three

I TAKE THE script from Cam as he thanks me profusely, wondering how much time I have before everything comes crashing down.

"Can you do all the lines except mine?" Cam asks.

"No problem." I sigh and take a look at the script. I'm already really familiar with it, since Coco's in the scene and I have to know in advance what's going on. I feel sorry for the best friend/sidekick, because her lines are pathetic. "Why didn't you have a table read with them at the studio?"

"Kate refused. She didn't have time. Jimmy said it'd be okay, that I'd pick it up fast."

"Okay, then." I scan to the last line before Cam's first one.

"I'm sooo glad you're here!" I squeal in my most sarcastic "Kate" voice. "Then it says she hugs you." I decide I won't go as far as acting out the stage directions. I mean, how awkward to just hug this guy, all alone in a trailer, five minutes after we've met.

He bursts out laughing. "She really sounds like that?"

"No." I give him a serious look. "Worse. But that's not your line. You don't have much time here."

"Okay." He grins. Dimples showing again. "Start over?"

"I'm sooo glad you're here!" I reach over and give him an air hug.

"I—"

The trailer door swings open, and Rachel pops her head in. "Camilo, they're ready for you." She looks at me. "Ellie, we've been searching for you everywhere."

"Oh, I was looking for Coco."

"In here?" She shakes her head. "Your dad already has her on the set."

"Am I fired?" I ask.

"Not exactly. At first Kate asked for you to be, but you're not actually on the payroll. Your dad is. He can handle Coco without you, you know."

I imagine Dad smoothing things over for me. Everyone loves my dad—even Kate.

"Then why were you looking for me?" I'm sure there's some sort of penance to pay.

"We need you to play Kate's friend. The actress we had lined up has already been let go."

She couldn't have finished more than a take or two in the time I've been in here. That has to be a record. What could she have possibly done wrong already? Besides, I am not an actress. I have a SAG card, but that's only because I've been an extra a couple of times and said a few lines. "And Kate is okay with this?"

"It was her idea. She said she's not wasting a whole day here without filming this scene while we find a replacement."

Rachel sighs. "Listen, Ellie. You're on shaky ground here. And remember, we're only filming the pilot. It's not like we can't find a new actress for the part if the show gets greenlit."

I stand there, frozen. Everything inside me screams run. But where to? The middle of the desert? And there aren't enough trailers on the set to hide in forever. "Isn't there anyone else here who can do it?"

"Yeah, we've got a ton of teenage girls here in the desert all lined up. Come on, you know the script. Let's go." Rachel turns and starts walking. End of conversation.

I gulp. Our entire livelihood could be in jeopardy if I don't do what Kate says. It's probably all a scheme to punish me for talking back to her.

Cam has been quiet the whole time and waits for me to follow Rachel before moving. "Like you said to me, it won't be that bad," he whispers.

Yep. I was lying. I'd also be lying if I said I wasn't scared. I am. Not of Kate, exactly, but of what she might do to Dad's career. Clutching the tiny silver heart that always hangs around my neck—Mom's necklace—I take a deep breath and stand tall. I have to take care of Dad.

Rachel touches Cam on the back as we walk. "Got your lines down?"

"Yes."

His accent is heavier than before. Nerves maybe? Or getting into his character? Not a bad idea. I have about five seconds to become "Emily," mediocre, adoring best friend of the fabulous Kate Montgomery. Let's see…how do I begin to act dumb, unattractive, and like a doting golden retriever following around its master?

"Can I see that script again?" I ask Cam.

"Sure." He hands it to me.

I scan Emily's lines. One reads, "We can't be stranded! I have a test tomorrow!" Really? That's the best the writers could do? I've been hanging around TV sets my entire life, and I've seen a lot of bad writing. Sometimes I go home and rewrite scenes in my journal, especially if it's a comedy. Dad and I can usually predict which shows are going to make it and which ones won't. This one is definitely doomed.

Rachel takes me to makeup and wardrobe and hands me my own copy of the script. Even though I'm supposed to be a little nerdy in the show, I'm a rich nerd, so they want me to change my clothes. The costumes designed for the last Emily don't fit me—I'm taller and thinner—so the wardrobe crew doesn't know what to do.

"She's going to have to wear something from Kate's wardrobe," Rachel says. "But nothing too cute or flashy."

It turns out Kate's wardrobe is made up of only cute and flashy. Reluctantly, Rachel allows them to dress me in a ballerina-type miniskirt, some high leather boots, and a gauzy shirt.

I memorize the script while the makeup artist does her work on my face. As she outlines my eyes, she stops and says, "You have the most gorgeous gray eyes I've ever seen." She applies a few coats of mascara. "I don't think I've ever seen eyes this color before. Where'd you get them?"

Get them? "From my mom, I guess."

"Well, they're stunning. You should play them up."

I mumble a thank you and go back to studying the script. Someone takes my hair down and runs a brush through it.

I hear someone comment that I'm looking too good. They decide to put my hair back in a ponytail and then hand me a tissue to wipe off some of the lipstick they just applied. I glance in the mirror. It's more makeup than I usually wear but not as much as Kate wears. Whatever they do is fine with me. All I want is for Dad to keep his job.

"Ready?" Rachel asks me.

"Um, sure. I guess so."

"You don't really fit the part." Rachel holds the door open for me. "Not the least bit frumpy or nerdy, but what can we do? Beautiful is beautiful."

It doesn't seem right to actually answer, so I just smile. I've been called pretty before, but when you live in LA, the land of the fake, it doesn't mean very much.

When we reach the makeshift set, I purposely avoid eye contact with Kate—and Dad. A stagehand helps me climb into the back seat of a light-blue Mercedes convertible, next to Coco. Logan's in the driver's seat, and Kate's sitting next to him. He turns around and seems to be appraising me. I guess I pass muster, because he raises his eyebrows at me and gives me his star-quality smile. The girl who was supposed to be playing Emily is nowhere to be seen. I wonder how she's getting back to LA.

The showrunner stands nearby. I met her a few weeks ago, and she seemed really nice. She walks over to the car and puts her hand on my shoulder. "Thanks for doing this, um, Ellie, right?"

I nod. She remembers my name—a good sign. Maybe she's one of those rare gems on top of the food chain in Hollywood who doesn't forget the little people.

"Do you need some time? Everyone's told me you know the script, but I want you to feel comfortable." She smiles, obviously unaware that Kate is rolling her eyes behind her back.

After the eye roll, Kate glares at me. I know it's a warning for me to get on with it. "I'm fine," I say. "I think I've got it."

I get up the courage to look at Jimmy while he addresses everyone. He doesn't seem mad.

"Okay, let's start from where we left off, and then we'll reshoot the earlier scenes," he says. "Kate, you're furious at Logan for getting a flat tire. Emily, you're a nervous wreck. Let's go."

The assistant director shows me where we are in the scene and then shouts, "Quiet on the set. Roll it."

"Rolling," someone shouts. An assistant says, "Twenty-one, take two," while another holds a slate in front of Kate's face and clacks it shut.

Kate gets out of the convertible and slams the door. "I knew I shouldn't have let you drive!" She looks at Logan. "It's flat. Now what?"

"I'll call my dad," I interject. *Another dumb line.*

"Earth to Ellie. Your dad's not supposed to know we're out here, remember?" Kate looks at me and shakes her head in exasperation. She turns to Logan. "You're going to have to change it."

"Cut!" Jimmy shouts. "Kate, it's *Emily*, not Ellie."

Kate groans. We do the scene over. She calls me Ellie *again*. And then again. For a seasoned actress, she's really losing it. Probably because she's seething over what I did earlier.

The showrunner laughs. "Hey," she says cheerfully, "I like the name Ellie. Let's make a switch." She scribbles something on her clipboard. "Everyone, scratch the name Emily."

"Whatever," Kate says. "Ellie. Emily. What's the difference?"

I press my lips together and take a deep breath.

The showrunner isn't finished yet. "On second thought, let's shorten it to *Elle*. It's a little more fitting. After all, this is Beverly Hills, and she is Kate's best friend. Ellie sounds a little..." She doesn't finish her sentence, but I can imagine what she's thinking. Ellie doesn't sound very well-to-do. My real name is Eleanor, which sounds more proper but is totally uncool.

The showrunner looks at Kate. "Can you manage to remember Elle?" Her voice is friendly when she says it, but Kate looks insulted. She nods her head and then rolls her eyes again as soon as the showrunner looks away.

After a few more takes, we finally get to the part where it becomes evident that Logan's character is incapable of changing a tire. "I'm going to call Mom's gardener," Kate says. She scrolls through her phone directory.

"Why do you have his number?" Logan narrows his eyes a little too much, and his nose scrunches up. He's supposed to look suspicious, but to me he's overdoing it.

"Are you kidding me?" Kate tosses her hair back and starts mimicking her on-air mom. "Kate, do me a favor. Call the chef and tell him I want sushi for dinner. Kate, call the gardener—there's a weed in one of the planters by the pool!" She huffs. "Why does she have a personal assistant anyway, if she's always asking me to do everything?"

Kate dials. She speaks to the gardener in perfect Spanish, just for effect, and then switches to English so the audience will understand. Before she hangs up she says, "And Pedro? Please don't tell my mom about this."

"Is he coming?" I ask. The script says I'm supposed to sound anxious, which goes completely against my nature. I know a good actress can play any part, but I'm so annoyed with my character that I say the line with confidence instead of fear. No one shouts "Cut!" I guess I'm getting away with it. Hopefully, when they watch the dailies, they'll see I didn't work out and find someone else.

"No," Kate replies.

I'm supposed to panic. Instead, I remain calm. Again, no one stops filming.

"He's sending his son," Kate says.

I glance over to where Cam stands waiting for his time to enter the scene. He's pale, and his eyes look huge. I want to give him a reassuring smile, but the cameras are fixed on me.

"You mean that adorable boy we saw last week? The one helping his dad prune your lemon tree?" I say it with interest instead of panic.

Kate doesn't miss a beat. "That's the one! But we need to walk a little until we come to a road marker so I can call the gardener back and tell him exactly where we are."

"Why doesn't Logan go?" I know I'm supposed to say it like I'm afraid to get out of the car, but it comes out more like I'm hinting that Logan should man up and do it for us.

"Why me?" Logan slides down in the front seat and props his feet up on the dash.

"We'll all go," Kate says decisively.

"I'm staying here with Coco," Logan says.

My dad signals Coco from where he's standing, out of the camera's eye. She leaps out of the car on cue. Later they'll probably add laughter in the soundtrack, so the audience realizes Coco has rejected Logan's offer.

"Come on, Elle. Coco will protect us." Kate gives Logan a look that says *I'm done with you.*

I get out of the car and follow Coco and Kate down the deserted stretch of highway, the camera dolly only steps ahead of us. The script says I'm supposed to stumble a little and almost fall, trying to catch up, so I do. My character is clumsy. Anything to make Kate look better. I know this is the part where Coco will run into the desert chasing a lizard, forcing Kate and I to run after her, get all messed up, and lose our way.

Everything will be pieced together and special effects will be added, but the crew needs enough film to work with. Kate and I take a breather while they get the footage they need with Coco and one of the lizards.

"You're not following the script," Kate says to me while makeup adds some fake dirt to our faces.

"I've said every word of every line." I purse my lips together so I don't cry out in pain as one of the makeup artists pulls a large section of my hair up and rats it with a comb.

"You know exactly what I'm talking about." Kate pushes the makeup artist's hand away when she tries to do the same to Kate's hair. "That's enough," she says to the girl. "We're lost in the desert—not caught in a tornado." She turns back to me. "I've got a date in LA tomorrow night, and I don't want to be stuck here reshooting this with Emily Number Three. Follow the script."

I suck in a breath and will myself not to respond. So that's the big rush. Kate has a date. I thought she was still with Logan. They must be "off" in their "on-again-off-again."

We walk over to the setting of our next scene, where we'll be resting in front of some giant boulders, having finally caught up with Coco. Time for the lizards to mess with us. The script says Kate handles the lizards with relative poise, while I freak out. I can flip out, no problem. I've witnessed enough actresses having breakdowns over not enough cream in their coffee—or too much. I've got "go berserk" in my repertoire, for sure.

Kate scolds Coco, and Coco puts her paws over her eyes like she's ashamed of herself. She's such a talented animal actress. I want to put my arms around her and tell her she's a good dog, but I'll have to wait. I see Dad's about to release a lizard on Kate. He's holding it in midair over her head.

"Stop!" Kate screams.

Jimmy yells, "Cut!" He looks at Kate. "What's the matter?"

"*Real* lizards? No one said anything about real lizards crawling on me! I thought you meant fake ones. Of course you meant fake ones!"

I resist the urge to tell Dad that I warned him this would happen.

Jimmy sighs. "We need a little of both, Kate. We'll be doing a lot of special effects with this, so I don't need a lot of footage. But I need a couple of takes with the real lizards to pull this off."

"They're harmless, Kate," Dad says to her gently. "I would never put you in any danger." He demonstrates by putting his finger in front of the lizard's mouth. The lizard puffs his red gill in and out but doesn't bite.

Kate's not impressed. "Absolutely not. Where's my body double?"

Jimmy snorts. "You don't have a body double. This isn't a 'stunt,' Kate. It's just a little pet crawling around, nothing else."

Jimmy probably shouldn't have used the word "crawl." Kate shudders. "Isn't this a violation of my contract? I insist on a body double."

The showrunner steps in. "I suppose we could get one here by tomorrow and reshoot." She sighs. "But I'd rather keep going. Why don't we ad-lib? Instead of showing the lizard crawling on both girls, have it crawl only on Elle."

Kate lets out a deep breath. "Works for me."

"Any problem with live lizards, Ellie?" Jimmy winks at me. He doesn't wait for an answer. "Kate, you see the lizard on Elle and slowly caution her. Something like, 'Elle, don't panic, but there's something on your head.' Elle, you freak out. Then follow the original script from there. Let's roll."

Dad sets a lizard on my head while I stay perfectly still so the camera can get a good shot. The lizard doesn't move either. Coco sits between Kate and me, and she's so well trained she doesn't take her eyes off of Dad even though she's only a few inches away from a reptile. She's on high alert. Dad slowly positions himself in front of her, and only her eyes move.

Kate is the only one out of sync with what's going on. She's staring wild-eyed at my head and doesn't look at all composed.

I feel the lizard move in my hair. Kate screams. Coco barks. I don't blame Coco, because usually when people scream on a set, it's a cue for a dog to bark. She should have waited for a command, but she's not perfect. But for that matter, neither are human actors.

The bark causes the lizard to leap from my head onto Kate's lap and then off into the desert. I forget that I'm supposed to flip out and instead watch Kate go berserk. She flies up and wildly flings her hands all over her body, like she's trying to brush the lizard off any place he might end up. Jimmy doesn't yell cut, and the cameras keep rolling.

"Ellie, help!" Kate screams, using the wrong name again. She grabs my arm.

"Relax, Kate." I'm laughing. "That lizard is halfway to Beverly Hills by now. He's gone."

Kate storms back to the paved road, having obviously quit the scene. I laugh again while the cameras keep filming.

It takes about a half hour and a promise not to redo the lizard scene to convince Kate to get back to work. We move on to the rescue scene. It begins with Camilo pulling up behind Kate's convertible in a stereotypical beat-up truck. He gets out and walks over.

"You're here!" Kate squeals, just like I'd told him she'd do back in the trailer, which seems like a million years ago already. She hugs him.

Cam walks over to the flat tire and manages to say all his lines correctly, although he repeatedly looks at the ground. Jimmy keeps rolling, and I think I know why. Cam's natural shyness must be exactly what Jimmy's looking for. He's not acting the part. He's can't-stop-staring adorable without a hint of arrogance. It takes a really talented actor to be that cute and appear on camera like he doesn't realize it. Sometimes it's just easier to use someone green.

When we finally wrap for the evening, the directing crew is jovial. To me it seems like everything went disastrous, but they seem pleased. I want to slip away as fast as possible so no one can talk to me. I still haven't heard the lecture I'm sure is coming from Dad, and there are probably ten other people mad at me in the vicinity—Jimmy, Kate, probably the showrunner, and every assistant director on the show. Before I escape, Rachel hands me the call sheet for the next day's shooting, along with a fresh script with notes scribbled all over it.

I glance down at the schedule. The plan is to leave location by tomorrow afternoon. If everything goes right, Kate will make her date. Normally, I couldn't care less, but I realize Kate's obsession with this mystery guy is the only thing keeping me from disaster.

four

I MANAGE TO get through a second day of shooting without receiving my punishment. It's like everyone's forgotten about my outburst. It doesn't hurt that Isa left after the first night, citing a migraine. Even Kate has been somewhat civil. When we wrap, she doesn't even ask me to watch Hairy. Instead, she sidles up to Dad and asks if he can take Hairy back in our camper with the show animals.

It's obvious Dad's happy to see me interacting with humans, especially ones close to my own age, because he insists I return on the plane with the actors. I should be glad—the plane's a lot faster—but this is exactly what I don't want to happen. How can I build my career as a handler if I'm stuck on the wrong side of the camera?

After I say goodbye to Dad and Coco, I walk to the departure area where the SUVs are waiting to take us to the airport. Cam heads our way, and it occurs to me that he wasn't on the jet yesterday. I wonder how he got to location in the first place. "Land or air?" I ask him as he saunters up.

"Jimmy wants me to fly, so we can talk."

"How did you get here?"

"I rode up with one of the trailer drivers."

"Oh." I smile at him. "And by the way, you're doing great."

"Are you sure?" He shoots me a nervous glance. "I'm thinking Jimmy wants me to fly back with him so he can fire me."

"Not a chance. He would have fired you by now and sent you back on a bus. Trust me. You're in."

Cam looks down and pushes the dirt around with his shoe. "I guess that's good."

He doesn't look convinced, but he's probably in shock over the entire thing. Showbiz is a little overwhelming for newbies. "You'll get used to—"

"Cam!" Kate walks up and puts her arm around his shoulders. "My new beau! Looking forward to the next scene?" She makes a duck face, her pink-glossed lips protruding in a mock kiss, and then climbs into the closest SUV.

I take in a breath to keep from laughing—and not because I think she's funny. Cam's eyes meet mine, and he looks more confused than amused. I've got this pilot script more or less memorized, and unless there's been another rewrite, they never actually kiss. I shrug my shoulders and nod toward the open door of the SUV. Cam slides into the middle of the back seat next to Kate, and I climb in next to him and pull the door closed.

"We were supposed to leave five minutes ago," Kate moans. "Where is everybody?"

Kate's date has to be the only reason she wasn't the last to show up like she usually is.

"Ellie," she says to me suddenly, brushing her arm against Cam as she leans over him to speak to me. A strong whiff of perfume hits me. "We need to make something very clear. You were totally out of character during the whole shoot. Did you even read the script? Emily, Elle—whatever her name is—is not cool. She's a nerd. Got it?"

"Don't worry about it. I'm sure they'll find a replacement for me when we get back."

"They won't. Not for the pilot anyway. It would cost too much to do over what we've done here in the last couple of days." She slumps down in the seat. "But yeah, the studio execs will definitely replace you...if we get picked up."

Why is she so sure? And why do I care?

"You, on the other hand, were fantastic." Kate puts her hand on Cam's knee and leaves it there for a minute. His eyes flicker over to mine, then out the window.

Logan opens the door. Through the dark windows, he probably couldn't see that the back seat was full. He grunts and slams the door shut. I watch him walk to another vehicle and hop in. Jimmy climbs in the front passenger seat of our SUV, and we finally take off for the airport.

Jimmy immediately gets on the phone with some studio execs while Kate keeps checking her cell.

"How long have you two been friends?" Cam asks Kate and me as we ride along. He's the only one who seems uncomfortable with the silence.

Friends? I purposely wait for Kate to respond. Even though Dad was the animal trainer for seven seasons on the show that made Kate a famous child star and I basically grew up in the wings of that very set, in the three-year interim between that show and this one, I rarely saw Kate. And whenever I did see her, she practically pretended not to know me.

"Yeah, Logan and I are just friends now," Kate answers absentmindedly. "We're not dating anymore."

"No, you and Ellie."

I decide to go ahead and answer. "My dad was the animal trainer for a show Kate was on, *Jet Set Vet*. It ran for seven seasons. Did you watch it?"

"Uh…" Cam hesitates.

I better let him off the hook. Kate thinks it was everyone's favorite show. She'll probably make Cam feel terrible if he's never heard of it. "Anyway, I was about six when the show first aired. My dad was allowed to keep me on the set during tapings, and I was tutored with the child actors who were on the show."

I pause to see if Kate wants to add anything. She doesn't even seem to be following the conversation. She's texting someone nonstop with this intense look on her face.

"Kate was two years ahead of me. So we were in the same classroom and had the same tutors, but we didn't hang out or anything." I think that about sums it up. There isn't much to our relationship, even though I've spent much of my life orbiting her world.

"What was the show about?" Cam asks. Kate is still engrossed with her text messages, so Cam will probably get away with that question unscathed.

"Kate's father on the show was a veterinarian in Beverly Hills, and he treated pets of the rich and famous. It was funny. We used a lot of animals in that show."

"Why didn't you go to a regular school, if you weren't a part of the show?"

"The hours are really long when a show's taping, and my dad wanted me with him."

"What about your mom?"

I give Cam a small smile, knowing he'll probably feel bad and start apologizing as soon as I answer him. It's the same every time. "She died when I was born." Wait for it...

"Oh." Cam doesn't make the usual apologies, and I'm glad. I hate endlessly hearing "I'm sorry," even though I know there isn't much else people can say. Instead, Cam says sorry with his eyes.

I take a deep breath. It's always a relief when it's out there. I quickly change the subject. "I loved growing up on the set. When I got older, I helped my dad more and more, especially with the dogs. I'm as much of a wrangler now as he is. Well, almost."

"It's amazing how well trained Coco is," Cam says.

"Thanks."

"How many dogs do you have?" Neither one of us is even trying to include Kate in the conversation anymore.

"Right now we have three. I trained Coco from a little pup. We also have Olive, a scruffy-looking terrier mix, and a German shepherd named Teddy, because he's just a big teddy bear."

Kate suddenly looks up from her phone. "You want to go to a party on Saturday night, Cam?"

Jimmy turns to face the back seat. His ears have always been highly sensitive receptors, hearing everything, even when you don't think he's paying attention. "That's a good idea, Cam. I'd like you to get around town a little. Rub elbows with some people in the industry. If the show gets picked up, I'll need you out there in the public eye. The girls are going to love you."

Cam's face turns red. He doesn't seem able to respond.

"Of course he'll go. I need an escort." Kate gives Cam a serious look. "Just friends, though, okay?"

I can't believe she just said that. What makes her think he wants to date her?

"I share a car with my sister. I'll have to ask—"

"I'll pick you up in a limo, silly. My people will contact yours for an address."

"No—I mean—I live pretty far out. I'll get to Mr. Gainer's house on Saturday, and you can pick me up there? Is that okay with you, Mr. Gainer?"

"You, too, with this 'Mr. Gainer' crap? Like I told Logan, just call me Jimmy. You kids make me feel old. And of course it's okay." Jimmy looks at me. "What about you, *Elle*?" He's obviously trying to be funny, using my "stage" name. Man

I'm about to decline, but Kate beats me to it. "Jimmy, that's so sweet of you to invite her to someone else's party, but I'm afraid I'm only allowed to bring a plus one."

"Bull—" Jimmy says.

"I can't. Really, I can't." It's sweet that Jimmy is trying to get Kate to include me, but it's so not necessary. "I already have plans."

"Of course you do," Kate says. She looks up from her phone and gives me one of her genuinely phony smiles.

Jimmy's phone rings, hopefully ending the conversation. Even though Kate ignores my existence unless she wants something, she knows I don't have a life. I'll never forget the day all of us kids from the show were hanging out on set after we wrapped the last episode of *Jet Set Vet* one season, and she invited everyone to a party she was having a few days later—except me.

I can still hear her words when someone mentioned she forgot me. "Only the actors," she said. "And besides, Ellie only hangs out with *dogs*." She looked at me with her angelic twelve-year-old face and added, "No offense."

It was true—*is* true to this day. I am pretty much friends only with animals. And a few adults. But it doesn't matter anyway. I'd never hear the end of it from Aunt Jess if she found out I went to a Hollywood party. She's told me so many times that my mom would've never wanted me to get involved in the celebrity scene. Not that I want to anyway. I've seen more than a handful of people completely self-destruct in this business.

But I love life on the lot, especially when an undressed set is taken over by set designers and turned into anywhere in the world. When a street goes from present-day New York City to the 1920s, all in a matter of hours. The large crews, the extras, the costumes, the makeup. The hustle and bustle. The animals. The joy when a show is a success, and even the "let's try something else" attitude when one fails. I can't imagine working anywhere else.

"You two have fun," I say as we come to a stop at the airport. "I really am busy this weekend." Before I can open the door, Logan does. He must have forgotten which side Kate was sitting on, because he looks surprised when he sees me and quickly goes to the other side to open Kate's door. I hop out of the truck and head straight for the plane.

"Elle, wait," Cam says. He sprints to catch up with me. "I'll sit with you."

I think about correcting him and telling him to call me *Ellie*, not *Elle*, but being called something different is kind of fun. It makes me *feel* different, like I can reinvent my life by just eliminating one tiny letter from my name. It occurs to me that the letter that's being eliminated is the letter *I*, but I push the thought away.

A line from *Romeo and Juliet* pops into my head: "What's in a name? That which we call a rose by any other name would smell as sweet." I have to disagree with the Bard on this one. There is a lot in a name. Otherwise, people wouldn't change their names all the time when they move to Hollywood.

I slow down and walk with Cam to the jet's staircase. We're the first ones inside. Cam follows me to the farthest seats in the back and sits across from me.

"I've never been in an airplane before." Cam runs his hand along the leather seat. "This is so cool."

Small planes make me nervous, but looking at it from Cam's perspective, this one *is* really nice. Kate appears in the doorway, followed by Logan, and they sit in the front. *Perfect.* But then Jimmy comes in and waves at Cam and me. "Come up here. I want a meeting with the four of you."

Cam and I move to the front. Part of me can't take this show seriously, but what if we don't get another job soon enough and Dad really does sell Animal Stars Inc.? I was so sure this pilot was doomed because the writing is so bad, but you never know. I look at Cam. He pretty much admitted his family needs the money. Jimmy will probably put him in another show if this one fails, but still, it looks like we both need this show to succeed.

I shake the thought away and give Jimmy my full attention. I need to finish filming the pilot, and then they can switch me out. I'll be back to animal wrangling in no time.

"After watching the dailies, the execs are optimistic," Jimmy says. He looks at me. "Ellie, they loved you. Seriously loved you. They ordered a rewrite of all the scenes we'll need to replace. You've got the part."

A sense of panic envelops me. *I don't want the part.* This could be a disaster. I consider the possible outcomes: We get picked up, and I'm stuck playing this dumb character for a gazillion seasons. Or the series is dropped, Animal Stars Inc. closes up shop, and we move to Salinas. Either way, my life is ruined.

I steal a look at Kate's face. It's expressionless. I sigh. As much as she annoys me, I have no interest in competing with her. I can't. And I don't want to.

"It's never too early to think about publicity," Jimmy says. "We'll have a meeting with all your publicists on Monday, but I want to strategize now."

Obviously, I don't have a publicist. I'm sure Cam doesn't either, unless Jimmy already provided him with one, which I highly doubt.

"The four of you should start appearing together around town. Cause some excitement..." Jimmy's eyes go to each of us. "If the studio sees there's an interest in your private lives, it could tip the scales in our favor if they're on the fence between our show and another one. Or maybe it could earn us a better slot or a larger number of episodes up front."

Kate nods. I look at Cam. Everything Jimmy's saying probably sounds foreign to him. I understand what Jimmy is trying to get across. I've been in the industry long enough to know how things work. But I also know if the writing's not good enough, it doesn't matter how popular the actors are in real life. A poorly written show will tank 100 percent of the time.

"I'm in every teen magazine, every month." Kate twists her hair up in a bun and leans back in her seat. "And most of the mainstream gossip magazines too. I'm the marquee actress. That should be enough."

There's no denying that Kate and Logan are the whole reason this spin-off was ordered to begin with. They were the "it" couple in teenybopper land, and their breakup has only intensified the attention. Everything they do is all over the internet nonstop.

"But Logan's had a lot of bad press lately," Jimmy says as the jet engines get louder.

We start taxiing. Cam stares out the window as everyone keeps talking. He and I smile at each other, no one else realizing this is a big moment for him. His first takeoff ever.

"All publicity is good publicity," Logan says. The standard cop-out, but basically true. "But let the record show, *Kate* broke up with *me*, not the other way around."

Kate rolls her eyes and then looks at Jimmy. "Please don't suggest we get back together."

"No. I actually like that you're apart. And if you get back together, hide it. Your fans will tune in to watch and see if there's hope. They're dying to have you two back together, and we'll tease them with the possibility, week after week.

At times you'll get close, but something will always come between you."

"Or *someone*," Kate says, raising a perfectly plucked eyebrow. "Cam? Are you following along?"

The wheels have left the pavement, and we're in that awkward stage of climbing, the part I hate most about flying. I never feel certain that the plane has enough momentum to stay up. Cam is understandably focused on our takeoff, not on our conversation.

Logan looks at Cam and then Jimmy. "I know the script has Kate's character confused. She's interested in the gardener's son—a little." Logan frowns. "But you're not really going to have her fall for him, are you?"

Kate smirks. "What's it to you? Are you trying to write the show now too? It's called a 'love triangle.' You probably studied it in your acting classes. Overused Tropes 101."

"Where does Elle come in?" Logan asks. "Maybe she and I should have something going on." He raises his eyebrows up and down at me. It makes me want to laugh. He may be clueless, but he's kind of funny.

"She's supposed to be my best friend, moron." Kate shakes her head. "I thought we could do this, Logan—work together professionally, be friends—but I don't know anymore."

"You don't have a choice," Jimmy says. His tone is serious. "Grow up. Both of you."

We're flying high now and about to enter a large, fluffy cloud. "Wow. Look!" Cam blurts. "We're going inside a cloud."

The three of them turn and look at him.

"It's beautiful, isn't it?" I say, ignoring them.

Jimmy resumes with no comment. "Cam and Kate are going to a party tomorrow. Why don't you all go?"

Kate opens her mouth, but Jimmy speaks first. "Don't even try, Kate. I know whose party you're going to. Jenny Simon's. I just spoke to her."

Kate crosses her arms. "Whatever," she says.

"What are you doing tonight?" Logan asks Kate.

"What's it to you?"

"Just wondering."

"I bet."

I guess I'm the only one who knows about Kate's plans tonight. I mean, I don't know exactly what she's doing, but it sure was important to her to get back to LA for her "date."

Jimmy ignores them and looks at me. "I'll have a car pick you up at your house. I'll talk to your dad too, okay?"

I nod.

"We'll plan our strategy at the studio next week. In the meantime, you have the weekend off. A rarity. Enjoy it." Jimmy opens his laptop and starts working. Meeting over.

five

I WAS EXPECTING Jimmy to send me an outfit. I wasn't expecting him to send me a stylist, a hair and makeup artist, and especially not Chris, one of the "talent" handlers from the studio. I put all three dogs in a sit-stay and invite the glam team into our living room, grabbing Coco's collar to prevent her from jumping on Chris like she does every time she sees him.

"Coco, sit." I pull her down, but she wriggles out of my grasp.

Chris taps his chest, signaling Coco to stand on her hind legs and put her front paws on his shoulders. He rubs her head and laughs. "You call yourself a trainer?"

"I never should have taught you that. What are you doing here?" I pull Coco off him.

"I'm your handler." Chris holds the door open, and the stylist wheels a small clothing rack into my living room. The makeup artist follows with her suitcase of supplies.

I laugh out loud. "I don't need a handler."

"That's not what I heard. Jimmy says you're cool as a cucumber one minute, then bam—you blow up."

"What!"

"See? No, seriously, Jimmy didn't say that. He just thought you could use a little direction. But Rachel did tell me how you lost it with Kate on location."

"You have no idea how she was acting—"

"Really? I used to be her handler, remember?" Chris raises his eyebrows and looks toward the stylists. "We'll talk about it later."

The wardrobe stylist unzips the plastic covering and reveals the clothes. "Mr. Gainer said you could pick as many things as you like. Lucky girl."

Long silky cords with price tags hang from each label. I lift one up, but the stylist brushes my hand away. "Uh-uh. No looking at prices. Boss's orders." She grabs a blouse and a pair of jeans from the rack. "Start with these."

I take them and stand there, not sure what to do next.

"Well, go try them on."

The makeup person looks around the room. "Where should I set up?"

"How about the kitchen table?" I walk toward the powder room. "Move whatever you want."

I go into the bathroom and change. Everything fits perfectly, which doesn't surprise me. No detail escapes Jimmy. I go out and model for them.

"Let's go one size smaller on the jeans." The stylist tugs on the back pocket. "Always wear your jeans snug. Even the best ones stretch a bit."

"We need something dressier for the party." Chris looks

through the rack, pulls out a short wine-colored lace dress, and hands it to me.

I sigh and go back into the bathroom. I can't help but look at the price tag. I mean, who wouldn't? I gasp. *Two thousand dollars!* For a casual little dress?

"Everything all right in there?" Chris says through the door. "You didn't rip it, did you?"

"I'm fine!" I slip it on and come out.

"Gorgeous. That's the one," Chris says.

The stylist pulls out a long white maxi dress. "What about this? It's the latest trend."

"Too old for her." Chris shakes his head. "What do you think, Tara?"

The makeup artist looks up from the pile of cosmetics she's organizing. "Definitely the short one. Looks good with her coloring too."

The stylist shrugs and pulls a number of tops off the rack along with the same jeans I tried on in the next size down. "If these jeans fit, I'll bring you a few more pairs to the studio on Monday. Try them on with these shirts."

One by one, I try every piece of clothing on the rack, except for the maxi dress, along with at least a dozen pairs of shoes. The one outfit I expected has turned into ten.

The stylist takes all the tags off and writes everything down in a notebook. "They're yours to keep." She slides the book into her tote bag. "I almost forgot." She opens a large cardboard box and unwraps three handbags: one black, one brown, and one white. "You're all set."

Chris picks up the black one and turns it in his hands. "*Céline.* Tish would be jealous."

"Yeah, right," I say. I've seen Chris's wife on only a few occasions, but each time she looked over-the-top stunning. Suddenly, I feel overwhelmed. "I wish I could give it to her. I don't feel right owning something this nice."

"Enjoy it while it lasts, Cinderella." Chris pats my arm. "Now change back into your rags so Tara can do your face."

During my makeover, Chris lectures me about the party. "Don't leave your drink unattended. I won't be there, so you need to take care of yourself at all times."

Don't leave my drink unattended? That's a little scary. My first party that doesn't include a bounce house, and I have to worry about being drugged?

"And don't talk details about the pilot with anyone. Got it?"

I nod and Tara groans. "Don't move." She wipes my face with a cloth.

"Sorry."

"Stick with Logan. He's coming to pick you up at ten."

"Ten? I'm usually in my pajamas by ten."

"Yes, ten. And don't let him take off and leave you at the party. Kate and Cam will be there too. Try and get along with her, all right?"

"Yes, father."

"I'm not old enough to be your father." He laughs.

"Are you sure?" I laugh too. I know he can't be more than thirty, but he's fun to tease.

The front door opens, and Dad comes in. Chris rises to his feet and shakes Dad's hand. "We were just talking about you, Tom. I'm giving your daughter advice on how to behave tonight."

"I can't believe I let Jimmy convince me to let her go."

"I'll be fine."

Dad pats me on the shoulder and sits in the chair across from me.

"The network loves her," Chris says.

"I heard." Dad rubs his eyes. I can tell he's worried—he knows Jenny Simon's reputation. But Jimmy promised he'd never let anything happen to me. I wonder how he can say that if he's not even going to be there.

Still, despite Chris's comment about not leaving my drink unattended, I'm not that afraid. I don't feel I'm corruptible. It's not like I've never been to a Hollywood event before. I have with Dad. We get invited to stars' homes every once in a while.

"I'm going to get a little work done in my room," Dad says. "Come in when you're ready so I can see how you look." He stands and shakes Chris's hand again. "*Handle* her with care." He chuckles like it's a joke, but his eyes don't match his smile.

The car was supposed to pick Logan up first and then me, but an empty limo comes to the house at nine forty-five, fifteen minutes early. The driver tells me Logan wasn't ready and told him to come back. I never understand it when a guy can't get ready on time. I mean, how hard can it be when your hair is wash and wear and there's no makeup involved? But whatever.

I tell the driver I'll be out in a minute and run upstairs to say goodbye to Dad. I've been ready to go for about two hours now, except for the shoes. They look like they have about a five-minute standing time limit, max. I slip them on and stop to check my appearance again in the hallway mirror. I like how she did my hair, mostly sleek and straight with wide, soft curls on the ends. My eyes look huge, even without the false eyelashes I convinced them I didn't need. I feel fake enough as it is.

Dad's door is only halfway open, so I peek inside and see him at his desk, staring out the window. His fingers fiddle with the pages of a script. I can tell it's an old one from before Mom died, because I can see the cardboard box is out from under his bed—Mom's old boot box, where Dad stashes all the scripts they used to work on together. I knock softly. "Dad?"

"Come in, honey."

"The car's here." I step inside the room.

"Did Logan come to the door?"

"Uh, I guess he wasn't ready, so we're going to pick him up now. It's not like it's a date or anything."

Dad is slow about putting down the script, but he finally does and turns to look at me. His eyes open wide. "Where's Ellie?"

"Very funny." I twirl in a circle, showing Dad the final result. Makeup, hair, dress, shoes, and purse.

"I've changed my mind on this—I'm not letting you out of the house." Dad smiles like he's kidding, but his eyes still have a worried look in them I'm not used to seeing.

"I've got to go." I kiss his cheek.

"Be home by midnight, or you'll turn into a pumpkin."

"It's already almost ten."

"I know. Just try to be home before dawn." He winks. "I'll be up waiting."

"Bye, Dad!"

I take the shoes off again in the hallway and carry them until I step outside, then put them on to walk the ten feet of gravel to get to the car. The driver opens the door for me, and I feel about five years older than I did a week ago. This must be what going to a high school dance feels like—except replace "high school" with mega-mansion and "dance" with A-list party.

I see Coco looking out the front window, her paws up on the glass, wondering where I'm going. I give her the wave command, and she lifts her paw at me as I get in the car.

I know, girl. What have I got myself into?

six

AFTER A LONG drive, we end up in the Hollywood Hills. We wind up a steep road and pull up to an intercom in a short, gated driveway. Before the driver has a chance to speak, the gates open, and we pull in. It's a modern, angular home that doesn't look like much from the front, but I can tell from my vantage point that the view in the back must be spectacular.

Logan makes me wait another ten minutes before he comes to the car.

"Sorry, Elle." He kisses my cheek as he slides in. "I thought it was silly for me to ride all the way to Burbank when the party is in the Hills anyway."

I wonder why Jimmy wanted the driver to pick Logan up first, when he lives so close to the party. Probably so I wouldn't be alone. It's sweet but just shows how Jimmy's not controlling things as much as he thinks he is. It doesn't matter what he arranges if no one cooperates.

"You look great." Logan leans forward and touches one of my loose curls. He reminds me of a Labrador retriever—no personal boundaries, but so amiable you don't really mind.

"You too."

"Did Kate say anything to you about her plans last night? She was so intent on getting back to town."

"Me? No."

Logan looks at his watch, a bold and obviously very expensive one. "I wonder if she's there yet," he mumbles as he turns to stare out the window.

It takes less than five minutes for us to get to the party. No wonder Logan didn't want to ride all the way to my house and back to get me. I stare at Jenny's home. It's huge—one of those McMansion compounds that keep popping up on the Hills, replacing the so-called "tear downs" Dad loves. I breathe deep and try to prepare myself to socialize.

Logan gets out of the car while the driver opens the other side for me. For a second it looks as if Logan's going to walk into the party without me, but then he turns back and takes my arm. His eyes dart everywhere, even though we haven't even entered the front door yet.

As soon as we step inside, Logan is off in a blur talking to people. I stand in the foyer for a minute watching him. He's laughing and joking and touching people, going from one cluster to the next. Yep, definitely a Labrador retriever.

Across the room, Jenny Simon stands next to a baby grand piano while Samuel and Samantha, from the singing duo SAM, sing her a tune. I know I should say hello to Jenny since she's the hostess, so I make my way to the other side of the huge living room, declining a glass of champagne on the way. I probably look older than sixteen, since I'm all dressed up and have makeup on, but not twenty-one. Of course, no one here cares how old anyone is.

I don't want to interrupt, so I stand a bit away and listen to SAM sing. Samantha sounds like an angel. They can't stop touching—or staring at each other—and they look like they could be brother and sister instead of America's hottest music couple, with the same wavy brown hair and big brown eyes. They're so talented and so in love. I heard they're getting married soon, but it's probably just a rumor. They can't be more than nineteen. No couple gets more media attention than they do—except Kate and Logan—but at least these two are the real thing.

Sam and Samantha finish their song, and Sam leans over and kisses Samantha on the mouth. She looks at him with adoring eyes. I'm not at all the romantic type, but my heart swells when I watch them. No wonder they're number one on the charts. People can't get enough of them. And they're good. Really good.

While everyone in the vicinity claps, I approach Jenny. "Thank you for having me," I say loudly, leaning toward her, even though I know she has zero idea who I am.

She pretends to know me, kissing both my cheeks. "I'm so glad you could make it!"

I smile, nod, and immediately slip out the sliding glass doors. It's much noisier outside. There are huge flower and candle arrangements everywhere, several bars and buffets, and a DJ playing music. I stare past the infinity pool that gives the illusion it's flowing straight down the hill and check out the view. We're in the midrange of the Hills, and you can see lights for miles. It's gorgeous.

The five minutes of wearability in these shoes has expired,

so I sit on a stone bench at the edge of the garden and search the crowd for a familiar face. I see a couple of actors whose dogs I've babysat, a producer I know, and a grip who somehow gets invited everywhere, according to studio gossip. At the studio, you can't avoid hearing gossip, even if you try. Maybe because everyone has to sign a confidentiality contract. Since "what happens on the set stays on the set," the crew can talk only among themselves. And they do.

I don't see Cam or Kate. And I don't see anyone I feel the urge to talk to. It's not that I'm shy, parties just aren't my thing. I'd rather be home watching old movies with Dad, cuddled up with Coco.

Logan finally makes it outside, and I watch him search the entire area. When he sees me, he waves but keeps on scanning the scene. I imagine he's looking for Kate. He talks to a few people and then comes and sits down next me.

"What are you doing, sitting all by yourself?" He nudges me with his shoulder. "You look all emo over here."

I laugh. "I am not 'emo.' I'm just thinking. You should try it sometime."

"Ha ha. Very funny." He shoots me a goofy grin. "Want me to introduce you to some people?"

"Maybe later. Look—there's Kate and Cam."

Logan freezes and watches Kate as she floats into the backyard, dressed in all white. She's holding Cam's hand and doesn't let go. They look like a couple. A really attractive couple. My stomach drops. I feel sympathy for Cam, or maybe it's something else. Am I jealous?

I turn to look back at Logan, and suddenly his face is pressed up against mine. His mouth is on my mouth, his hands in my hair. He doesn't stop, and I'm so taken aback I don't move.

This isn't what I imagined my first kiss would be like, but like I said, I'm not a romantic. It's not something I've dreamed about, but still, I didn't want it to be like this. Logan finally lets me breathe.

I rub my lips, trying to get his slobber off me. "What are you doing?"

"I'm sorry—" He starts to apologize, but within seconds his lips are back on mine. I've gone from never-been-kissed to mauled in a matter of moments.

This time I push him off me. "Stop it." I jump to my feet. "I can totally see why Kate dumped you!"

The kiss was probably all for naught, because Kate has her back to us. Cam, however, has let go of her hand and is making his way over. Logan stands up next to me and puts his hand on the small of my back. I have the strongest urge to elbow him in the ribs. Cam arrives and kisses my cheek and shakes Logan's hand.

I feel a little shaky after what just happened. I've been kissed—and I haven't even been on a real date yet. I've heard actors and directors give dissertations on the differences between a real kiss and a stage kiss, but give me a break—stage kisses have their effect just like any other kiss. Otherwise, how can you explain the unlikely odds that costars often end up together, at least for a while? They pretend they can separate truth from fiction, but I don't buy it half the time.

Logan is speaking to Cam but looking at Kate. It's pathetic. "Excuse me a minute..." Logan says, walking off. I sit back down on the stone bench and catch my breath. I can only imagine what Cam thinks. He sits next to me, staring at the water in the fountain, silent.

"I want you to know something about Logan and me," I begin.

"It's none of my business."

"I want it to be your business," I whisper.

Cam turns and looks into my eyes. His are dark, yet soft. Intense and deep, yet lighthearted too. "I'm listening," he says.

"I was sitting here, alone. Jimmy arranged for Logan to escort me, but he disappeared the second we walked in the door—until right before for you walked back here." I laugh a little, trying to make light of it. "Then as soon as he saw you and Kate, he grabbed me and pretended to kiss me."

Cam doesn't laugh. "Pretended to? I think he actually planted one on you pretty good." He touches the side of my chin gently, like he's assessing the damage. "Do you mind if I go punch him?"

"Not at all. But there was probably something written in the fine print of your contract—not to mess up Logan Canfield's mug, no matter how much you want to."

This time Cam laughs. "We could leave them here."

"I think Kate likes you."

"She's nice, but not really my type." He puts his hand on top of mine and squeezes it, then moves his hand to his knee. I'm still a little shaky, but now I'm not sure what's causing it. I stare at his hand, wishing it would move back.

"You want to get out of here? Jimmy told me to call his driver when I wanted to leave. I can escort you home." He looks around. "But I guess I have to tell Kate."

We both look for her, but she's disappeared—and not with Logan. He's sitting on a barstool in the cabana talking to a producer.

Cam shrugs. "I guess I'll tell Logan. Any messages?"

"None that don't entail pushing him in the pool."

"That's tempting. I'll call Jimmy first." Cam walks to the farthest edge of the backyard, probably because it's so loud where we are. He paces with the phone on his ear for what seems like forever. He's frowning when he comes back.

"Jimmy asked me not to leave Kate under any circumstances. He told me he couldn't tell me why but asked if I could please do him the favor. He said it's important." Cam sticks his phone in his pocket. "But he's sending a car for you."

Disappointment falls on me like an unexpected curtain call.

"Great!" I squeak out a little too forcefully. I'm an actress now—I should do better than that. "I'll go wait out front."

"I'm staying with you until it gets here. Come on." Cam takes my hand in one smooth motion, like it's the most natural thing in the world.

His hand is warm and holds mine firmly. It feels way more exciting than the kiss Logan forced on me.

Instead of cutting through the house, we take a stone path that leads from the backyard to the front. It takes us by a small, heavily landscaped patio area on the side of the house. Through the bushes, I spot Kate sitting on a short stone wall. A guy is facing her, his back to us. There's something familiar about him, but I can't immediately place him.

Kate sees me and puts her finger to her lips. She shakes

her head. The boy disappears, and Kate pops out of the foliage. "Cam! You deserted me! I was looking for you."

Somewhere during all of this, Cam has let go of my hand. Kate slips her arm under his and melds her body against his side.

Cam stiffens but doesn't move. "Elle's leaving. I'm walking her out."

"So early?" Kate keeps her arm locked on Cam's and starts walking toward the front of the house. "I'll join you."

I walk behind them on the path, like I'm a cameraman following them with a dolly—not part of the scene. Cam turns his head back and motions for me, sticking out his empty elbow.

I smile and keep on walking behind them, ignoring the gesture. The path isn't wide enough anyway, and I'd feel like a fool.

The car is already there when we reach the front. The driver probably never left to begin with. Cam pries himself away from Kate, opens the door for me, and kisses me on the cheek. As I get in, Cam's hand moves from my shoulder and slides down my arm and then grasps my hand until the last second, as if he doesn't want to let me go. Our eyes meet one last time, and he flashes me that nervous smile.

"Bye, Ellie." Kate waves, pulling Cam back by the arm with unnecessary force. "See you Monday!" But the tone of her voice doesn't match her expression. She's no better actress than I am.

seven

ON MONDAY MORNING, I get to the studio an hour before my call time. I need to find Jimmy before anyone else gets here to see if there's any way I can get out of the pilot. Maybe they can cut enough to make it look like only Logan and Kate drove into the desert. Then they can shoot the scenes they were going to reshoot with me with a new actress. It wouldn't take much rewriting, but it would add time to the schedule. I know how tight the budget is, but still, there's hope he'll listen to me.

I walk down the hallway toward Jimmy's office and see Kate standing right outside the door. I stop cold and watch her. She's obviously eavesdropping. I continue down the hall so she can't get away with it, but when she sees me, she puts her finger to her mouth and waves me away. Normally I wouldn't care what she wants, but her eyes are begging me to remain quiet. She looks like a frightened puppy—a look I've never seen on Kate before, not even when she's acting. I inch closer even though she puts her hand out like a stop sign.

I hear Jimmy and a couple of writers talking—about me. I take a deep breath and brace myself.

"Seriously, Jimmy. The notes from the studio and the network on the dailies we sent all say the same thing. They loved Elle, but they're over Kate. We saw the same sort of fallout in the last series Kate was in. Her star is descending. We need to face it. She's not the lovable child actress she once was."

Papers rustle. "Look at this," someone says. "I quote: 'Elle was my favorite part of the show. She was funny, refreshing, and adorable. I almost wish she was the main character instead of Kate.' Maybe we have something here."

They're silent for a moment, and I'm afraid they'll hear my heart pounding. Kate looks at me with wide eyes. I frown so she knows I'm not happy about what they're saying. As much as I can't stand her, I still don't like to see anybody hurt. And there couldn't possibly be anything actors hate to hear more than that their star is falling.

Jimmy finally breaks the silence. "I see what you're saying, but you all know this is Kate's show. Written *for* her. *About* her. It would be like *The Fresh Prince of Bel-Air* without the Fresh Prince. No one knows Ellie."

I recognize the showrunner's voice. "Ellie wasn't following the script very well, either. Let me rephrase that. She followed the dialogue precisely, yet somehow managed to change the character completely. Elle's personality was specifically written to balance Kate's, not compete with it."

I glance at Kate. Her expression softens, and she lets out a slow breath.

"But isn't that more interesting?" someone asks. "If it's Ellie they want…"

Kate pales.

"I don't know," Jimmy says. "Two strong girls in the same show? Would they even be friends in real life?"

"It's never been done before. And there's a reason for that," a studio exec says. "Who will bear the brunt of the jokes?"

The showrunner laughs. "Logan."

"I've got another idea," Jimmy says. "Of course Logan's the buffoon of the show, but why not work with the natural tendencies of both girls to add conflict? They *are* different. Let's be frank—we all know Kate has turned into a monster. Ellie is sweet but no pushover. She'll grow in popularity if the series gets picked up. Then we'll do a spin-off if it tanks—with Elle as the lead."

There are good reasons why people shouldn't eavesdrop. Kate has gone from white to red to green. I reach out to touch her arm, but she pushes my hand away. I need to walk in and interrupt them so Jimmy doesn't dig himself in any deeper. I walk toward the door, but Kate grabs me and pulls me down the hall. I guess that works too. We turn the corner.

"If you breathe a word of this to anyone," she hisses and squeezes my arm, "I swear I'll—"

I pull away. "Listen, Kate, I'm not going to tell anyone." At least she's not crying. I can admire that. "Let's just pretend this never happened."

Kate's icy-blues stare daggers at me. "I have a lot of power in this town. I got you into this show, and I can take you out."

She used to have leverage, that's true. But like Dad always says, Hollywood is new every day. It always operates under the law of *what have you done for me lately*? "I didn't ask to be in the show. I'll see you on set." I turn to walk away.

Kate grabs my arm again. "Wait, Ellie, I'm sorry. We've been friends a long time…"

Friends? Wasn't it just a few days ago that she pretended to barely know me?

"We can work this out. Together. I can help you."

Kate's quick change proves how desperate she is. As much as she talks a big game, she clearly needs this show to succeed. Maybe even more than I do.

I need to think. I need air. There is nothing I would rather do than tell Kate to jump off the fake bridge on stage two, but this pilot has to be picked up. For Dad. For me.

"You have nothing to worry about." I pull my arm from her grasp and walk toward the exit. Isa enters through the door before I can get out, and the hairs on my arms stand on end. If Kate tells her mom about this, I'm doomed. I wave my hand and squeak out a pathetic "hi" as I pass her in the hallway.

As soon as I get outside, I jog to our trailer, hoping I don't run into anyone else on the way. It's still early, so I sit in the trailer waiting for my call time, debating how I should play Elle. I could do what I am supposed do—act the part the way it was originally envisioned, be the nerd Kate wants me to be. But now that I know how the network executives feel about my character, I need to handle this right. All I want is for the show to get picked up—but without me in it. Is that too much to ask?

Visions of lettuce leaves and hunched-over backs flood my mind. Breaking glass and slammed doors. Angry words and endless guilt trips. Dad with sad, empty eyes. I can't move to Salinas. I'll run away if I have to.

There's a knock at the door. Call time. I open it to find Logan standing there. Before I can get a word out, he slips in and shuts the door. "Hey," he says. "Can I come in?"

"You're already in, aren't you?"

He laughs and scans our trailer. Papers and books are piled on every flat surface. Dog dishes and bags of various animal foods line the walls. It occurs to me that no one ever comes in here, and I'm glad they don't. My cheeks feel hot.

"I need to talk to you." He runs his hands through his hair.

I pick a pile of clutter off the bench in the breakfast nook and motion for him to sit. "Speak," I say, like I'm giving a command to a dog.

Logan grabs my hand. "Sit with me."

I sit a few inches away from him, because there's not much room. "Yes?"

"I think Kate's cheating on me."

"Wow. And I thought you came to apologize. Silly me!" I take a deep breath. Why is he telling me this? And if they're broken up, how is that cheating?

"Do you know anything?" he asks, ignoring my comment.

"Me? Kate hates me. We're not exactly confidants." And besides, I don't really know anything. "I thought you weren't together anymore."

Logan runs his hands through his hair again. He stares into my eyes, making me very uncomfortable. "Can I trust you?" he asks.

"Um, sure."

"We *are* together. We're pretending not to be because Jimmy was so happy about it, but mostly because of a role I'm auditioning for, a made-for-TV movie on another network about a guy with a messed-up love life. They're hoping to make a series out of it. My agent thinks the producer will give me stronger consideration if I'm single—so the girls will think they have a chance with me." He raises his eyebrows.

I try not to laugh, but I can't help it. He really believes he's irresistible.

"What's so funny?" Logan laughs too.

"Nothing, actually." It feels like *Born in Beverly Hills* is falling apart before my eyes. "What about *this* show? You're under contract."

"Chill. I'd be shooting the movie next month while we wait to see if this show gets the green light. You know what the odds are. If this show doesn't get picked up, I need something in my back pocket."

"Of course." I exhale, wishing Dad and I had something in our back pocket. "I'm sure you have plenty of projects waiting for you."

"You have no idea. My agent screens dozens of calls a day."

I try not to roll my eyes. "If you and Kate are together, then why did you kiss me to make her jealous?"

"I didn't. I kissed you because the producer was watching."

"Well, you shouldn't have kissed me at all. That wasn't okay, Logan. I didn't even see it coming."

"Sorry. I didn't think you'd mind." He makes a sad puppy dog face.

I shake my head at him, ready to set him straight, when there's a knock on my door.

Logan makes a gesture like his neck is being slit and then waggles his finger back and forth like he's not here. Despite how angry I still am at him, it makes me want to laugh. He slinks to the back of the trailer and squats down, motioning for me to answer the door. I open it a crack.

"Report to Makeup in five." Rachel hands me an updated call sheet and a new script. "And tell Logan to stop hiding and get to stage three. Now."

"What do you mean?" My voice turns to an awkward high pitch as I try and fail to play dumb.

She shoots a pointed glance to the back of my trailer before hopping on her golf cart.

"Got it!" I shout, a little too loudly.

Logan peeks between the blinds and watches her drive away. Then he comes close to me, grabbing both my hands.

His eyes plead with mine. "If you hear or see anything, please tell me."

"You love her that much?" The words come out unexpectedly. "Sorry—"

"Love her? I thought I did. But now I just want the truth."

"Would you even recognize the truth if it hit you on the head?"

Logan looks at me like he's seeing me for the first time. "A little cynical, aren't we?" He puts his hand on the doorknob, then turns back. "I like you, Elle."

I shake my head as he slips out the door. I should still be mad at him, but he's just so clueless I can't stay angry. I look down at the day's schedule, skimming to see if I have any scenes with Cam. He has only one today, in the late afternoon, and I'm not in it. But I do have one with Kate right before. I'll definitely see him.

I scan all of replacement scenes in the schedule—all the places my predecessor filmed before the desert scene. Luckily, there weren't that many. I know there was supposed to be a scene in the beginning where Kate and I first see Cam by her pool, but I guess they need only Kate and me there to fix it. A little cutting and pasting, and it will be as if "Emily" never existed.

I want to pull my hair out. I should be working on the other side of the camera, directing Coco. But my chance to open my mouth and not get into this mess in the first place has come and gone.

WHEN KATE AND I reshoot our scenes, I play the middle ground. I try not to change my character to the point of upsetting Kate, while still adding enough spunk to please the network heads. I must be doing a good job, because the shooting goes quickly, with very few takes. We wrap for lunch, and everyone's in a jovial mood.

"I'm done for the day, right?" I confirm with Rachel.

She looks at her master list. "Yep. But stick around a while in case we need you, okay?"

Not that I'd leave anyway. I have to stay on the lot until Dad finishes with Coco.

I fold up my schedule and put it in my back pocket. Logan is sitting in a director's chair, watching me. He gets up and walks over. "Lunch at the commissary?"

I glance around the stage, looking for Cam. I was hoping he'd be hanging around by now. "I think I'll just grab something at craft."

Logan follows me to the craft services table and grabs a plate. "Everything's so healthy," he mutters.

"You haven't made any requests?" I pick up a small plastic container of fruit salad and some Greek yogurt.

"Naw. I gave up junk food." He settles on a turkey sandwich, opens it, and tosses the lettuce and tomato in the trash. He grabs a packet of mayonnaise and opens it with his teeth.

"I think I'll take this back to my trailer." I smile at him and attempt to slip away.

He squirts out the mayo and wraps up his sandwich before following me out the door. He really is like a retriever. Down, boy!

We get close to an outdoor picnic table. Better to eat here than to have him back in my trailer again. I doubt there'd be anything I could say that would stop him. "It's so beautiful out. I guess I'll eat here."

He sits next to me. Not across from me, like a normal person, but right up close. I inch away a little and open my fruit.

I see Cam walking toward our soundstage. He's wearing a white T-shirt and jeans and looks absolutely adorable. I'm so afraid he'll only say hi and keep walking, but he comes straight over. He smack-shakes Logan's hand in some kind of ritual boy greeting and then sits across from us. "Hi, Elle."

My heart skips. "Hi!"

He smiles at me, and all I see are dimples.

I smile back.

"We're done for the day," Logan says.

I wish he wouldn't use the word "we," even though what he says is technically accurate. Why can't Logan have a dentist appointment to go to or something? It's almost impossible to be alone with Cam.

Rachel must be my fairy godmother, because as soon as the thought crosses my mind, she pulls up in her golf cart. "Logan, we need you on set. Your close-up didn't turn out right. Hop on."

"That's impossible. Plus, I'm eating." Logan points to the empty piece of foil wrap where only the crusts he removed from his sandwich remain.

"Bring it with you. It has to be done now," Rachel says. "We need to set up a new scene."

Logan groans but gets on the cart with her, leaving his garbage behind. I don't know why it makes me want to laugh. Maybe that's why he landed in a sitcom.

Cam stands as they drive away. "I better get to wardrobe."

So soon? "Good luck today." I force a smile. *Please don't go yet!*

"But I wanted to ask you..." He exhales.

Yes?!

"Do you want to hang out? Like if we finish early one day?" His voice is hopeful.

Yes! "Sure."

"Okay, see you."

"Have fun." *Yay!*

I do a happy dance inside and watch him walk away.

eight

I SHOULD HAVE told Cam that finishing early—both of us, on the same day, at the same time—would be about as likely as Kate not complaining on set for more than one take. I squirm in my chair and try to focus on the latest shot playing out on the monitors. I swear we'd be finished shooting if Kate would just go with the flow, even just a little.

I've been so sure—about ten times now—that I'd hear *that's a wrap* any second. Finally, I hear something almost as good. "We'll fix it in post."

We wrap, and I check my call sheet again. The afternoon's been scratched due to a script revision. I wish I could join the writers in the writer's room and give them some of my suggestions. Not that they haven't improved the script—they have—but so many ideas keep popping into my head, and I wish I were allowed to share them with someone.

Cam's eyes meet mine from where he's standing next to Kate. He tips his head toward the exit.

"See you tomorrow!" I call out to whoever's listening and head for the door. It's a good idea to leave the premises as soon as possible, before someone changes their mind and remembers some shot they wish they had taken.

Rachel stops me and hands me the next day's call sheet. "This is tentative. Someone will get a script to you sometime tonight if all goes well." She hands one to Cam, too, but tells Logan and Kate to stay put.

"You're joking, right?" Kate says.

Logan plops down in a director's chair and winks at me.

"See you later!" I give Logan the slightest wave goodbye. It doesn't seem like a good idea to actually leave with Cam in front of everyone, so I signal him with my eyes and go out the door first. As soon as I'm out of sight, I lean against the outside wall of the stage next to ours and wait until Cam comes around the corner. I feel like grabbing his hand and dancing him off the studio lot. I stick my hands in my pockets to keep myself from touching him.

Cam looks at me with his big eyes and flashes me his nervous smile. "Spend the afternoon with me?"

I nod and grin back at him. "But we have to return these clothes to wardrobe first, or they'll kill us. I'll meet you by the picnic tables in five."

CAM IS THERE before me, leaning with his back against the table, texting someone. Since he's not looking at me, I can stare at him all I want: his dark hair still styled from the set but no longer perfect, his long lashes shading his eyes as he looks down at his phone, his broad shoulders back in his white T-shirt. He's adorable, true, but there's something else about him that makes my heart beat faster.

I plop down next to him. "What should we do?"

"Hi." He looks up from his phone. "Do you mind if we pick my nephew up from preschool? I used to do it every day for my sister until I got this job. He misses me."

I force myself to smile. "Sure!" I wasn't counting on sharing Cam with anyone—or hanging out with a preschooler—but I'll make the best of it.

Cam sends one more text and then stands. He holds his hand out to help me up. His touch makes me feel all jumpy. I need to stop reacting to everything like a puppy! I totally get how the cliché *puppy love* came into existence. I reluctantly let go of his hand as we walk toward one of the parking lots.

His car is small and probably ancient, but the white exterior looks freshly painted and clean. He unlocks the car on my side and opens the door for me. It's spotless inside and smells like mint.

"What's your nephew's name?" I ask after we've driven awhile.

"Santos."

I've never met anyone with that name before, but I've had enough Spanish lessons to know it means "saints."

"He's four. And he's really cute."

I'm sure he is, if he's related to Cam.

We stop at a red light, and Cam picks up his phone from the center console, turns it on, and hands it to me. "I have a niece too. She's a year old." The background picture is a close-up of a darling, chubby baby girl with a huge smile and a head full of dark curls. "Alma," he says, with his own gigantic smile.

Alma. *Soul*. Must be a religious family. There's also a plastic card with a picture of Jesus surrounded by a glowing halo taped to the dashboard. Cam catches me staring at it.

"It was either that or a moving plastic statue of Saint Christopher standing upright on the dashboard." He laughs. "My mom."

There's a moment of silence, like there often is whenever someone says the word "mom" in my presence. It's awkward. Moms are everywhere. Mom is a common word. But some people avoid it around me. I don't want Cam to do that. "Santos lives with you?" I ask, trying to keep the conversation going so he knows it doesn't bother me.

"Right now he does. My sister's husband lost his job, so they moved in with us. What about you? Is it just you and your dad?"

"After my mom died, my dad's younger sister—my aunt Jess—lived with us for a while. My dad paid her to be my nanny. He needed to work and said he couldn't bear to put me in day care. Not that I remember. I was three when she moved back to Salinas to marry her high school sweetheart."

"Do you see her very often?"

"Enough."

We're quiet for a minute, and I think about Aunt Jess. I'm not sure why, but I don't like being around her. She's so unhappy. Dad says it's because she's bitter, but that she wasn't always that way. He says when she lived with us, she was happy. I try to conjure up a happy Aunt Jess, but there is no happiness on the lettuce farm. Not for her or for anyone.

"Sounds like a romantic ending." Cam glances at me and then looks back at the road.

"Au contraire. I guess I shouldn't have called him her high school sweetheart. She fell in love with someone else while she was my nanny, but he broke her heart, so she ran back to her hometown and married a boy she'd dated in high school. They had two kids, but when the youngest was still a baby, the guy left her for a coworker. Left the state and didn't even pay child support. She moved back into my grandparents' house, and she's been there ever since."

"Wow. That's more like a tragedy."

Telling the story to someone else makes me realize how sad it really is. "You're right. If it were a movie, we'd have to write in a new love interest. Or have the first one come back. No one would come to see such a hopeless plot."

"Do you always think in movie terms?" Cam laughs.

"I guess I do, actually." I take in a deep breath and exhale. Cam glances at me but doesn't ask me what I'm thinking about, which is good, because it would be too hard to explain. I wish more than anything that I could rewrite Aunt Jess's life so that she wouldn't mess it up, and Mom's so that she'd still be here. But I can't. Life is not a fairy tale, not even close.

Cam pulls into a church parking lot. "This is it. Come in with me?"

"Of course." I get out of the car, still thinking about Aunt Jess and her depressing movie of a life. Dad's on the verge of casting us in her show, and I can't let that happen. I push the reel from my mind.

Inside the building, we go up to a receptionist's desk. There's a bench behind it with a row of little kids sitting on it, and all four of them run to Cam shouting his name like he's a rock star, hugging him around his knees.

"Hey there." He hugs them back and tousles their hair. Then he picks up one of the boys, the smallest one, and holds him on his hip. The boy squeezes Cam around the neck with a big smile on his face. Dimples must run in the family. He's practically a mini Cam.

Cam signs Santos out, and we head back to the car. "This is my friend Elle," Cam says. Santos looks at me with his big eyes, framed by even bigger eyelashes. I lean down to his level, and he dutifully kisses my cheek.

I smile at him. "Hi."

"*Helado!*" Santos chants as Cam secures him in the back seat. "Want to go to the *parque*, Cam?" he adds.

"We usually go to the park," Cam says to me, "and get ice cream." He smiles. "Is that okay with you? We have a routine."

We go through a drive-through and Cam orders us three soft-serve cones, which we eat in the parking lot as Santos tells us about his day between bites of ice cream. He gets some on his nose and giggles. "Cam, we made animal masks! Look in my backpack!"

While dabbing at Santos's face and hands with a napkin, Cam listens intently to every word and then reaches for the backpack. He gently pulls out a paper plate with a string stapled to the back that looks like it's supposed to be a lion. He holds it in front of his face and turns toward the back seat roaring. Santos screams, and we all laugh.

Santos kicks his feet against his car seat. "*Me toca a mí!* My turn!"

After giving Santos the mask and a good tickle, Cam pulls

out of the parking lot and heads up the hills. After a few miles, with Santos roaring—and Cam and I pretending to be afraid—we pull into a park.

"Have you ever been here?" Cam asks me as we get out of the car. "It's actually a dog park."

"No, never." I look farther up the hillside and see the Hollywood sign in the distance. A few dogs and their owners are milling around in the grassy areas, but other than that, it's pretty empty.

Santos takes off and runs straight to the playground, leaving his lion mask behind. I sit on a nearby bench and watch while Cam pushes him on the swings. Santos lets go of the chain with one of his hands every few seconds to wave at me, then quickly grabs it again. It's so cute.

A little girl is playing on the slides, and suddenly Santos wants to get off the swing and join her. Cam hoists him out of the swing and sets him down. As he dashes over to the slide, Cam walks back to me.

"He's adorable," I say.

Cam smiles, his dimples showing. "Want me to push you in the swings?"

"Yes." My heart skips.

I haven't been on a swing in forever. Cam pushes me a little, and I swing my feet back and forth. "Let me see how high I can go by myself," I tell him.

Cam sits on the swing next to me while I pump my legs as hard as I can. Cam nearly falls off the swing laughing.

"What's so funny?"

"I've never seen anyone work so hard to barely move. It's like you're swinging in slow motion!"

I let my legs dangle. In seconds, I'm already motionless. We both laugh. "This is harder than I remember." I twist the swing from side to side, and it moves closer to Cam so that our legs almost collide. Our eyes lock, and my heart pounds. I look down.

"What time do you have to be home?" Cam lets his knee touch mine and then glides back.

"I'm totally free!" It's weird to be able to say that. Ever since pilot season started, I've been occupied every second. Even before we started filming *Born in Beverly Hills*, I had so much to do on the lot. Dog sitting. Helping out on other shows. "Since Coco wasn't needed on set today, my dad went to look at a wolf cub on a ranch up in Fresno. He won't be home until late."

"A wolf cub? What for?"

"A possible show about a Native American boy who lives alone in the mountains with only a wolf as a companion."

"That's cool. But for a show, it'd be boring."

"I know. It'll never make it. But that's what it's like in television. So many shows made, so few picked up. You have to get used to putting your heart into things that come to nothing." I look into Cam's eyes. I'm putting my heart right now in his hands, and I'm scared. What if it comes to nothing too?

Santos comes running back to Cam, his eyes welling up with tears.

"What's wrong, buddy?" Cam lifts him onto his lap.

"I want my mom."

"We'll see her soon." Cam rocks the swing in a soothing motion. "What happened?"

"She called me *burro*." Santos points to the little girl.

"Are you a *burro*?"

I look at Cam. I'm in the animal business, so I know a burro is a donkey, and I know how it might be used in English to insult someone. I assume it means "stubborn," but Cam mouths the word "stupid" to me, and I frown. I can hear Grandpa Pete's voice in my head. *Stupid, stupid, stupid.* It's a popular word around the lettuce farm.

Cam turns Santos around on his lap so they're facing each other, with Santos's legs coming out the other side of the swing like a crab. "Look at me," Cam says. "You are smart."

Cam pushes off the ground hard with his legs and starts swinging higher and higher. "*Inteligente.*" He tickles Santos. "Tell me you're smart."

"I'm smart," Santos says shyly.

When they slow down, Cam stands with Santos still wrapped around him. "It doesn't matter what anyone else says you are. You decide who you are." He lets Santos slide to the ground, and he goes running back to the little girl.

I thought Cam might stop him or go with him to talk to her, but he sits back down on the swing and watches.

"That was sweet," I say.

"My mom did that with me when I was little. If we were put down by anyone, even ourselves, we had to take it back." Cam laughs. "She still does it."

We drift on the swings watching Santos and the little girl. They look like they're having fun again. Cam drags his feet along the ground. "Eat dinner at my house? And then I'll take you home?"

"I wouldn't want to impose. Your mom's not expecting me."

Cam glides his swing closer to me. "Impose? If my mom found out I didn't invite you to dinner when I had the chance, she'd never forgive me. You'll see. At my house, there's always room for more."

nine

CAM'S MOM SCOOPS a giant serving of carnitas onto my plate—for the second time. I'm about to stop her, but she looks so happy, I can't do it. There are a lot of good Mexican restaurants in LA, but I've never eaten anything as delicious as this. Anywhere.

"Gracias," I tell her. "This is so good!" She beams at me and rattles something off to Cam in Spanish.

There are nine of us squeezed around a dining room table meant for half as many people, so close our arms are practically touching. Four dining room chairs, a high chair, and four lawn chairs have been forced to fit. I scan the faces, trying to remember all the names Cam mentioned when he introduced me: his mom, Rosario, his dad, Ernesto, his sister, Carmen and her husband, Juan, Santos, baby Alma, and his grandma, whom Cam introduced only as Abuela.

Cam was telling me the truth that day in the trailer when he said he lived with a house full of people. No wonder he didn't practice out loud. There's literally nowhere to be alone.

After dinner, Cam's mom puts music on in the kitchen and dances her way back to the table to clear it. It's not Spanish music, like I would have expected, but current pop. Cam takes a stack of plates out of her hand. "Go sit down and rest, Mami. You did the cooking. We'll clean up." She smiles at him, holding both his cheeks in her hands, and then kisses him on the forehead.

I join in the cleanup, glad no one stops me because I'm a guest. Cam washes, I dry, and his sister puts the dishes away while Juan and Ernesto keep the kids occupied. Instead of resting, Cam's mom and grandma put the food away and tidy up the kitchen. The music is so loud, I wonder if the neighbors mind.

Cam and I carry the lawn chairs back outside, walking through the living room and out the sliding glass door. "Here's where I sleep," he says when we go back through the living room to get the other two chairs. I see a pillow and blanket neatly folded up on one end of the couch.

"You don't have a room?"

"I used to. It's just for a while." He shrugs. "The four of them need it more than I do."

We arrange the other two lawn chairs on the patio and then sit. Mariachi music floats from the house next door, along with the sounds of people laughing and talking in Spanish.

I feel content and at home, even though I'm about as gringa as they come. I pick up Cam's little dog and put him on my lap. He's a scruffy little mix of who-knows-what named

Paco. He's cute in the ugly kind of way that only animals can get away with. He has an overbite and three colors of wiry hair going every which way. I *love* him.

"Do you think you could train Paco to be in the movies?" Cam laughs. "He's a monster." Cam reaches over and musses up the long hair on Paco's head. "He won't listen to anybody."

"He just hasn't been trained by the right person."

We're both quiet for a minute, and then Cam scoots his chair closer to mine. "May I kiss the right person?" He leans closer to me, but instead of kissing me, he actually waits for my permission.

I freeze. It's sweet that he asked but embarrassing at the same time. Couldn't he just kiss me? Like Logan did the other day, only for the right reasons? I try to speak but nothing comes out. Instead, I let out a deep breath, and Cam kisses me on the cheek.

Paco leaps up between us and starts licking my face. I laugh nervously. "Somebody needs some obedience training." I hold Paco down and avoid Cam's eyes.

"I guess I should get you home."

"I guess," I say but I don't move.

Cam gets up, so I set Paco on the ground and stand too. For a minute, I think Cam might try to kiss me again. A real kiss. I hold my breath, but he takes my hand and leads me back into the house to say goodbye.

WE GET TO my neighborhood way too soon. It's already dark, and there aren't many streetlights where I live. Cam puts his brights on. "I didn't even know an area like this existed so close to the city. How much land do you have?"

"We have three acres, with a house and a barn where we keep our animals. You'll see. It's not that big." We turn a corner. "It's the next one on the right."

Cam pulls up and shuts the car off. There's no one here. Bill would have fed the animals at least an hour ago and locked up. "Come on," I tell him. "I'll let the dogs out, and then I'll give you a tour of the barn."

I take the key to our house out from under the dirt-filled but plantless flowerpot and open the front door just enough for the dogs to escape. Coco, Teddy, and Olive fly out the door and jump all over us like they haven't seen a human in decades. After I introduce Cam to Teddy and Olive, we all head to the barn. We go inside, and I take a battery-operated lantern down from the wall. "We don't turn all the lights on at night. It spooks the animals."

I show Cam our biggest stars—first Wilbur, our potbellied pig that I adore as much as a dog but Dad won't let me keep in the house anymore, and then Gus, our surly goat. Next, I show him our cow, our donkey, and our six hens and one rooster. Then I show him the aviary with our regular and exotic birds, and in the last room, the raccoons, ferrets, rabbits, two turtles, the infamous lizards, and one snake.

I take Cam out the rear door of the barn to meet our only horse, Scarlet. She trots up to the fence and whinnies, expecting a treat. "Sorry, girl." I stroke her velvety muzzle. "I don't have anything with me tonight." Cam reaches out and pats her neck, and she nuzzles him hard in the chest. I'm impressed, because he doesn't back away.

"Have you been around horses before? Most people are skittish at first." I search his adorable face, wanting so badly to reach out and touch it, because it looks as soft as Scarlet's nose.

"No, but I don't see any reason to be afraid of her." Our eyes meet, then lock, and I feel my heart melting into the sawdust we're standing on.

I get the courage to take Cam's hand and lead him to my sacred ground under the jacaranda tree. I show him the large rock that marks Belle's grave, the only dog that overlapped my life and Mom's.

Even though it's Belle's resting place, it feels like it's Mom's too. "Belle was my mom's dog, and my dad says she never left my side when I was a baby. She died when I was seven, and I was so upset I cried for days." I think I pretty much stopped crying in general after that, because I used up all my tears.

Cam puts his arm around me, pulling me into him, and I rest my head on his shoulder. He feels strong and safe. It's all I can do not to turn and face him. To give him another chance to kiss me.

Both of our phones sound at the same time. If it were just mine, I'd pretend I didn't hear it, but this is too loud to ignore. We dig in our pockets, the spell broken. It's a group text from Rachel with the latest script attached.

"I better get home, so we can both be prepared for tomorrow." He glances around the yard. "And I imagine there's no sleeping in around here."

"Not with our rooster," I say, laughing.

Reluctantly, I walk Cam to his car. "Thanks for bringing me home."

"Thanks for showing me everything."

We both stand by his car, neither one moving, in an awkward silence.

"See you tomorrow," I finally say, taking a step back.

"See you."

Cam gets in his car and closes the door, waving one last time through the closed window. I wave back and watch him drive away, wishing he had given me my first real kiss. A kiss I knew was coming.

One that actually meant something.

ten

THE STUDIO PRESSURES us to finish the pilot in the next two days. They already have a test screening set up with a public audience for next week, and the postproduction team needs time to polish everything in the editing room. With all the changes, it's already taken way longer to finish the pilot than the studio allotted for.

We film until late both nights, but Cam and I never get off at the same time. In most of the scenes, either I'm alone with Kate or he's alone with Kate. But because of Coco, I able to make an excuse to hang around the set whenever she's on the call sheet. Dad says I don't need to help him, because I'm working too much already, but I can't stay away.

I probably *should* stay away, because the script plays heavily on the budding romance between Cam and Kate, and it's hard for me to watch. I know it's just acting. There are lights and cameras and a bunch of people staring at them, but there are moments when it seems real. What if he falls for her?

On the last day of filming, I sit in the stands where studio audiences sit during live tapings instead of my usual director's chair and watch the last scene that needs to be reshot. I'm so glad it's almost over. We'll have all the free time in the world while we wait and see if our show is chosen to make some episodes for next season. Hopefully I can spend some time with Cam before Dad and I head off to Salinas for "vacation."

Logan and some other cast members are sitting around me. This last scene is between Cam and Kate. Everyone's waiting for the final wrap, because afterward there will be a mini wrap party with the whole crew.

Time to celebrate.

And then wait.

Jimmy tells Kate and Cam to get back on their marks. "Keep in mind what we're going for here," Jimmy says. "We need chemistry. Last time it was a little weak. Improvise if you have to. Roll."

The slate clicks. I've read the whole script, like I'm expected to. Everyone should understand the dynamics between every scene. This is a pivotal one. Kate is supposed to realize that she's falling for Cam even though she also has feelings for Logan's character.

It's a classic trope: Who should she pick—poor boy or rich boy?

Cam pretends to wipe some sweat from his forehead with a red bandana, although it's really just mist from a spray bottle. It's cold as ice in here.

Kate reaches up and takes the bandana from his hand and then acts as if she's dabbing sweat from his cheek. "The rose bush, it's—"

"Bella," Cam finishes, reaching for her hand. Even though I think this part of the script is as phony as it gets, I'm mesmerized by Cam's facial expressions. His eyes. The sincerity behind them. He's come out of his shell. He's actually a really good actor. I hold my breath.

They're supposed to "almost kiss." It says so right in the script. But thanks to Jimmy's permission to improvise, they slowly move closer and closer until they actually do kiss. My heart clenches, and I feel like every ounce of oxygen has left my body.

Because the one who improvises...is Cam.

He leans in, like he has in every take, but then instead of pulling back, he traces her cheekbone with his fingers gently, and then ever so softly, touches his lips to hers.

"Cut!" Jimmy shouts.

Everyone is dead silent. I force myself to exhale. This is a show. Only a show. I've been watching TV shows tape since before I knew the alphabet. I need to get a hold of myself.

I look over at Logan. At least I'm not the only one who looks gutted by the romantic stage kiss we just witnessed. He looks like he swallowed a giant chipotle pepper. Isa, on the other hand, looks thrilled.

"Well," Jimmy says. "That's one way to do it. But let's try it again the way the script was written. We'll decide later."

I can decide right now—less is more. Hasn't that always been one of Jimmy's mantras? I get up and leave the set. I can't watch it again—even without the kiss. I slide out the stage door before it's too late, while everyone is still discussing the scene and no one minds me opening it.

I walk through the lot toward our trailer as silly tears well up in my eyes, which is totally not like me. I'm reminded of a conversation I overheard years ago between Dad and Grandma when they thought I was sleeping.

"She never cries," Dad said. "Not what I expected when I found myself having to raise a girl on my own."

I remember Grandma chiding him. "Not every female is emotional." Then she laughed. "But I know what you're saying. She's like the Tin Man."

"If she only had a heart," Dad sang, and they both laughed. "I'm only joking," Dad said. "She has a big heart. Especially when it comes to animals."

I remember thinking about *The Wizard of Oz*, my mind whizzing. They don't think I have a heart? Well, at least I have courage. I think that would be more important to have in this world.

Now here I am, almost crying over absolutely nothing. I know Dad and Grandma were just kidding. Of course I have feelings. But I'm not a drama queen. I prefer comedy. I'm probably not actress material. Unless I'm typecast, limited to playing only the sarcastic comedian in a sitcom. This is so *whatever*.

I feel better and decide to turn around and go back toward our soundstage. Ellie Quinn is not a wimp.

They've already wrapped when I get there. People are hooting and hollering and giving out high fives. There's a miniparty right at the snack table, because some of the crew can't make it to the official wrap party at Jimmy's house later. I didn't even get the chance to ask Cam if he was going.

I should just ignore the kiss, find Cam, and ask him if he wants to go to Jimmy's together—like *together* together—before Kate sinks her claws into him. Before I get the chance,

Jimmy waves me over. "The president of Epic Machinations wants to meet you."

"Hello, Ellie." She shakes my hand.

"Hi, I'm Ellie," I say foolishly. She just said my name, duh.

Before I can mess up any further, Dad approaches with Coco. "Excuse me. Sorry to interrupt. Ellie, we have to go. I just got a call from Aunt Jess. It's Grandpa."

eleven

GRANDPA APPEARS FRAIL—until I look in his eyes. How does an old man dressed in a thin hospital gown, unable to even use the bathroom by himself, still seem so powerful? He used to remind me of a Rottweiler or a Doberman that's been trained to scare people—but now he's more like a Jack Russell terrier, albeit a mean one.

Aunt Jess was there when we walked in, of course, like a one-person lapdog. She probably stayed all night in that blue vinyl chair just to make sure her martyrdom was accounted for in case we somehow arrived at the hospital before she came back.

I hear a moan coming from behind the curtain in the bed next to Grandpa's. The divider is pulled completely around, giving them both privacy, but it still felt awkward passing through the other man's side to get to Grandpa's bed by the window.

"That jerk's been hollering all night," Grandpa says gruffly. "Can't get a good night's sleep around here."

Aunt Jess glares at him and puts her finger to her lips.

"I don't care if he hears me!"

My face feels hot. The poor man.

Dad holds Grandpa's hand and quickly changes the subject. "How are you feeling?"

"Terrific. That's why I'm in the hospital." Grandpa pulls his hand away.

"Ellie, get Grandpa some ice? Ask where to get it at the nurse's station." Aunt Jess hands me a tall cup. I'm glad to leave the room. The same tension that permeates the farm has now been compressed inside a ten-by-ten-foot box, making even breathing a noticeable act.

I take the cup and walk toward the nurses' station, keeping my eyes away from every open door I pass. This isn't Grandpa's first heart attack, and it's not the first time I've walked down a hospital hallway. I know that each room holds its own grief—except for where the healthy babies are born, and their moms are still alive to hold them.

It must be so much harder for Dad to step foot in a hospital. He knows firsthand what it's like to gain someone and lose someone in a place like this. I swallow hard and touch Mom's necklace.

A nurse shows me where the ice is. After I fill the cup, I have nowhere to go but back to the room, as slowly as I can manage to walk and still move. Jess feeds Grandpa some ice chips while Dad stands next to the bed. I don't want to take the last chair, so I lean against the windowsill and study everything in the room—except Grandpa.

Aunt Jess says to Dad, "Let's go to the cafeteria and get some coffee." She touches Grandpa on the shoulder. "We'll be right back."

I stand up to follow them, but she says to me, "Stay here, and text us if the doctor comes."

I nod and sit on the chair next to Grandpa's bed and try to conjure up a smile. I want to say something, or rub his arm, or pat his hand, but I'm not sure I should. He closes his eyes without trying to speak, so instead I take the blanket and pull it higher on his chest to keep him warm. He falls asleep, and I'm relieved.

WHEN WE FINALLY leave the hospital, Aunt Jess goes to pick up Brett and Annie from a friend's house while Dad and I get food for everyone. On our way to the farm, we pass field after field of produce. Migrant workers are everywhere, putting away equipment, unloading baskets, and riding away in pickup trucks as dusk sets in. They move with a weary stiffness under soiled, heavy clothing, and I feel the familiar pang of sympathy that has haunted me my entire life.

Two young girls walk along the road, reminding me of Yesenia, a girl who came to the farm with her family every harvest season. Because she was too young to work in the fields, she played in the house with me whenever Dad and I came to visit. I can still hear Grandpa's harsh voice arguing with Grandma, saying we weren't running a babysitting service. And I can still remember the year when I waited and waited, but they didn't show up. I never saw her again.

The heaviness stays with me as I set paper plates on the

table and arrange the takeout boxes of Happy Chou Chinese Food in the middle. I put a serving spoon in each one, because if I don't, Brett will take the very mouth-slobbery fork he's eating with and dig in for seconds. Not only Brett, but all of them will except for Dad. I wonder why he's not more like them, and I imagine maybe it's because of my mom. Maybe she magically transformed him in the years before I was born. It's a nice thought, so I go with it.

I divvy up the fortune cookies and then look in the fridge for something to drink. Milk doesn't seem to go with Chinese food, so I decide on ice water. There's nothing else. Odd, since usually there's enough soda around here to fill the water tower at the studio.

The ice maker has been broken for as long as I can remember, so I open the freezer to take out the ice trays, hoping they're not empty as usual. They are. Who empties an ice tray and puts it back without water? I fill them up and stick them in the freezer for later.

"The car's unpacked." Dad walks in the kitchen and puts an arm around my shoulder. "Looks good!"

He was strangely silent on the way here, which was fine with me. I can only imagine the guilt trip Aunt Jess took him on when they went for coffee, and I wouldn't want to hear it for myself. His forehead is deeply creased, his eyes tired. I know we have to be here. I know it's right. But I wish more than anything we were back at our own place. In our own lives.

Dad opens his mouth to speak but then closes it again and stares out the window. What is it about this place that feels so suffocating? It was a million times better when Grandma was still alive. It's like she took everything good and kind with her, and the whole place turned into a movie set for *The Grapes of Wrath*—or rather, *The Lettuce Heads of Wrath*.

I go back to setting the table. I hear a car pull in but don't bother turning around. My chest tightens and guilt washes over me. Aunt Jess was like a mother to me, the only mother figure I had when I was little, except for Grandma, whom I didn't see very often. It shouldn't be so hard to want to be with her.

The kids come screeching in first, followed by Aunt Jess carrying a twelve-pack of soda. *Orange soda.* The thought of it makes me nauseated. She puts a few in the freezer and the rest in the fridge. I hug Annie and then Brett.

Annie takes a teen celebrity magazine out of her messenger bag and shows it to me. "Look, Ellie. Kate's in here!"

"Where did you get that?" Jess asks her. "You know I don't like you reading that garbage."

"Let me see!" Brett grabs it out of Annie's hand, and she screams, "Give it back!" Aunt Jess does nothing. Brett runs out of the room with the magazine, and Annie flies after him.

They've been in the house for only two minutes, and they're already fighting. I storm after them. He can't just get away with it. I grab him around his waist. Animals are so much easier to control than children. I hold him while Annie tries to pull the magazine from his grip without ripping it. He won't let go, so I tickle him. I know it's the wrong thing to do. It's like I'm encouraging him to misbehave, but what other power do I have over him? He squirms and laughs enough to weaken his grip, and Annie takes the magazine and runs. Just as I was afraid of, he tears after her to get it back. Of course he does. I've made it into a game.

Dad comes to the rescue and grabs Brett around the waist, swinging him in the air. "Time to eat, buddy."

I exhale. At least Grandpa's not here to crush everyone down. I'd rather deal with Aunt Jess's permissiveness and intermittent outbursts than Grandpa's yelling and constant insults—his need to control all of us and his methods of doing so. I glance at the patch in the living room wall that's been there for years, a constant reminder of Grandpa's unpredictable rage. It's true that he's never turned it on me—not full force anyway—and he breaks and punches things, not people, but it makes me want to run and never come back.

I put my arm around Annie, and we head back to the kitchen. She tucks the rolled-up magazine under her arm and takes it to the table, where Aunt Jess promptly takes it away and shoves it under her own plate. "Get your head out of Hollywood."

Annie looks down, color spreading across her cheeks, and a pit forms in my stomach.

"Water?" Brett looks in his glass. "I hate water!"

"So dump it out." Aunt Jess scoops some rice onto her plate.

"Mom, get me some orange soda." Brett slides his water away from him, spilling on the table.

Annie says what I'm sure all of us are thinking, "Why don't you get it yourself?" He's eight years old, not two. It takes the eleven-year-old to point that out.

"Mom," Brett goes on. "Get it."

Aunt Jess gets up and goes to the freezer. Of course she does. She always gives in. Dad says it's because she can't deal with it. Can't deal with her life in general. She snatches the ice cube tray before I can stop her, and water goes flying all over her pants and the floor. She throws it down, cursing, and stomps out of the kitchen.

We're all quiet for a moment.

Brett finally breaks the silence. "Annie, get me a soda."

I can't believe it. "Don't you dare do it," I tell her. I get up and grab a roll of paper towels, feeling responsible for the water all over the floor although I don't know why.

Brett finally gets up and opens the fridge.

"Those are still warm," I say, opening up the freezer. I take out a soda can and hand it to him. Positive reinforcement. He got up. He pops the top open, and I pat him on the head like a good little dog. Maybe he can be trained after all.

I'M THE FIRST one downstairs in the morning. I'm used to waking up early to the feed the animals, but there are no animals on the lettuce farm. Not even a dog. I picture Rascal, the German shepherd mix that Grandpa put to sleep after he bit too many people, and my throat tightens. I will never forgive him for that. It wasn't Rascal's fault. Grandpa trained him to be mean by antagonizing him with sticks. I miss all the dogs so much, and I've been away from them for only one day. Even if I could bring Coco here—which I can't, because she belongs to Bill too—Aunt Jess said she doesn't want any dogs inside the house because she's allergic, which is a total lie because really, hardly anyone's allergic to poodles.

I heat up some of the leftover Chinese food, which I couldn't eat last night with all the tension, and pull up a chair. Annie's magazine is still lying upside down on the table. I might as well read up on the latest spin about Kate. I turn the magazine over and drop my fork. The headline reads "Samantha's Heartbreak." There's a huge close-up of Samantha Rey from the duo SAM, her face stricken.

I know Hollywood well enough to realize the picture might have nothing to do with the story. For all anyone knows, she could have just stubbed her toe or heard a sad story from a friend when a paparazzo just happened to have a camera ready. But the caption startles me. "Inside Scoop: Cheating Sam Breaks Samantha's Heart with Kate Montgomery."

My heart sinks—because I believe it.

He must have been the boy in the bushes with Kate at the party. Even though I saw him only from behind, I'm sure of it now. I'd had a flash of recognition that night, from his hair and his clothes, but I couldn't connect it before. I'd seen him earlier at the piano. It explains a lot—Kate's mysterious date the night after we returned from location and her strange behavior. How could she do such a thing? And how could Sam do that to Samantha? What a jerk!

"What's the latest gossip?" Dad sits down across from me.

"You're not going to believe this. Do you know SAM?"

"Sam who?"

"Sorry. Not a person Sam—SAM the singing duo. They're this really cute teenage couple, both named Sam, who formed a group. You know, like Alex and Sierra? They're actually boyfriend and girlfriend. You can tell how in love they are...were." I can tell he doesn't get it, so I try to think of an example from his era. "Like Sonny and Cher? They're super popular."

I slide him the open magazine and show him the story

about Kate. There isn't any actual photo evidence to back up the claim, just a picture of Sam and Samantha ripped in two, with a picture of Kate superimposed in the middle. Like she's splitting them apart. "If this is true, and I think it is, everyone will hate her."

"Jimmy must be having a heart attack."

"Not funny," Aunt Jess says, walking into the kitchen.

"Oops," Dad says. "You're right. Have you talked to Dad this morning?"

She pours herself a cup of coffee and sits down. "Not yet. I need to be highly caffeinated. How long can you guys stay?"

Not long. Please, Dad.

"As long as you need us." Dad leans back in his chair. "Bill has everything covered for now. After we get the results back from the pilot screening, I'll know more."

I know the time has come. We need to tell Aunt Jess the truth about the pilot, before she sees *me* in one of these magazines. I've already been on a few internet sites that Aunt Jess would never look at, but unless this pilot fails now, just being connected to Kate could push me into the celebrity news cycle in a heartbeat. Dad looks at me, and I nod.

"Honestly, Jess, I don't think we'll get picked up. But if we do, there's something you should know." He straightens his back. "Ellie's got a part in the series."

"What do you mean, 'a part'? She's directing Coco?"

"No. She's acting. Doing really well too."

I knew she wouldn't like it, but her reaction is worse than I expected. She throws her hands up in the air. "This is wrong—any way you look at it! What are you doing, Tom? Trying to ruin your daughter? Name one teenage star you know who isn't a complete disaster by their midtwenties. Just one!"

"I can name several," Dad says.

"And I wouldn't recognize any of their names, because they aren't famous enough yet to have their egos out of control! You've been in this business twenty years. You know what happens—to *all* of them."

I feel the need to interject. "It won't happen to me—"

"That's what they *all* say!" She's yelling now. She goes on to list about a dozen child and teenage performers who have gone off the deep end, alive and dead. I know she's basically right. So many of them *are* corrupted by fame. I probably wouldn't believe me either if I were her. But I could name a few who are normal, really nice people.

"Calm down, Jess," Dad says. "She's only a secondary character. It just sort of happened, and I'm sure this pilot won't get picked up. I'd bet on it. Besides, I've got good news for you..."

Dad turns to me. "I wanted to tell you first, after we found out for sure about the pilot, but with this news about Kate there's no way it will get greenlit." Dad reaches for my hand. "I'm sorry, honey, but Bill agreed to buy out our half of the business."

"What do you mean?" I knew he'd talked about the possibility before, but I never took it seriously. "What about the wolf show?"

"If it ever gets made, which I doubt, Bill will do it. There aren't enough shows being made using real animals anymore to keep both of us working full-time with all the competition."

"What about our house and the barn—and our *animals*?"

"Slow down. Bill will pay rent for the facilities. The house can stay empty for a while, until we decide to sell it."

Why wait? In case life here is unbearable? News flash: it will be.

"So you'll be coming back to Salinas?" Aunt Jess asks. Her hands are tightly clenched around her coffee cup.

"As soon as we get the official news that the pilot's been scrapped." Dad's phone beeps. He picks it up, then scrolls through his messages.

I try as hard as I can not to cry, but I can feel the tears building. I'm not the Tin Man now. I must have had a heart all along, because I can feel it breaking into kibble. This can't be happening. I look down at the magazine. If there was any hope at all of Kate's pilot being picked up, it has certainly been shattered by her home-wrecking ways.

"You don't need to look so glum about it," Jess says directly to me. "It's life. Sometimes you have to eat the crap sandwich."

I look down at my plate. I don't know where to look, or how to look, because Aunt Jess is obviously focused on my every facial expression. I pretend to eat my food, the way actors do in a restaurant scene, but there's no way I could actually eat it. I feel sick.

"You're just like him," she continues. I look over at Dad, but she corrects me. "Not like your dad—like your grandfather—only quiet about it. And I guess your mom was like that too."

When I don't ask what she means, she nods her head like I've just confirmed everything. "Quiet but stubborn."

Dad's phone rings, and I'm not surprised it's Jimmy. It was only a matter of time. They talk for a few minutes while Aunt Jess and I listen to Dad's side of the conversation. It's enough for me to know I'm leaving Salinas a lot sooner than I thought I was.

"She'll be on that flight." Dad hangs up and looks at me. "Emergency meeting at the studio tomorrow for the lead actors. That means you."

Jess harrumphs. "I thought you said she's a minor character."

"They said they need her." Dad's eyes are bloodshot, and there's stress in his voice. "I need to stay here," he says to me. "Jess and I can drop you off at the airport on our way to the hospital. Jimmy's sending a car to pick you up at LAX."

I always want to leave here as soon as possible, but not without Dad.

"Who's going to stay with her at the house?" Aunt Jess asks, as if I need a babysitter.

"I stay alone all the time."

Dad looks at me. "Once."

"Well. Once overnight. But—"

"She's only sixteen, Tom." Aunt Jess shakes her head at Dad. I'm practically seventeen, but I'm sure that doesn't matter.

"Bill is almost always there, working and taking care of the animals. And we have alarms. And dogs." Dad turns to me. "Do you want me to find someone to stay with you?"

"No. You know I'm not afraid. I'll sleep in your bed with the dogs and...a couple of other animals." I can't help smiling a little as I imagine bringing Wilbur into the house to sleep on Dad's queen-size bed with me.

"This isn't something to smile about, Ellie." Aunt Jess gets up and puts her mug in the sink. "I'm going to get ready for the *hospital*." She walks out of the kitchen.

Will this be my new abnormal? Constantly scrutinized and judged, monitored to prevent any display of happiness? I frown at Dad, and he squeezes my hand. I don't bother defending myself to Jess, and with Dad, I don't need to.

twelve

WHEN I GET to Jimmy's office, Kate is sitting at the table with her publicist, her agent, her lawyer, and Isa. Jimmy, Logan, Cam, and one of the show's producers sit on the other side of the table as if this were some sort of standoff. I wave and say hi to everyone at once, my eyes locking on Cam's. He waves and smiles at me.

I grab an empty seat at the foot of the table as the head publicist from the studio and her assistant walk in. The assistant hands an accordion file to her boss and then takes the chair next to me. Supposedly, they've come up with a plan to stop the damage the press is doing to poor little Kate. I'm probably the only one here who knows she's actually guilty.

Jimmy opens the discussion. "We'll get to the rumors about Kate in a minute, but first I'd like to go over the surveys from our sample viewers."

Rumors? I saw her in the bushes with him. And Jimmy probably had an inkling too. Why else would he tell Cam not to leave her side no matter what?

Jimmy thumbs through a stack of papers. "First, the good news. We got a sixty. That's excellent. However, they were very negative toward Kate's character. And that was *before* the breaking news about SAM."

Breaking news, all right. She broke up a couple, and a band, in one fell swoop.

"It's the writers," Kate says. "We need better material. I've done the best I can with the scripts." She crosses her arms in front of her and pouts.

"No one thinks it's *your* fault, sweetheart," Isa says.

I know the writing could improve, but I don't think it's the reason Kate comes off as a brat on the show. Maybe it's getting harder for her to hide her true character, since she doesn't seem to know how to treat people in real life.

Isa's not finished. "I told you it was a mistake to change 'the friend' character." After she says it, she looks straight at me, as if I've caused the whole problem. "She's competing with Kate. She's younger—has that sweet, *innocent* look." She says the word "innocent" like it's poison. "She's too pretty, too comedic, too…cheerful."

"What are you trying to say, *Isa*?" Kate hisses at her mom. "She's prettier than your own daughter?"

"You know exactly what I mean. Not *prettier* than you…too pretty to be your sidekick. And more attractive on camera, which I understand since she's younger, but nonetheless—"

Jimmy interrupts. "And as I told you earlier, Isa, the network loves Elle. And now we can see the test market viewers do too. I don't think that's our problem. This is about Kate's image—on and off the screen. But we'll get to that in a minute. I have more good news to relate."

He turns to Cam. "You were an instant hit. You have to read these comments." He skims through his paperwork. "Listen to this one: 'the gardener's son was dreamy, and so sweet!!!'" He looks up. "Three exclamation points! Then she wrote, 'I'd tune in every week just to watch *him*, for sure!'" He flips a page. "Here's another one: 'I love the Camilo character. I melted every time he said a word. Every time he appeared on screen! I love, love, love him!!!!' Four exclamation points and a heart scribbled next to it. I have dozens of these."

Logan sits up in his chair. "What did they say about me?"

"Don't worry, Logan, you did better than we thought you would. You had a decent likability rating. You just didn't cause quite the stir Cam did." He looks over at Kate's publicist. "Now let us hear your grand plan to turn this disaster around. We've got a strong supporting cast and a weak main character who just got messed up in the scandal of the year. How can we solve this?"

"This is bigger than just Kate. This affects everyone. The publicity departments at the studio and the network met with me this morning. I'll defer to them." She leans over and pats Kate on the hand.

The studio's head publicist rises from the table and passes out a sheet of paper. "We've written a statement to give the press. We really believe this will end the story in a matter of days."

I look down at the paper expecting to see a public apology, or at least a denial, written as if it's from Kate, but the first thing I see is a statement from Cam Rodriguez.

> Kate Montgomery and I have been dating since we began filming the pilot for *Born in Beverly Hills* in April. We're very much in love. I can promise you the allegations that Kate has been seeing Sam Beckford are completely false.

There's another statement from Kate, but I can't read any more. I'm seeing stars, and not the human kind. I can't look at Cam, even though I know it's not true. Well, it can't be completely true, but what about the kiss? Maybe something happened between them while I was gone.

The head publicist has been standing behind Cam. She puts her hand on his shoulder. "Normally, I'd have talked to you first, alone, but I know you're new to this sort of thing. I wanted Jimmy and your supporting cast to explain things to you."

"Explain what?" Cam looks around the table. "This is a lie. I didn't write this."

I breathe a sigh of relief as the producer chuckles. He says to Cam in a kind tone, "We all need to work together on this. You want *Born in Beverly Hills* to be a success, don't you?" He looks up at the publicist. "Excellent. We need to get Cam out in the public eye as soon as possible. Get him on some celebrity news shows. If they love him as much as the sample audience did, they'll believe him. His popularity and sincerity will carry Kate."

"I'm not going to release a false statement," Cam says.

The assistant chimes in, "Kate is receiving hate mail by the bushel. Fans are blowing up social media sites in outrage. She's the most despised woman in America right now."

Kate squishes her face into a snarl. "I wouldn't go that far." Then she smiles at Cam. "Please? It's almost true."

"What part of it is true, Kate?" Cam pushes his chair back.

Logan stops him from getting up. "Cam, you need to do this. For all of us."

"Why me? You're her boyfriend. Can't the two of you get back together? It'd be the perfect solution."

The network publicist says, "Not going to work. Logan doesn't have the credibility, or the sincerity, to pull this off. And no one would believe Kate was with Logan during the SAM fiasco, especially when they see this." She pulls out an eight-by-ten black-and-white photo and slaps it on the table. There's a collective gasp. It's Logan and me in what looks like a major make out session.

"This was taken at the party on the same night Sam is said to have cheated on Samantha. One of our employees took a 'selfie' from the other side of the pool and purposely angled it to get this shot. He sold it to *Meteorite News* in an exclusive, but not before sharing it through a text with another employee, who shared it with me." She slides it down the table for everyone to gawk at. "The guy who took the picture's been fired, and I contacted *Meteorite* and asked them not to publish it, which we all know is not going to happen. They've been sitting on this, but they won't wait much longer."

My stomach drops, and my face burns. Logan better explain to everyone what happened. What really happened.

Kate glares at Logan. "I guess we're even, then."

"Not even close," Logan says. "I kissed Elle because I needed to for a role. You...you actually went behind my back."

"You *needed* to? Ha!" Kate rolls her eyes.

I expect her to turn on me next, but she doesn't seem that devastated. Maybe this isn't the first time she's seen the photograph. She's probably known all along. I guess I need to explain for him. "It's not what you think—"

The publicist holds up her hand. "It doesn't matter. I don't want to hear it." She stashes the photograph back in her file. "The whole thing works to our benefit. For maximum exposure, we could use an ongoing conflict to keep us in the tabloids."

She tells us a long story of how one show she worked on had super high ratings because of a continuous feud between two female stars. "We need to take care of the 'Logan' issue, so we don't have any fans feeling sorry for him and blaming Kate. The best way to do that is to have Logan and Ellie get together. Then she and Kate can be rumored to be at odds with one another—the current girlfriend versus the ex. We accomplish everything with this scenario. Kate is forgiven for the original breakup with Logan, because he's now happily dating Ellie. Kate is redeemed about the SAM breakup, because the fans will believe she's been dating Cam the whole time, and she can ride on Cam's skyrocketing popularity. And the cherry on top: a rumored, on-set war between our two leading ladies."

She's smiling like she found the cure to a terminal illness. "We're one-upping the love triangle. We've got a love square. The only two who will never have any romantic ties will be Ellie and Cam!"

Oh yay! My heart feels like a sandbag.

Isa actually applauds the publicist. "It's genius!"

"We want all four of you out there in a big publicity

push. We want rumors. Paparazzi pictures. The works." The publicist finally sits down, her face glowing. It's a classic "plant and deny" scheme. We'll plant enough rumors to keep us in the news but deny all the negatives.

Cam looks at everyone in the room. "No."

Isa pleads with him. "Cam, darling, look at me. She's been receiving death threats."

Jimmy rolls his eyes. "You don't have to do this, Cam, but I seriously advise you to go ahead with it. If it makes you feel any better, things like this are done all the time."

Cam shakes his head, and Kate must realize she has only one card left in her pocket, because she looks at me. "Ellie, please talk to your boyfriend. Tell him it's okay."

Cam's forehead wrinkles in disbelief. "She won't do this either."

My heart clenches. He needs to understand. I can't lose this show. I can't lose my entire world and move to Salinas. "Please, Cam. Just do it."

He doesn't need to say anything. His eyes are even darker than normal, and the look on his face needs no interpretation. He stands up and leaves the room without uttering another word.

"Give him a couple of hours," Jimmy says. "I'll see if I can convince him."

"If not—threaten to fire him," Isa says.

The studio publicist rises to her feet. "Tread carefully. We can't lose him. Not unless you have another drop-dead gorgeous Latino teenage actor waiting in the wings."

I walk out the door after Cam, and Kate calls out to me, "Thanks, Elle!"

I don't look back.

I catch up with Cam and grab his arm to slow him down. "Wait."

"Is this normal to you, Elle?" His eyes are piercing.

"No. You don't understand."

"Elle, I thought you..." He stops and takes a deep breath. "You and I..."

"Cam, I don't want you to make that statement, either. The last thing I want is for you to start dating Kate for appearances. But..." I look in his eyes. "The *real* last thing I want to do is leave Los Angeles. Leave this job." *Leave you.*

He looks at me like I'm a stranger and keeps walking toward the parking lot so fast I have to practically jog to keep up. "Cam, if this pilot fails, my dad is going to sell his half of Animal Stars Inc. Our careers will be over." *I'll be forced to live out the rest of my years on a lettuce farm with mentally unstable relatives. No soft fur or wet noses pressed against my cheek.* I blink, trying to stop the tears from coming, but they won't be stopped. *We'll lose our animals, our sanity—our souls.* "I'll lose...*everything.*" A whimpering sob comes from deep inside me, and I take a long breath to keep from choking.

Cam slows down and looks at me again. Knowing him, he probably can't stand to see a girl cry, because he stops and puts his arm around me. "Let's go for a drive."

I nod my head, because I'm afraid if I speak I'll cry again, and I don't want to cry anymore. I don't want to make him feel guilty, either, like Aunt Jess would if she were me. Everything revolves around guilt with her, with Grandpa, and with Dad too, because he feels it too much and gives in because of it. Cam holds my hand and opens the car door for me. Always so sweet. He makes me feel safe, and I don't want to lose that.

We drive to Lake Hollywood Park, where we took Santos what seems like eons ago. It's dusk now, but several people and dogs are still milling around. We walk for a while in silence and then sit on a bench, the giant Hollywood sign staring down on us from high up on the hill.

A couple, obviously tourists, comes by and asks if we could take their picture with the Hollywood sign in the background. Cam does the honors while I watch. They're so excited to be as close as they are to the iconic sign, although it's still pretty far in the distance. I focus on the famous letters, and my mind is like the Frisbee I toss to the dogs, spinning, sailing, back and forth. Such a complicated place—Hollywood—a dream and a nightmare rolled into one. But I have to play by its rules, or I can't play at all.

By the time Cam sits back down, I know what I have to do. I can't let my feelings interfere with what has to be done.

"Nice people," Cam says. "A real couple. Free to be who they really are in the world. That's what I want for you and me."

"That would be great, but it's not reality."

"I think you need to check the definition of reality."

"Cam, I know you don't get this, but—"

"Don't talk down to me. I get it, I just don't need to do things their way."

"That's just it. You *do*." I put my hand over his, and he doesn't pull it away, but I feel him stiffen. I keep my eyes on the hill in front of us. "I never set out to be an actress. All I want is to be a professional animal wrangler, but with all the new digital effects in movies, our industry is shrinking. And most TV shows don't bother using animals—it just complicates things. I have no choice. Kate's show might be the only offer my dad and I have for a long time."

Cam remains completely silent. I hope he understands my logic. I have a lot at stake here. Finally, I spit it out. "I'm going to do what they asked."

"You're actually going to 'fake date' Logan Canfield?"

"Yes. And if you do the same with Kate, everything will work out." I look down and quietly add, "And we can still be together."

"Where? In some underground world I don't know about? I'm sorry, Elle, but I don't see things the way you do." He looks away from me. "Why do you let everyone mold you into what *they* want?"

The last part feels like a stake to the heart, but I *will* stand my ground. I'm saving Dad here too. I have to do what I have to do. What's wrong with a little compromise?

"You expect life to be fair, because you are, Cam. But it doesn't work that way. That's like walking into a lion's cage and being surprised when the lion tries to eat you, because you weren't going to eat him."

"They're not lions."

"That's where you're wrong."

Cam exhales. "I don't want you to lose your business. I won't quit, because I signed a contract, and I'll honor it—on my terms. If they want to fire me, they can. So you go ahead and date Logan all you want."

"I don't *want* to date him, okay? Don't be a jerk about it." I feel like pulling my hair out. "What about Kate?"

"I'm not going to release that ridiculous statement, but I won't comment if she releases hers. If any reporters ask me anything, I'll say I don't discuss my personal life. It's no one's business anyway. I'll go on as I have been with her, as friends. People can think what they want." He looks into the horizon. "It doesn't matter anymore, anyway."

I know what he means by that last part. He's done thinking of me as a potential girlfriend. Honestly, his sense of honor was endearing at first, but now it's getting a little annoying. He needs to understand—this is how things work.

"You didn't seem to mind kissing her the other day."

My words hang in the air like something from a blooper reel. A line that wasn't in the script, and there isn't an answer for.

Cam's eyes are intense, searching mine, a mixture of emotions I can't quite read. "Let's go," he finally says, standing up. "I'll give you a ride home."

WE DON'T SPEAK the entire way to my house. When we pull into my driveway, I want to cry again—for the millionth time in a week—because I thought that the next time Cam dropped me off, he'd kiss me. Instead, his hands clutch the steering wheel like a stunt man ready to drive a car off a cliff. "See you," he says, releasing a giant breath. I know if I lean over, he'll kiss me on the cheek, because Cam is Cam. But I'm no longer Ellie—I'm Elle. And Elle knows how to deal with the real world. How to face cold, hard facts.

I had to do what I had to do, but I hate what it's costing me.

thirteen

SINCE DAD IS still in Salinas, Jimmy sends a car to pick me up and get me to the lot by six the next morning. I unlock our trailer, not used to doing this alone. No Dad. No Coco. Bill has taken over as her trainer in Dad's absence, and I can't take it. She's my dog. I was supposed to help handle her in this pilot.

I know she belongs to the company—the company that's never been all ours and is soon to be none ours if I can't make this work. But to me, she's always been mine since the day we got her from the shelter, only six months old and already a wreck. I can still see her matted fur, how she flinched every time we touched her. How it took us ages to get her to trust us. A lump forms in my throat. It's what Dad and I do best. It's what he and Mom did together before me. I center Mom's necklace at the base of my throat. Dad will have to deal with this new charade to save his dream. To save us.

When I called Dad last night and told him everything, he didn't take it very well and asked me to quit. That's the problem—he's too willing to give up, to quit on us, to give in to Aunt Jess. He was especially upset about the picture of Logan and me kissing. If Dad is this upset, I can only imagine the reaction Aunt Jess will have when *Meteorite News* publishes it. I thank my unlucky stars that Dad finally relented, even if it took an hour of pleading from me and a phone call from Jimmy. I hate putting Dad through all of this, but I know it's what's best for him too. Why can't he see that?

I put my stuff down and head to makeup. I'm here to do a photo shoot with the cast for promotional materials, and then after lunch, there will be a "premiere" of the pilot at the studio theater. This could have been a fun day, but how can it be with Cam still angry at the studio—and at me? Kate will have to deal with him now. He's made it perfectly clear he's done with me.

Halfway to makeup, I run into Logan. He shoulder bumps me. "Hey, girlfriend."

"Hey." I slow down to walk with him.

"I wanted to ask you something." Logan stops. "Why did Kate call Cam your boyfriend yesterday? Is he?"

"Nope." It's true. I can't even say he *was*. He was an *almost* boyfriend. "I liked him, we hung out a couple of times, but that's it. Come on, we're going to be late." I pull him along. "How are *you* doing—with all this news about Kate?"

"I'm so over her. For real this time." He puts his arm around me.

This time *I* stop. "Logan, we're on the lot. You don't have to pretend."

"What if I'm not pretending?" He does that eyebrow wiggle thing he always does, and I can't help but laugh.

I wriggle out from under his arm and start walking again. "I thought you needed to pretend you were single. For that part you were trying to land."

"My agent promised them we'll break up before they start filming. You'll have to be the one to do it, though. I need to play the sympathy card."

"You're such a jerk."

He puts his arm around my shoulders again. "Save that for our breakup, babe. We're in our honeymoon stage."

I shake my head. Even though he's such an idiot, he cracks me up.

Logan takes his arm down but walks so close to me I'm practically tripping on him. We get to makeup, and he stops outside the door. "They don't need me for another forty-five minutes. See you later, babe." He puts his hand on his chin. "Hmm, does that feel right? Sweetheart? Honey? Pookie?"

I hit his shoulder, laughing. "Dork."

"Naw, you're definitely not a dork." He leans closer to me.

I shake my head again and open the door.

"Babe, definitely," I hear him say as he walks away.

Kate is already in one of the makeup chairs with her hair set in huge rollers, scrolling through her phone with a bored expression on her face. I leave one empty chair between us and sit. I'm glad Ricky, my favorite makeup artist, is here today. He always makes me feel better.

Ricky looks over at me. "I'll be with you in a minute. In the meantime, brush out your hair and wipe your face down with astringent."

"You work fast." Kate looks up from her cell and directs her stare at my reflection in the mirror.

"I have to," Ricky says. "I'm the only one here today."

"Not you. *Elle*." Kate gives me a wry smile. "I heard you and Logan talking."

"It's not what you think. He's just—"

"Kidding around? No one knows Logan Canfield better than I do. He likes you. It's okay, Elle. I'm happy for you. And I can get him back anytime I want to. *If* I ever want to."

She sounds calm and totally serious. I have no idea how to answer her, so I don't. I pull down my ponytail and start brushing my hair.

Kate continues. "You did me a favor yesterday. I won't forget that. We're in this together now, so let's be friends."

"I thought we were supposed to be enemies," I say. "To boost ratings."

"Frenemies are much more interesting." Kate laughs. "Seriously, though. You need me. I can teach you a lot."

That's all I need, lessons from the evil princess.

"Let these rollers cool for a few more minutes," Ricky says to Kate. "I'm going to start Ellie." Ricky takes a comb and parts my hair into sections. He grabs a roller.

"You're not going to style her hair like mine, are you?" Kate scrunches up her forehead.

"Not exactly," Ricky says. "But I need body in her hair for the shoot."

"Don't take this the wrong way, Elle, but you need your own signature look." Kate smiles at both of us. "Ricky, why don't you make your life easier and give her one of those slick ponytails? All plastered back with gel."

I hate that look.

Ricky holds my hair back and looks at my face in the mirror. I try to send a message with my eyes. *Please no!*

Looking up at the clock, Ricky sighs. "I am short on help today. Let's go for it."

Kate sits back in her chair with a satisfied look on her face. "You're going to love it." She picks up a magazine and starts flipping through it. "Now I'll start brainstorming a new fashion look for you."

"That's okay. I'm sure Jimmy will make sure I get the right clothes." I take a deep breath. I feel like telling Kate to mind her own business, but having her as a "friend" is better than butting heads with her all day.

Kate's face softens. "It's the least I can do. Did you hear about the plan for the Golden Globes next week? I've got three dresses I'm deciding between. I'll let you wear one of them. You'll be stunning."

Hmm. Red flag. Why is she being so nice? "I wasn't invited to the Golden Globes."

"They didn't tell you? I'm taking Cam as my date, and Logan is taking you. We'll go separately of course. Our publicists are strategizing what each of us should say in our red-carpet interviews to get our plan rolling. The timing couldn't be better."

"Does Cam know about this?"

"Yep. We've been texting about it since yesterday. You and Cam are beyond lucky. You'll get national exposure before your first show even airs. And a few days after the Globes, we have an *Inside Hollywood* interview with all four of us to promote the show." Kate checks her teeth in the mirror and then puckers her lips. "Oh, and don't forget—Saturday's my half-birthday. Party at my house!"

Half-birthday? Are you kidding me?

It's amazing. It's like she did nothing wrong. Everything is fixed for her with a magic publicity wand. And what's her real game here? Am I suddenly "in" because I did her a favor, or is she planning something even more sinister?

Kate goes back to her magazine while Ricky mists my hair with water. Next, he takes a spray gel and applies it to the top and sides of my head, spreading it with a fine comb down to the nape of my neck.

He holds my hair back with one hand and looks at me in the mirror. "I hope wardrobe doesn't kill me," he says. "You might need to wear leather with this hairstyle."

"Nonsense," Kate says. "It's classic. She can wear anything with it. But like I said, you really do need your own signature look."

I imagine she wants me to *look* as horrible as possible, no matter how "friendly" she's acting. The truth is, I don't care. I only care that we get picked up. If looking like a biker chick keeps me from moving to Salinas, so be it.

Kate puts down her magazine. "Finish me up, Ricky. I'm dying here."

Ricky brushes my hair straight back and pulls it into a ponytail so taut it hurts. "Don't worry. It'll loosen a little in a minute. Now sit tight until I finish Kate."

"Sit tight?" I laugh. "No pun intended?"

They both look at me, oblivious to the joke. "*Tight*," I try again. "My ponytail?"

"Funny," Kate says dryly. "No wonder you and Logan get along. You're both comedians."

"I should have said 'no bun' intended," I add. Ricky laughs this time, and Kate rolls her eyes. He puts the finishing touches on Kate's cheeks and then dusts her face with one last layer of powder. When they're both satisfied, she gets up to leave.

"Go dramatic on her makeup to match the hair," Kate says. "Black liquid eyeliner. Red lips."

Yep, totally sinister. And the "look" she's so kindly recommending is probably a joint mother/daughter scheme with Isa to make sure I don't look better than Kate in the promo—no matter what.

"I got this," Ricky says.

"Of course you do. Ciao! I'm off to wardrobe." She glances at me one more time. "You're welcome!"

Fake!

As soon as the door shuts behind Kate, Ricky pats me on the shoulder. "You okay with this look?"

"Whatever. I mean, I trust you."

"Don't be *whatever*, Ellie. Be you."

"Isn't that what acting is, being a character?"

"The best actresses bring a little of themselves into every role." He looks at my face carefully. "You could carry it off...the defined eye, red lip look. But I've got something else in mind. The hair is severe enough. Let's do a smoky eye with a light lip."

I bite another "whatever" back. "Sounds great!" I don't want to be whatever everyone wants me to be, but what choice do I really have? I'm trapped. Tied up like a dog on a yard stake.

When I get to the photo shoot, Logan, Kate, and Cam are laughing and horsing around. I guess Mr. Do-Good

Cam doesn't hold grudges either. Not with Logan and Kate anyway. He stops laughing when he sees me. His eyes cloud over, and he looks away quickly.

"Oh yeah." Logan whistles and eyes me up and down. "Come to daddy, babycakes."

Wardrobe did not put me in leather. Well, except for soft brown leather boots. I'm wearing a high-necked cream lace blouse and a peachy-pink flouncy skirt. My lips are the same color as my skirt, my makeup tastefully done while still striking. I should have known Ricky would pull it off. I even like the hair.

A frown flashes across Kate's face before a closed-lipped smile takes its place. She hooks her arm around Cam's. If she can't get to me through makeup, I guess she'll get to me through Cam. Cam doesn't take his arm away from Kate but leans in and kisses me quickly on the cheek. All politeness and ice. "Hey," he says.

"Hey."

I feel a wet nose nuzzle my hand and turn around. Coco! Bill stands a few feet away, holding a rolled-up leash. It should be Dad handling her. Or me. I get down at her level and pet her. My baby. I feel water building in my eyes, and I force it back. I can't ruin my makeup. It took forever to apply, and Ricky would kill me.

I wave at Bill, and he gives me an understanding look. None of this is his fault.

The photographer whistles for attention, and Bill calls out, "Heel!" Coco whips around, leaving me. I swallow hard and take my mark.

Isa struts up and purses her lips as her hawk eyes pass over me, confirming everything. She doesn't even try to fake it with me like Kate does. I watch Kate to see if she makes eye contact with Isa, but of course she doesn't—she's too good at acting to make such a rookie mistake.

The photography crew adjusts our poses and tries to get us animated. If I don't pull myself together, this will take all day. Promotional materials are taken seriously around here. "Pretend like you're having fun! You all look like someone stole your Lamborghini," the head photographer shouts, chuckling at his own joke.

Logan puts his arm around me and whispers, hot in my ear, "Lamborghinis can be replaced."

It was a very loud whisper, obviously not intended for my ears only. I ignore it but pose for the camera as if just standing next to Logan makes me deliriously happy.

Kate will not be outdone. "Let's get a shot of Cam and Logan both holding me up—horizontally. Logan gets my *feet* of course. Elle can be standing slightly off to the side since she's not of equal importance."

I am 100 percent positive that the crew would like to tell her they don't need her input and 100 percent positive they will take it. They do. Fine with me.

Cam puts both of his arms around Kate's rib cage. She glances up at him, her blonde curls flowing across his chest. She flashes her brilliant white fangs at him, then puckers up and gives him an air kiss. He smiles back at her—a genuine smile—and it guts me.

I stop looking and focus on where I'm supposed to stand. The only part of Kate's instructions the photographer changes is to have me stand behind them, not "off to the side," to keep the shot tight. Bill has Coco sit facing the camera in front of us, centered.

Logan reluctantly lifts Kate from under her knees and then pretends he can barely hold her up. "Whoa…Nelly." He grimaces and then smiles at the camera while Kate tosses her head back and fake laughs for the shot. He drops her legs without warning, and she actually kicks at him on the way down. Cam's nephew and his little preschool buddies are definitely more mature.

The photographer insists that they do the same shot with Logan holding the top part of Kate's body, because after all, in the pilot, Logan is her first love interest and Cam is still basically an unknown entity. Kate performs with equal flourish, then glares at Logan after the flashes stop.

We take several shots of the four of us arm in arm, me on the end, naturally, with Kate flanked by both her guys. Gag. Of course, it's Logan who has his arm locked with mine so that Kate and Logan, the "big" stars, are in the center. I wish it were Cam holding on to me so I could feel him close to me one more time.

Logan drops his arm from Kate when we're done with the pose and lowers the arm he has around me to my waist, pulling me in against his hip. I smile, determined to play along. Is it really torture to be given special attention by America's most adored teen actor? Cam doesn't seem to notice or care. He's not acting as "fake chipper" as the rest of us, but he certainly isn't pushing Kate away.

"We need one of me and Elle in a lip-lock!" Logan announces, dipping me back and pretending to go in for a kiss.

"We've already got *that* shot," Kate remarks. "Don't we?"

"Not part of the script," the photographer says wryly. "That's a wrap."

"See you at the screening. Ciao, ciao!" Kate waves at the whole of us and drags Cam away by the arm, clearly staking her ownership. I turn to look for Coco, but Bill has already slipped away with her, without even a ciao.

"Ready, babe?" I feel Logan's hand on my arm.

"For?"

"The screening. We can go together." His eyes are following Kate and Cam as they disappear between Soundstages eight and nine.

The screening isn't for another couple of hours, and fake deal or no deal, I need a break from Retriever-boy. "I'll see you there, bo—babe!" I pat his arm. "There's someone I need to talk to."

I wander on foot to my favorite street on the lot, a fake, quiet suburban neighborhood that looks like the happiest place on earth. Pastel-colored, wood-sided façades line the sidewalk. There are picket fences, porches with swings, and flowering trees.

I go straight to my favorite fake house and sit on the fake steps in my fake outfit to talk to my real mom—who's not really there, but I fake it anyway, like I have for years.

"Mom..." I actually whisper out loud. The street is perfectly quiet, since it's not a real place and no one is using it. "What should I do about Dad? About Grandpa?"

She doesn't answer. Maybe because the voices in my head won't let her. Aunt Jess's voice condemns me. Dad's censures me. Kate's criticizes me. Cam's convicts me, but Jimmy's convinces me.

It's no use.

THE ATMOSPHERE IS less than festive when I get to the screening. Maybe it's because my favorite members of the crew are all busy working on other shows. They can't wait around until we get picked up, and there's no guarantee they'll be part of the new crew if we do. And the people who have to wait, who will be part of the production no matter what—if we get picked up—probably didn't feel like coming all the way to the studio when they're no longer getting paid to be here.

I say hello to a few people from different departments around the studio. Jimmy invited anyone and everyone on the lot who was possibly free, and that's a good thing. The more people, the better the pilot will seem. There's nothing worse than an audience consisting of a handful of people who've already seen the dailies, done all the postproduction, and won't be able to laugh at a joke they've already heard a dozen times even if it's the funniest thing on earth.

Logan is standing at the front of the room, and as soon as he sees me, his face lights up. He excuses himself from the group of execs he's schmoozing and practically jogs up to where I am, his blond hair flopping behind him. *Down, boy.* I brace myself like he's going to jump up on me or lick my face.

"Hi, babe," he says, swinging me around. He leans in like he might kiss me on the mouth, so I turn my head and give him an air kiss on the cheek before he gets the chance. "Excited to see yourself on the big screen?"

"Thrilled," I say.

"Are you being sarcastic?" Logan looks at me quizzically, and I feel guilty. I should have a better attitude.

"No, really, I'm excited. Want to find a place to sit?"

"Seats for the cast are in the front. You're in the club now, babe."

I know what he's saying, and I never thought I'd see the day. I'm a "below the line" girl whose name is suddenly "above the line." Sometimes I don't know how to act—and I don't just mean on set. I'm used to helping actors while staying out of their way as much as possible. Now I'm one of them.

Logan walks me down the aisle with his arm around my waist, and we sit next to the actress that plays Kate's mom on the show. "How are Won and Ton?" I ask her. I haven't dog sat her two little overfed pugs since I started acting in the show. "Sorry I haven't been able to take care of them for so long."

"I think it's for the best. With age creeping up on them, and I know how that feels"—she laughs—"they're better off home with the nanny."

Jimmy sits on the other side of us, followed by a couple of studio execs. Cam and Kate come down the aisle at the same time and sit next to each other farther down the row. I can't help but wonder where they're coming from and if they came together. Are they boyfriend-and-girlfriend-together? My stomach drops, and I take a deep breath. There's nothing I can do about it.

The lights go down, and the screen comes on. A few people cheer as others rush to sit down. My palms start to feel damp, and my heart races. I'm going to see myself act, and it might be hard to watch. Heat spreads across my cheeks. Few of us have seen the final product, and I pray it's better than I'm expecting it to be.

I know from experience no one will laugh harder than the cast. Just watching themselves on screen seems to be an overwhelming delight. It's the reaction of our guests who have nothing to do with our production that interests me.

Our intro comes on, and the laughter is immediate, even though it's not particularly funny. The best part is when Coco runs up at the end. It's a weird feeling, watching myself. It's like it is and isn't me. I feel a total disconnect from the girl I see on the screen.

We get to the desert scene, and I hold my breath, wondering if they included the footage of Kate flipping out over the lizard. I hope they did, because it's truly the funniest scene in the whole pilot. Logan bursts out laughing as he watches himself put his feet up on the dashboard and refuse to get out of the car. He looks over at me, and I smile, but it's hard to laugh out loud at any of this.

Finally, we're at the part where Kate and I are sitting on the rocks with Coco, but the only thing that didn't get cut was Coco chasing the lizard and the two of us running after her. I look over at Kate, and she smirks at me. The power of the number one star in a show. I sigh and watch as we end up back at the car and she makes the phone call that will bring Cam to the rescue.

There's an obvious split where a commercial will go, then suddenly we see Cam arrive on the scene. He looks just as good on film as he does in real life, and he's beyond adorable in person. Sadness washes over me. His whole life is about to change. He will never be just Cam again. I hope he doesn't change with it.

I watch the rest of the pilot mesmerized, my mind swirling. It ends with the kiss. The kiss between Kate and Cam.

I'm not surprised—the network isn't stupid. I swallow hard as the entire theater erupts in applause. I gently put my hands together in a half-hearted clap.

Someone shouts, "I love it!" But I know the reaction from the crowd doesn't mean anything. Every viewing I've ever seen in here gets the same response. We're all a part of show business, and we support everyone's show no matter what we really think of it.

I whisper a quick goodbye to Logan and sneak out before the lights come on, thinking I can avoid everyone, but Kate follows me out.

"Hey, Elle. Stop."

What could she possibly want? She has everything now, even if the pilot tanks—a fake story in the press to rehabilitate her career, her very own frenemy, and now Cam.

"I'm heading out. My dad's out of town, so I need to get home to feed the animals." It's a lie, but it sounds good.

"We're going out to celebrate—you need to come along." Kate squints at me in the sunlight.

This dumb "appearances" thing again? Haven't I done enough? "No, I can't."

Kate shakes her head at me. "Why do you sabotage everything? You didn't play the part as it was written. You kiss my boyfriend in public. You somehow manage to get Ricky to doll you up like you're the main attraction for the promo shoot. Do you want this pilot to fail?"

"No, I don't it want it to fail, Kate. That's the only reason I'm here at all. If you must know, I couldn't care less about acting—or this pilot—but I want it greenlit even more than you do."

"Why?" Kate puts her hands on her hips and waits for me

to speak, but I can't get the words out. Cam comes up behind her, and I know just what to do.

"He can tell you. He knows my reasons."

I lock eyes with Cam. He has every reason to be mad at me, but his eyes hold more pity than anything else.

Pity... the last thing I want from him, or anyone.

I start walking, and I don't look back.

fourteen

BEING FORCED TO attend Kate's birthday party is bad enough, but having to arrive four hours before it actually starts is just plain cruel. Nonetheless, here I am at five o'clock in the afternoon, standing in front of the double glass doors of her Malibu mansion, holding a present, because her people sent a message to my people—or more accurately, my "person," a.k.a. Chris—asking me to hang out before the big birthday bash. I said no, but Chris insisted. He says Kate and I need to bond.

I turn and look at the driver, who is waiting for me to go inside. This is so weird. If she really wanted to hang out with me, why didn't she ask me herself? I feel like getting back in the car and asking the driver to take me home, but instead, I ring the doorbell.

Hairy gets to the door first. He's barking like crazy, and I can see his tail wagging through the distorted glass. An umbrella handle pushes him away, and the door opens.

"Good afternoon. Elle?" A maid in a classic black-and-white uniform holds the door open while at the same time batting at Hairy with the umbrella. "Come in."

Hairy twirls in frantic circles, barking while she tries to quiet him. I hand the present to the maid and reach down to pick him up, which is only rewarding his bad behavior, but hey, I'm not here to train him. He licks me wildly all over my face while the maid looks on in horror.

"It's okay. Hairy and I go way back," I tell her.

"Kate said to send you to her room. Up the stairs, go right, third door on the left."

"Thanks. Can I bring Hairy?"

"Be my guest."

I carry Hairy up the giant marble double staircase. I go to the right, count three doors, and knock. "Come in!" Kate shouts from inside.

I push the door open and set Hairy down. He runs to the bed where Kate is propped up with her laptop against a huge white upholstered headboard. She pulls Hairy up on the bed. I know I don't have much experience "hanging out" at a friend's house—even though I can hardly call Kate a friend—but this is so awkward. Why in the world has she summoned me? To gossip while we braid each other's hair?

Kate closes her laptop. "What are you doing here?"

I open my mouth to speak, but before I get anything out, Kate bursts out laughing. "I'm just kidding. Have a seat." She motions to the bed.

I sit on the side, my legs dangling over. Hairy jumps all over me, so I hold him on my lap.

Kate crosses her legs and leans toward me. "The first thing

we're going to do is plan what to wear to the Globes." She gets up and goes into her huge walk-in closet, or rather, her adjacent room for clothes. "Shut your eyes," she calls out.

I only partially close them as Kate rolls out a garment rack holding three designer gowns. "I've got it down to two now, and I need only one backup. It's between the Versace and the vintage Chanel. Open your eyes."

I can't even feign interest. "They're open."

"So that means…you can wear…this one!" Kate hands me a long silvery gown. "It will go perfect with your gray eyes." I take it from her and examine it. There has to be something embarrassing about it. Or a trick seam that will unravel with the slightest tug. Surprisingly, it looks fine. It's actually gorgeous.

"Well, try it on." Kate goes back into her closet. "I'll find you some shoes to go with it. How lucky for you that we wear the same size in *everything*. Well, almost everything. I'm sure my bras would be too big for you."

I look down at my chest and frown. "*Whatever.*"

I quickly remove my clothes and step into the dress before Kate has a chance to come back with the shoes. She emerges with a pair of silver stilettos and tosses them on the bed. "Turn around." She zips up the back of the dress and then tugs at the waist.

"Fits like a glove. Here, come have a look." She drags me over to the enormous three-way mirror in the corner of her room. It allows a complete view from every angle.

"It's perfect for you. You're welcome." Kate retrieves the stilettos and shoves them at me. "Put these on, and we'll see if you need it hemmed."

I put the shoes on and turn back and forth in front of the mirror. It's still a tiny bit too long.

"I can have it fixed for you. We'll get ready together here before the show. Just come over in sweats, and I'll have everything ready."

It sounds like a setup. I'll come and the dress won't be finished. The one she'll replace it with will be hideous. Does it matter? "Sure," I say. "What time should I come?"

"Be here by ten. Believe me, it'll take at least that long to get ready." Kate calls someone on her cell. "We're ready for our snack now." She hangs up without a goodbye.

Within minutes, the same maid that answered the door comes in with a tray of fruit, cheese, nuts, and lemon ice water. She sets it on the coffee table in the sitting area and walks immediately back out of the room. Kate doesn't thank her, so I yell toward the door, "Thanks!"

Kate hands me one of the glasses and then picks up the other. "Cheers!" she says. "Here's to a new friendship."

I clank my glass against hers and take a tiny sip, wondering if there's poison in it.

"Why are you being so nice to me?" There. I said it.

"I told you, we're friends now. And trust me, you're going to need me. You're about to walk your first red carpet."

"Chris said he was going to tutor me on that."

"Chris?" Kate sets her glass down and starts putting fruit on a small plate. "He's a guy. Guys have different rules. The studio execs were idiots to give you a man as a handler."

"He's—"

"He's a doll!" Kate pops a grape in her mouth. I wait as she eats it. "But listen, you need to be prepared. I wish this was the Teen Choice Awards or something to ease you in, but this is the Golden Globes. If you aren't red-carpet ready, you'll be humiliated."

I'm hungry, so I make myself a plate and sit on the floor with Hairy. I feel pretty certain now that Kate isn't trying to poison me. "How so?"

"Have you ever watched any of the entertainment shows the day after an awards ceremony?" Kate continues. "Either your dress was too safe, or it looked ridiculous. They'll rip apart your hairstyle, your choice of accessories. It used to be if you were a teen star, they'd go easy on you, but not anymore. Did you hear what they said about Teresa Biltmore after the Oscars last year?"

"No."

"She wore a multicolored ruffled dress, and Deidra Hendrix quipped, 'Blindfold the kids and find a stick!'"

"Wow. That's mean."

"There is no 'mean' in Hollywood." She pauses. "Except for my mother." Kate laughs when she says it, but her voice catches on the words. "She's a witch. You're so lucky you don't have a mom breathing down your neck."

I put my plate down and get up. "What a terrible thing to say." I've done everything I can to make this pilot work, but this is too much.

"Wait." Kate grabs my arm. "I'm sorry. Please."

I pull my arm away and grab my bag. "My mom died the same day I was born. That makes me lucky?"

"I know. It slipped out. I swear, I'm sorry. I'd just rather have a dad like yours than ten moms like mine." Kate is actually crying now, so I sit back down.

I wait for her to stop crying. I have no answer to give her.

Kate rubs her eyes with the sleeve of her hoodie and sniffs. "You have no idea what it's like to be me. I can't even choose my own friends. Remember that girl from *Jet Set Vet*, Tiffany Arrington? When I was eleven, Tiffany was my best friend. Her parents cooked real food, and she even had *siblings*." Kate loses it again on the word siblings, then pulls herself together. "I spent a whole week at her house once while Isa disappeared with one of her boyfriends, and I gained three pounds. She never let me go to her house again—ever. She kept making excuses why I was 'too busy' until they stopped asking."

"How did she know you gained three pounds?"

"I had to go to her bathroom every morning before breakfast and weigh in—naked—on her scale until I was thirteen and her shrink told her it might backfire. That it might *cause* me to have weight issues instead of preventing them. But back then, she knew about every ounce I gained or lost."

I suck in a breath. I can believe anything about Isa, but I can't believe Kate is confessing all of this to me.

"I mean, Mom was right in a way. They eventually ended up moving to *the Valley*. Tiffany wears these terrible bangs now, and she's can't snag a part to save her life—"

"Kate—"

"I'm just kidding." She bumps my shoulder. "Sort of."

We laugh, but then she starts tearing up again. "Since then I've never had another *real* friend. Everyone coming tonight either wants something from me or would sell a story about me to the tabloids behind my back if it meant they got their shot at fame."

Awkwardly, I reach over and pat her arm. It's hard to feel

sympathy for Kate, but maybe that in itself is reason to try. Besides, I get it—the not-having-friends part. It's something we actually have in common.

Kate looks directly at me and sniffles. "And do you even *know* who my father is?"

The truth is, I haven't ever thought about it. I rack my brain to see if I have some memory of him ever being mentioned, but nothing comes to me.

"You don't, do you? *Nobody does.* That's because my mother pays him monthly 'child support' to stay away." A sob comes out. "He's an unsuccessful Canadian producer she had a one-night stand with back when she tried—and failed—to become an actress herself. Like I said, you have no idea what it's like to be me."

"No, I don't. But if you don't like how your mom is, why do you act like her?"

"I don't."

"Do you *not* think breaking up SAM was mean?"

Kate puts her head on her knees and then looks up. "He was a challenge. I get almost everything I want, so what I can't have is…what I want, I guess. I know how messed up that sounds."

"Yeah, it is messed up. Trust me. Do you realize how much you hurt Samantha? That was so wrong. And are you even seeing him anymore?"

She shakes her head. "As soon as somebody really likes me, I lose interest. Like with Logan."

"That's also really messed up."

Kate frowns, and I hope some of what I'm saying is getting through. I want to ask her about Cam. If she decides to pursue him, and he likes her back, he'll get hurt. Maybe I should warn him.

Hairy is curled up, sleeping at Kate's feet, and I remember she wanted to trade him in for another dog. As if he were a boyfriend she was tired of. "You kept Hairy..."

"What are you talking about?"

"You were going to give him away, remember?"

Kate rolls her eyes and pulls Hairy onto her lap. "I didn't really mean it. I just get so worked up around *Isa*—as she prefers to be called—that it's usually easier just to agree with her." She stands up. "Let's go down to the beach for a little sun. I need twenty minutes a day so I can avoid a spray tan for the Globes. Another warning for you: once a girl's spray was too orange, and Deidra was super cruel. She said she looked like an Oompa Loompa from *Charlie and the Chocolate Factory*."

I make a mental note not to let Kate spray tan me, no matter what. When we get down to the beach, we walk along the shore until we get about fifty yards from her house and then sit down by the water and look out at the horizon. The salty wind blows my hair back away from my face, and I breathe in the cool air. The waves crash softly, and seagulls float overhead. It's so peaceful.

I take a stick and draw a line in the sand and then poke the stick down as far as it will go. How ironic, since I can't seem to draw any lines that I won't cross in real life. "Don't hurt Cam," I say.

Kate looks at me. "You still like him?"

If I say yes, I'm certain it will make her want him even more. "No." I move the stick in circles, wondering if he told her everything after the preview. If he did, she hasn't let on.

"Cam's a nice guy. He's different. I'm not going to hurt him," Kate says, definitively.

I want to believe her—I really do. I only hope those aren't her famous last words.

fifteen

AFTER THE BEACH, Kate and I get ready for the party. It was *supposed* to be just Kate getting ready, but as soon as she found out I was going to wear the same outfit I showed up in, she insisted I wear something of hers. I was wearing a sundress, which is a big deal for me because I almost never wear dresses, but Kate said it was too casual. So here I am in one of her minidresses—a flashy, bright royal blue one none-theless—curling my hair with a curling iron as I wait my turn to have my makeup done by Kate's personal makeup artist.

When everything's done, I look at my reflection in the mirror. On the show and for photo shoots, I have to wear a lot of makeup for the camera, but it doesn't look very good in real life. It just looks fake. The job the makeup artist has done on me for the party makes me look totally different. I actually like it.

"You look gorgeous," Kate says. "You're welcome."

"Thank you," I say, and I mean it. She may be annoying, but getting ready with her like this has actually been fun. Maybe this is what it's like to be at a sleepover with a friend, something I never got to do when I was a kid.

"Logan's going to drool." Kate smiles at my reflection in the mirror.

I laugh. Drooling is a word I would definitely equate with Logan.

Instinctively, I touch Mom's silver heart and then catch Kate staring at it. "Do you want to wear some of my jewelry?" she asks. "I've noticed you always wear the same thing. Boooooring! You can't wear that to the Globes. No offense or anything."

"It was my mom's," I whisper and catch my breath. I can't believe I'm actually sharing such personal info with Kate.

Her eyes meet mine in the mirror, and the genuine sympathy I see in them can't be faked. "It's perfect," she says. I look away so I don't choke up.

We stay upstairs, waiting for the maid to come up and give Kate the latest report. As soon as there are at least ten guests, and Cam and Logan are among them, Kate and I will make our grand entrance. I'm wearing the highest heels I've ever worn before, so I practice walking across the carpeted floor of her bedroom.

"Walk like this," Kate says, floating across the room in even higher heels than I have on.

I try to imitate her but end up walking like a robot. We both burst out laughing.

The maid knocks on the door, and it's game on. We walk down the hall giggling. As soon as we get to the top of the stairs, Kate puts on a serious face, which only makes me crack up even more. For a second, I think she's going to get mad at me, but then she laughs as we go down the stairs, me hanging on to the railing for dear life.

Everyone has gathered in the kitchen, and we enter the room to a chorus of "Happy half-birthday!" I stand aside so the swarm of Kate's guests can get to her.

Logan saunters up to me immediately. "Kate's worked her magic on you, I see." He lifts one of my curls off my shoulder. "Make sure you don't pick up too much from her." He glances at Kate and snorts.

"Like you, for example?" I raise my eyebrows. I've never flirted much before, and I suddenly realize the power in it. For the first time, it feels like Logan's actually interested in me. Or the new me. Or the *fake* me.

Logan pulls me into his chest and whispers in my hair, "Are you sure you can handle me?"

I'm absolutely sure that I can't. While I furiously try to come up with a clever answer, Cam comes over to say hello. He's as cold as he was at the photo shoot, but as the politest guy on the planet, I expect nothing less from him than a greeting with a kiss on the cheek. He doesn't disappoint. His kiss doesn't even make contact, but mine accidently lands an inch from his mouth. I jerk away.

"You're beautiful," Cam says with so much sincerity my heart breaks. He always says things just a little differently than everybody else.

Logan puts his arm around me. "Mine, amigo."

I feel like pushing him off me, but what for? Kate doesn't wait a second before retrieving Cam. She floats over and grabs him by the hand. "I want you to meet someone." She doesn't even look at Logan and me as she drags Cam off.

"You're no match for her," Logan says.

"What are you talking about?" I force myself to laugh.

"It's written all over your face."

My cheeks grow hot. What kind of actress am I? I slip my arm through Logan's, pretending he meant something else. "Who says either one of us wants you?" I try to give him a flirtatious look, but the confidence I felt only minutes ago has evaporated. "Want to get something to eat?"

"I'll let you feed me grapes."

I laugh. For real this time. How does Logan say something so observant one moment and then come up with something so ridiculous the next? "Come on. I'll throw some at you," I answer back.

Logan takes my hand. The show must go on. The food is outside at a buffet table by the pool, and it takes us about twenty minutes to get to it, because Logan stops to talk to everyone he knows, not letting go of me for a second. He introduces me to anyone I haven't met before as his girl-friend. Between how he's been treating me around the studio, our picture kissing that will be out soon in the tabloids, and now this, it almost feels like we're not acting. The lines are blurring, and I'm not sure anymore where show business ends and real life begins—or the difference between what I want and what the network wants.

As I fill my plate with food, I see Chris on the other side of the pool with his wife. They're talking to Isa and an exec-utive from the studio. I wave at Chris, and he nods at me with obvious approval. My eyes wander to Isa, whose look says just the opposite. I'm not sure if Isa is bothered by the fact that I'm wearing Kate's clothes or that I exist altogether.

After we eat and socialize for a while, Logan takes me by the hand again and leads me to a path that winds around the pool and out to the edge of the property. I can't help but wonder how many times he's done the same thing with Kate. It's late now, and a chilly ocean wind whips around us. Logan takes off his jacket and puts it around my shoulders, and then he pulls me into his arms. I turn so he can't kiss me and then rest my head on his collarbone, looking out on the moonlit waves of the Pacific.

Maybe he's not as bad as I thought he was. He is being awfully sweet. He kisses the top of my head. "Don't change too much, Elle."

It's a strange thing to say, I think, since if I don't change, I won't fit in. It makes me wonder what Logan would be like—or Kate for that matter—if they hadn't grown up in the spotlight. Do they even know what "normal" is? What it's like to walk down the street like everybody else, no one following you or taking your picture? I don't want to think about how my life—or how I—might change because of this. I'm playing the part so Dad and I won't have to give up our lives and move to Salinas, yet this role means my life will never be the same.

My cell phone buzzes. I gave it to Logan to put in his jacket pocket earlier, and even though I promised Dad I'd answer it anytime, anywhere while he's gone, I don't even look to see if it's him. Instead, I look up at Logan and think about letting him kiss me. Really kiss me, not the version of me who is just a prop, like I was the first time. Logan kisses my ear and then my cheek. All of it feels wrong, but why should it? I've lost Cam anyway, and this could turn the Logan-and-Elle-are-dating lie into the truth.

Warning bells go off in both my head and my heart. I've learned that they'll go away if you just ignore them, and if you do it enough times, they won't come back. But I'm not sure that's a good thing. Maybe Aunt Jess was right—we're all only one choice away from ruining our lives. I pull my head away just as Logan's lips come close to my mouth.

"What's the matter, pookie?" Logan leans into me.

I step back. "Just friends, okay?"

Logan bursts out laughing. "Did you recently escape from a convent? Friends kiss, Elle. Common procedure. No ties. No drama."

"Not me."

"Okaaaay." His eyebrows scrunch up, but then he rolls his eyes and seems to let it go. We hear someone shouting that it's time for cake and to gather around to sing happy half-birthday.

I start to remove Logan's jacket, but he stops me. "You can still wear it—even though you don't want to kiss me." He smirks and winks at me.

I punch him on the arm, and we walk back toward the party. He takes my hand again, and I can only imagine what we look like to everyone as we come into view. Our hair messed up by the wind, me wearing his jacket, hand in hand. Like a real couple. I purposely avoid all eye contact, which I'm sure makes me look guilty of something, but no one seems to notice or care. Especially not Cam, who is trying to light Kate's candles with a giant barbecue lighter. The breeze keeps blowing them out, and he and Kate keep laughing.

Cam asks everyone close by to build a wall with their hands around the candles to block the wind. Logan joins in, never one to be left out of anything, but I sit and watch. After Cam gets them all lit, he says, "Make a wish, Kate." His Spanish accent slips out unexpectedly, and it sounds more like *weesh*.

"Yeah, Kate, make a *weesh*," Logan repeats. Cam doesn't even notice, or if he does, pretends not to. With Logan, it's hard to tell what's mean-spirited and what's just Logan being Logan.

"I wish—"

"Shh!" Cam puts his hands on Kate's shoulders. "Don't ever wish out loud, or it won't come true."

Kate laughs. "Don't worry, Cam. My wishes always come true." She blows the candles out and then pecks him on the mouth. Everyone claps.

Except me.

Cam not only lit the candles, but he's now cutting the cake too. Next he'll probably feed her. Wasn't he the one claiming he *wouldn't* play the role of Kate's boyfriend? So that means he's either caved in or not acting. I'm not sure which is worse.

I can't wait to get out of here, but then I remember—I don't have a ride. The driver dropped me off, but he never said how I was getting home.

Logan tells Cam he wants a big corner piece with lots of frosting. I could ask Logan if he wants to leave after the cake, but I'd prefer not to be alone with him anymore. I can't trust him—or myself.

My phone buzzes again, and my heart drops. With everything going on, I forgot to see if it was Dad who called earlier. He's supposed to be coming home tomorrow. Of course it was him—he's literally the only person who calls me. I grab my phone from Logan's jacket pocket and catch it on the last ring.

"Dad?" I walk away from everyone.

"Hey, Ellie." Dad's voice is calm, but he sounds tired. "We had to take Grandpa back to the hospital tonight. He's not doing too well."

"I'm sorry, Dad," I whisper. "I'll find a way to get there."

"Listen, honey, you don't need to come, yet." Dad's voice cracks. "It's really late. Just hold tight. If he gets any worse, I'll get you a flight in the morning. You can go back to sleep. But keep your phone by you."

The music gets louder, and some of Kate's friends are dancing to, of all things, a SAM song, and whooping and hollering. I think about hitting the mute button or covering the phone with my hand.

"Where are you?"

I suck in a breath. "I'm at a party. At Kate's."

"A party?"

"She's at a party!" I hear Aunt Jess interject in the background. "You've got to be kidding me."

Dad sighs but doesn't reprimand me. "I've got to get back to Grandpa. Be wise. Love you."

When I hang up, I see it's just after midnight and that I missed two calls from Dad—the first one at a quarter after ten. If I'd have answered, I could be halfway to Salinas by now. A tear slips down my cheek. I'm not sure why I'm crying, whether it's about Grandpa, or Dad, or my own selfishness.

I know what I have to do. Grandpa could die. A terrible thought crosses my mind, that if he did, we wouldn't need to move to the farm. I choke. My heart clenches in a panic. I don't want him to die. As much as I hate every minute I have to be in that house, he has to live. I walk back toward the party. Logan is still eating cake at a table with Cam and Kate, so I sit in the empty seat next to Logan. "Are you leaving soon?" I ask. "I need a ride to a bus station."

"*A bus station?*" Logan looks at me like I've lost my mind.

"I need to get to Salinas. Family emergency."

"Is that in Mexico or something?" Kate asks.

"No. It's about five hours from here." I want to add, "it's where your food comes from," but I stop myself.

"Why don't you fly?"

"There isn't time. My grandpa...he could be dying right now. By the time flights start running in the morning, it might be too late." I will my eyes to remain dry, my voice steady.

"You're taking her, right?" Cam says to Logan.

"I don't have a car. I came with friends."

Kate makes a face. "Hello? There are drivers all around, people!"

"I'll take you." Cam stands.

"Thanks." I practically choke with gratitude. "You can just drop me off at the nearest station."

"To Salinas." Cam's eyes are intense.

Kate throws her hands up in the air. "Step up, Logan. Elle is *your* girlfriend."

Yeah, the lines have completely merged. I've got my first "real" boyfriend.

"I've got an early appointment at Spa Paradiso tomorrow. I can't reschedule. The Globes are in two days." Logan looks down at his watch. "Make that tomorrow."

I look at Kate, ready for her to protest, but instead she nods like she totally gets it. "You're right. You'll never get in if you try and reschedule." She should know. And what could be more important than a facial before hitting the red carpet? Evidently nothing, even if you're a guy.

Kate sighs and grabs Cam's hand. "Take her in my Mercedes. No offense, but it'd take twice as long to get there in your car." She looks at me and then back at Cam, not letting go of him. "But hurry back."

"Thank you," I whisper.

Kate doesn't answer or even smile. Does she actually have genuine feelings for him?

Logan takes my hand in his, copying Kate. "I'm sorry, pookie. If I didn't have that appointment at eleven o'clock in the freaking morning, I'd have my driver take you."

I give him a weak smile and stand. He looks at me as if everything he's saying makes perfect sense. As I'm walking away he yells, "Elle, wait!"

Has he changed his mind? I turn around.

"Can I have my jacket back?"

Wow. I take my phone out of the pocket and toss him his jacket. Kate doesn't look very happy, but she leads us into the house and gets her car keys.

A few minutes later, Cam and I plug the address into the GPS of Kate's Mercedes-Benz. Estimated time of arrival: 5:30 a.m. As we pull away from Kate's compound and make our way to the Pacific Coast Highway, I'm afraid I'll fall asleep, and I don't want to.

I need to stay vigilant.

I close my eyes, just for a moment, and pray that Grandpa will live.

sixteen

"**YOU WANT TO** talk about it?" Cam takes his eyes off the road and looks at me.

Talk about what? You and me? You and Kate? I feel shy around him now, as if I no longer know him. I finally have him all to myself for the next five hours—exactly what I wanted during all those endless days on set—and I don't even know what to say.

"How long has your grandpa been sick?" Cam reaches over and touches my shoulder before putting his hand back on the steering wheel.

I know he's only comforting me, but if we were in Dad's pickup truck with the bench seat, I don't think I could resist sliding all the way over. "Since my grandma died a few years ago. She always made sure he ate right and took his blood pressure medicine."

"He's probably sick from a broken heart. From losing her."

I should be touched by Cam's romanticism, but instead I want to laugh. Grandpa doesn't have a heart. A long-forgotten image of Grandma and Grandpa dancing in the kitchen floats into my mind. He was as gruff with her as he is with everyone else, but I guess it's true—she could soften him like no one else. "Maybe you're right."

"Who takes care of him now?"

"My aunt tries, but he's stubborn. And with his age... and the stress of the farm..." I swallow hard. It's like I'm making the same arguments Aunt Jess does when she pressures Dad to help her.

"Why doesn't he sell it?"

"My dad has been asking him to for years. His answer is always the same, 'When pigs fly.'"

Cam laughs. "You mean cows?"

I look at him. "It's a saying, meaning it's not going to happen."

"In Spanish we say, '*El día que las vacas vuelen*,' the day cows fly."

I laugh, too, imagining a herd of cows with wings gliding through the sky. I put my head back against the seat and close my eyes. It's hard to open them again, but I do. I don't want to miss a minute with Cam.

"You should sleep," Cam says.

"No, I need to keep you awake."

"I'm fine." Cam glances at me. "I can tell you're tired."

"I'm okay." I feel like resting my head on his shoulder, and I wonder what he'd do if I did. I need to snap out of it. I can't repay Kate's kindness by going after her boyfriend—if that's what he is now—in her car, when she's doing me a favor. I do my best to keep my eyes open, but after a while my head is bobbing, and I find myself nodding in and out.

"Ellie, please." Cam takes off his jacket, one arm at a time, and tosses it to me. "Ball it into a pillow and get comfortable. Everything will seem worse when you get there if you don't get some rest."

Reluctantly, I form a makeshift pillow and lean it against the door. I see Cam reach for the armrest on the driver's side and click on the lock sign, double checking the doors. My heart melts. I stare at his profile in the dark, as adorable as ever.

He looks back at me and smiles. "Good night."

I curl up with my legs on the seat and put my head on his jacket. I don't know how I'll be able to sleep, because all I can do is breathe in his scent: laundry soap with a hint of men's cologne, and the slight smell of smoke from the firepit. I feel like I'm cuddling with him, like I'm already dreaming. "Thanks, Cam. For doing this..."

He reaches over and pats my foot. I close my eyes and let myself fall.

"WE'RE HERE." Cam jiggles my shoulder gently to wake me up.

I keep my eyes closed a few seconds longer, wishing he would kiss me awake like Sleeping Beauty. Time to face reality. He's not my boyfriend. He did me a favor, because that's who he is—a full-fledged Boy Scout. I sit up. "Sorry I slept so long."

"You needed it." Cam looks out the windshield at the hospital. "Do you want me to go in with you?"

I want to say yes, but instead I say, "You better get Kate's car back to her."

Cam glances at me but looks away again as soon as our eyes meet. "I'll wait here until you text me. In case they left… or something," he says quietly.

Or something? If I need you? If I'm too late? "You should take a nap."

"I will, right here, until you let me know everything's all right."

"Okay." I open the door and grab my purse. I look ridiculous in a wrinkled cocktail dress this early in the morning, but does anyone care about rumpled dirty clothes when someone might be dying? I run my fingers through my hair in a hopeless attempt to look presentable and get out.

I walk into the front entrance of the hospital and show my ID at the desk. The receptionist looks for Grandpa's name on the computer and writes his room number on a badge for me. There's no good place to pin it on an open-shoulder garment, so I attach it to the top of the bodice and shiver. It's cold in here. I take the elevator to the third floor. Every step feels like it takes an eternity.

When I get to the room, I see only Jess and Grandpa. I stop at the door to assess the situation and watch to see if his chest is moving. His skin reminds me of a colorless lettuce leaf, veiny and translucent. I look to the machines he's hooked up to. It shows a heartbeat. I made it.

I remain silent and walk in. Jess turns and sees me, her eyes narrowing as she notices what I'm wearing. I hug her, and she hugs me back for only a second, her body stiff. "Don't wake him up," she mouths.

I nod.

Jess takes my arm and leads me out into the hallway. "Your dad's somewhere in the hospital on his laptop, looking for a plane ticket for you. Probably the cafeteria. You better stop him before he buys something."

"Okay. I'll text him. How's Grandpa?"

"He needs some sleep. If he wakes up, you can talk to him." Jess shakes her head. "Why in the world would you show up here wearing that?" She gestures to my flashy, over-the-top minidress.

"I'm sorry. I was at a birthday party."

Jess lets out a deep sigh, shakes her head again, and goes back into Grandpa's room. I'm just as embarrassed as she is by my appearance, but there's nothing I can do about it now.

I stay in the hallway and text Dad. Then I text Cam and tell him he can go. Cam doesn't reply, but Dad does. "I'm in the chapel. First floor." I look in Grandpa's room at Aunt Jess but decide not to disturb her.

I make my way to the elevator and take it back down to the lobby to look for the chapel. I see signs pointing to the right, past the front door. But Cam still hasn't answered, so I go back out into the parking lot to tell him he can leave.

When I get to the car, I find Cam sound asleep with the windows open. There's perspiration on his forehead, even though it's still the coolest part of the day. I open the door, and the alarm goes off. I jump in, pull the key out of ignition, and shut it off.

"That's one way to wake a guy up." Cam sits up and runs his fingers through his hair. "How is he?"

"Still with us. Thank you for getting me here. I guess it wasn't an emergency after all."

"That's good."

"Sorry to make you drive all this way in the middle of the night." *And take you away from Kate.*

"Don't worry about it. I'm just glad your grandpa's okay." Cam squeezes my hand. He's always touching me, and I wish he wouldn't. Doesn't he have any idea how much I like him?

"You can go now. I'm going to spend the day here. If everything stays the same, I'll fly back tonight. The studio would have a fit if I missed the Golden Globes."

"Elle..." Cam shakes his head. "They don't own you."

"My grandpa's fine." I'm not sure that's true, but suddenly I want to leave as urgently as I wanted to come. I'm hoping he'll say he'll wait for me. That we can ride back together. It's selfish of me to keep him here, but what if there's a way we can start over?

He doesn't say anything, so I remind him that he hasn't slept very much. It's true. I don't like to think of him driving back alone, tired. "I think you should stay for a while. You could go back to the farm and sleep."

Cam looks at me for the longest time. Sometimes I wonder if he knows what appropriate eye contact is. His eyes are deep and unreadable. I'm the first to look away. I glance back at the hospital and take a deep breath, willing him to say yes.

"I've got to get back." Cam puts his hand on the steering wheel, like he's ready to take off if I'd just get out of the car.

I lean over and kiss his cheek, closing my eyes, wishing this were a movie. If it was, he'd pull me into his arms and tell me he loves me. That Kate doesn't mean anything to him.

"See you tomorrow. Thanks again." I put my hand on the door slowly, still hoping.

"De nada. It's nothing. See you." Cam starts the car.

It's nothing. *De nada.* One of the first things my tutor taught me in Spanish class. The equivalent of *you're welcome.* It feels like he means that we are nothing, that him taking me here means nothing.

I finally manage to open the door. I can't move any slower. I get out, close the door, and wave. Cam waves and then turns to enter something into the GPS. I don't look back toward the car until I'm almost ready to walk in the hospital doors. When I do turn and look, I see that Cam is watching me, waiting for me to go inside. We both wave, and he finally backs out of the parking space and pulls away.

I go in, and the automatic doors close behind me, cementing that it's too late to say the things I want to say. The attendant nods at me when I point to my badge. My face feels hot as I realize how lame that was—like he's going to forget a girl in a shiny royal blue cocktail dress who stepped outside for a minute.

When I pass by the gift shop, I remember Chris said today was the day *Meteorite* was releasing the pictures of Logan kissing me. There's a newsstand just inside the door of the shop, so I force myself to go inside and look for it. Even though I can't stand the thought of it, I might as well see it for myself. I pick up the latest issue. Thankfully, it's not the front-page story. I scan the article titles splashed across the cover and find "Inside: Logan Canfield's Secret Love Affair." I flip through the magazine until I come to the picture. It's grainy, and you can't see me very well, but I know infamy spreads as fast as fame. Probably faster. The caption reads, "An insider on the set of *Born in Beverly Hills* confirms that

Logan's mystery girl is Elle Quinn. According to a source close to the couple, Elle stole him right out from under Kate's nose." No one outside the studio has seen me on TV, but my name and image have already been plastered on internet gossip sites for the last couple of weeks, and now this. I buy a copy and shove it my bag.

The chapel is only a few steps away from the gift shop, so I stop and lean against the wall before I go in, trying to pull myself together. The attention in the press will go away if there's nothing more to feed it. It's not too late to reverse this. Taking a deep breath, I slowly open the chapel door and peek inside. The place is empty, except for Dad sitting in the first row with his head down, like he's praying. I walk down the center aisle and sit next to him.

Dad reaches over and grabs my hand, and we lock eyes. His are pink and watery. He doesn't say a word about my attire, but that's so him. He knows me. Trusts me. My heart clenches. In all the times Grandpa has been in here, I've never seen Dad like this. "Did you talk to him?" he asks me.

"He's sleeping." I stare at the stained-glass window. "Dad, I need to tell you something." I take in a breath and exhale. "If the network passes on the show...it's okay if we move here." I don't really mean it's *okay*, it would never be okay, but I'd do it for Dad.

He hugs me but doesn't answer. Maybe he's shocked. "Come on. Let's go see him." Dad holds his hand out to me. "Seeing his granddaughter in such a pretty dress should cheer him up."

His comment makes me feel worse. It's the sweetest thing he could possibly say—and the exact opposite of Aunt Jess's reaction. It's been about two seconds since I agreed to move to Salinas, and thinking of her response makes me realize I made an obvious mistake. But I can't take it back now. Not under the circumstances.

Grandpa opens his eyes and looks at me, and then he closes them again. At least he knows I came. The doctor comes and checks on him. When he finishes his examination, he asks Dad and Jess to go out into the hallway. I follow them.

Dad puts his arm around me. "Dr. Richards, this is my daughter. Pete's granddaughter."

Dr. Richard shakes my hand and then looks at Dad and Jess. "His blood pressure is back to normal. I think he'll be all right if he stays on his medication and takes care of himself."

If we take care of him, he means.

"We'll keep him a couple more days to make sure everything's under control."

Nothing is under control, I realize. Not under my control. Or Dad's. Or anyone's, ever.

An orderly wheels Grandpa out of the room to get some tests done. I tell Dad and Jess that I'm going down to the cafeteria to get something to eat, even though I'm not really hungry. I need to think. I meant what I said to Dad in the chapel, but I still know it would be a mistake.

I buy a fruit cup and a bagel for Dad—poppy seed with a slab of butter, just the way he likes it—and head back to Grandpa's room. Every solution I come up with seems futile, as if there's no way out of the inevitable.

When I come back up, I stop as I hear Aunt Jess and Dad arguing in the room.

"If we sell it now, Brett will never get the chance to own

it—because you're being selfish. We need to hold on to it. It's been in the family for four generations, and you just want to throw it away."

"He's eight years old. How do you know he'll even want it when he grows up?"

"Well, I'd like him to have the choice!"

"What about what Ellie wants?"

"Open your eyes, Tom. She'd be better off. Do you see how she came in here this morning? Do what's best for your daughter for once."

"Really, Jess? I've always done what's best for Ellie—from day *one*." Dad chokes on his words, and I know he must be thinking about how he let Mom choose for me to live, even though it cost her her life. I've always known it, even though no one talks about it.

"And look at what that cost. Did either of you consider what a terrible burden living with that guilt might be for her?"

"She didn't ask to be born. How could it ever be her fault?"

"I know that. You know that. But it can't be easy for her."

My stomach twists, and I feel sick. I've always known that my mom died giving birth to me, but Dad never let me see it as my fault. I turn and leave and go back to the elevator. I push the button and wait. It seems like it's taking forever. When the elevator finally opens, Grandpa is inside, ready to be wheeled out and taken back to his room.

I sigh. "Hi, Grandpa," I say and smile at the orderly. Grandpa doesn't even open his eyes, but still, I follow them back to the room. And when we get there, I smile at Dad, too, as if I didn't hear a thing.

seventeen

LOGAN AND I walk slowly toward the handler on the red carpet. She's holding a clipboard and hustles over to us. "Please pose for pictures over there"—she points to a long row of step-and-repeat screens—"and then wait for me to pass you on to Deidra."

Logan puts his arm around me. "This is going to be fun," he says. "Watch how I rile up Deidra during our interview."

"Great," I say, distracted. Even though I practiced posing in my bathroom this morning before I went to Kate's, and Kate made me practice a dozen more times as we got ready, practicing and doing are two different things. I feel fear taking over my body and turning into sheer panic. Immediately, I'm sure I'm going to look like one of those nervous, awkward people who look ridiculous as they pose in front of the dozens of cameras. The worst are the ones who look like they're trying too hard.

I think of the acronym Dad taught me about fear: False Evidence Appearing Real. My body is telling me I'm a baby antelope about to be eaten by a pack of lions, but it's not true. I'm a girl, in a very pretty dress, who is perfectly fine. I'm standing in front of some vinyl paper screens, not the jungle. Some other humans have a job to do, which is to point glass and plastic apparatuses at me and click while I smile and pose. No big deal.

I take deep breaths in and out and stride hand in hand with Logan to the screens. A complete calm comes over me, and I smile at everyone. We pose together for several pictures, everyone screaming our names, and then I'm asked to step aside so Logan can have some shots alone. He is the famous one after all. I stand off to the side and watch.

A large group of fans cordoned off several yards away from us have been cheering Logan since we got out of the limo. I laugh, thinking there could be real danger for me when it comes to Logan's fans. Kate was right about that. I've already seen hate messages from jealous teenage girls about me on Twitter. It doesn't make me scared or mad. It makes me really sad to know there are girls with lives so empty that they love boys and hate girls they don't know.

And speaking of hate, I'm glad Kate doesn't hate me anymore. She was almost nice today, and she was really helpful again. She didn't try and sabotage my makeup, and the dress turned out perfect. It's weird, but I think we could actually become real friends someday. Maybe.

Isa, on the other hand, was a hovering nightmare. Kate eventually had to kick her out of her room. I thought she was going to kick her literally. It's true. It's not so easy being Kate Montgomery, daughter of Isa No-Last-Name-Required.

After every photographer gets a shot of Logan, the handler escorts us near a platform where we chat with Chase Donovan and his supermodel girlfriend, Lily Carter, while we wait for our turn with Deidra. I've never been starstruck, but now that I'm interacting with celebrities as a peer and not a peon, I find myself tongue-tied. Luckily, they're both super-friendly and nice as can be. Lily squeezes my hand goodbye when the handler comes back for them, and I watch as they climb the step to where Deidra awaits. We're next. Fear tries to return, but I successfully push it down. Deidra's claws are only words. I know words can hurt, but only if you accept them as truth. Besides, she's always nice to your face. If she wants to sink her teeth into me, it will be tomorrow on her own show.

"You can go up now." The handler nods and speaks into her headset. She nudges us along. "Logan, steady your date on the stairs, please."

Logan offers me his arm. I hold the hem of my dress up on one side so I don't step on it. We're halfway up the stairs when Deidra shrieks, "Here comes my favorite guy!"

Deidra looks into the camera, holding the microphone to her mouth. "This is the moment we've been waiting for—Logan Canfield with his new girlfriend, Eleanor Quinn. Come here, you two!"

Logan kisses Deidra on both cheeks. "You look beautiful, as always," he tells her.

Deidra beams at him. "Logan, how does it feel to be up for a Golden Globe at nineteen?"

"It's amazing."

"Talk about amazing, look at this dress!" Deidra points her microphone at me. "Who are you wearing?"

"Georgi Ivanov." Kate made me practice how to say it a dozen times, and then I double-checked with Chris in case mispronouncing it was part of some scheme of Kate's. But she was correct, and it's Chris's job to know.

"It's gorgeous! Did he make it especially for you?"

Yeah, right. You so know better. I'm glad Kate prepared me for this. Well, sort of. She told me Deidra might ask, and she told me whatever I did, to *not* tell her how I got it. She advised me to dodge the question if it came up. To joke that it was "just something I had in my closet." That doesn't sound authentic, but the authentic me vanished into thin air weeks ago. I decide to be bold and sort of tell the truth. "Borrowed from a friend!" I smile sweetly. I didn't name the friend, and no one would dream it's Kate's, except for her stylist, who obviously knows.

I can hear a voice in Deidra's earpiece telling her to break for commercial. That should do it. We'll need to move on so Deidra can prep for the next interview. But Deidra seems to ignore it—she's staring toward the limo drop-off area. I follow her eyes, expecting to see Kate. But it's Samantha. Alone. No Sam.

But that's not what makes Deidra pause. Samantha looks stunning as she steps out of the limo...wearing my dress.

"We need to go to break, but don't you two move! I'm not done with you yet!" Deidra's voice is sickly sweet, and she can barely contain her glee. It's what every celebrity reporter dreams of: a disaster unfolding on live TV. My stomach drops. So this was Kate's diabolical plan—something that would never occur to me. I wonder how she knew what Samantha was wearing, but who am I kidding? She's

Kate Montgomery, and like she said the day she gave me this dress, she always gets what she wants.

Fight or flight? How can I make the best of this? I grab Logan by the arm and whisper in his ear. "Samantha Rey is wearing the same dress I am. We need to bolt."

"Yeah, well, about fifty dudes are wearing a black tux like mine." He laughs.

I glare at him. "You know it's different. What should I do?"

"Be glad you were here first?"

Deidra has her back to us as she speaks in hushed tones on her headset. I know I have only seconds. If I disappear, it might make everything worse. I glance back at Samantha, wondering if she'll be the one to walk away, even though it was already too late the moment she stepped out of the limo. Cameras were already flashing, and the tapes were rolling.

"Back in four, three, two, one…" Deidra grabs Logan's arm and readies herself for the opening shot. "We're still here with Logan and Elle. Elle, you said you borrowed this dress from a friend? How wonderful to have friends with current designer gowns to lend. What's her name?"

I exhale. It's amazing how easily they can trip you up if you leave any opening at all. I should have stuck with Kate's line, even though now it's clear why she didn't want me to tell the truth—then the whole world would know Kate has it out for Samantha, first stealing her boyfriend, then stealing her dress. This is not the place to ad-lib. There are no second takes. No edits or voice-overs. No cutting rooms. "You don't know her." Crap. I shouldn't have lied. Not because lies are immoral, but because they are easily exposed. Chris lectured me on that very thing last week. Avoidance of questions is accepted, but lies are uncovered and thrown back in your face to embarrass you. I look for Samantha again. She's posing for the cameras in front of the screens, and there's quite an uproar as more and more people realize what's going on.

"What's happening down there?" Deidra asks coyly. The cameras focus on Samantha. "Looks like Elle and Samantha have the same friend. We might have a live version of 'Who wore it best?' on our hands." She turns back to me. "Stay right here."

My heart beats faster as I weigh my options. I could expose Kate right now on live television, but what would be the point? I actually thought we were becoming friends. Now I just want to avoid stooping to her level.

Logan is no longer standing so close to me. Feeling his body leaning into mine was comforting minutes ago, if slightly annoying. Now there's a growing gap between us. I suck in a breath as Deidra instructs her helpers to escort Samantha up on the interview platform. In one second we'll be standing side by side on live TV, wearing the exact same gown. My face starts burning.

"Have you two ever met?" Deidra asks. She holds the microphone near Samantha's mouth.

Samantha's face is flushed too, and her hands are trembling. Cameras flash all around us. She gives me a big hug and grabs hold of my hand. "You look beautiful, Elle. I love your dress!"

"It looks better on you," I say, squeezing her hand. "Congratulations on your nomination. I'm rooting for you tonight." I don't wait for permission to leave. I grab Logan's arm and start walking down the steps like it's exactly what I've been cued to do. He follows, and no one tries to stop us.

It's too loud to hear what Deidra says next to Samantha, and it doesn't really matter. Strangely, I don't care what anyone thinks. I feel a surge of elation at the thought. I look at Logan and laugh. He doesn't join me.

"You're right. That *was* embarrassing. Where did you get that dress?" Logan is walking us down the red carpet at an inappropriate clip, nodding at groups of people he knows without stopping to chat.

"Kate."

"I wonder who she was trying to hurt, you or Samantha? Or me?" He walks faster.

"Why choose only one when you can have all three? I wonder how she knew what Samantha was wearing tonight." I pull hard on his elbow to slow him down. I'm walking in stilettos, after all.

"I suppose her stylist found out and then got Kate a new dress and told her not to wear the one you're wearing. Who knows? Kate has her ways, believe me. It wouldn't be that hard. Especially for her."

He drags me inside the building to a corner. "You're not staying, are you?"

"Why would I leave?" I know this is embarrassing—I'm the one in the matching gown—but his reaction stings.

Logan shakes his head. "Well, you probably don't have a designer ball gown in your purse. And I'm not going to sit next to you all night while the cameras focus on your dress and then pan over to Samantha Rey and zoom in on hers— over and over again. I know how this works."

"Oh." I frown and look down. The sparkle on the dress, so beautiful before, now just seems to mock me.

"Hey, I'm sorry." Logan holds my chin in his hand. "Why don't you go home and change, and I'll have someone pick you up for the after-parties."

I nod my head because I can't speak. He gets on his phone and arranges for my disposal and subsequent retrieval. My eyes burn, and I squint trying to keep from crying. I force myself to think of a distraction. Kate and Cam enter the building hand in hand. Not the kind of distraction I needed. I take a deep breath.

Logan puts his phone back in his jacket. "All set. Do you mind walking back out alone? I haven't had a chance to mingle."

"No problem." My throat feels like it's closing up.

"I'll see you later on tonight, then." Logan kisses me super quick on the cheek and almost pushes me along. "Go out that side exit and look for the same driver who brought us here."

I'm barely halfway to the door before Kate grabs my arm. "Elle, I swear I had no idea. I can't believe this happened."

It doesn't take Logan more than a second to intervene. "Tell us your story later, Kate. Elle's leaving."

"She isn't going anywhere." Kate slips her arm through mine and glares at Logan. "Why would she leave?" She waves her assistant over. "My wrap, please."

The assistant opens her giant handbag and pulls out a nylon pouch. She unzips the pouch and unfolds a pale gray silk shawl with tiny beads embroidered all over it. It shimmers in the light.

Kate takes it from her and artfully wraps it around my shoulders. "Voilà. Problem solved."

Cam is standing a few yards away talking with someone. I look over at him, and our eyes meet. I look away. "Okay?" I ask Logan.

"I guess." Logan shrugs. "I know you did this on purpose, Kate."

"Believe whatever you want. I could not care less." Kate turns to me. "I had nothing to do with this." She squeezes my forearm. "I swear." Her eyes are pleading, and for a second I want to believe her. I can't say I totally bought her pretending to be my friend, but somewhere along the line, I must've started to.

Logan puts his arm through mine and glares at Kate. "Let's go to our seats."

I let him lead me to the entrance of the ballroom. An usher in a tuxedo walks us to our table. Logan was right. We will have cameras looming on us all evening. Right away my nose starts itching because I know I can't scratch it. I can't frown, roll my eyes, or make any facial expressions other than serene or happy. Chris also told me to watch every word I say because people will try to read my lips. I sit down, cross my ankles, and pull the shawl all the way across the front of my dress.

Logan leans into me and whispers in my ear, "Remember, I'm announcing the award for 'Best Original Song' tonight. While I'm up there, the camera will be panning to you constantly. If Samantha wins, you'd better look happy."

"I will be happy. I love Samantha." As I'm saying this, I see Samantha being led to her seat in another section, and I try to make eye contact. I want her to know I had nothing to do with the dress fiasco. I stare at her, but she doesn't look over.

An usher brings Cam and Kate down to their seats next to ours, and Logan stands up to hug and kiss Kate and shake Cam's hand. I wave at them but stay seated. The music starts. I glance at Cam, but just when he looks back, Logan puts his arm around me, so I look away. By the time I dare take another peek, Cam's staring straight ahead with a serious look on his face.

Logan takes his arm down from my shoulder and holds my hand. I fight the urge to pull it away. Like it or not, he is my so-called boyfriend. There's nothing I can do about it tonight, so I might as well enjoy the show.

About a half hour in, Logan gets the signal to go backstage during a commercial break. "Break a leg," I say and almost mean it literally.

A few minutes later, Logan walks onstage carrying a large golden envelope. He saunters over to the podium and cracks a few canned jokes from the teleprompter. I laugh dutifully, knowing full well I am being scrutinized, live, by millions of people. I smile until my face hurts. Logan reads the names of the nominees from a cardboard square and then opens the envelope. "And the winner is...Julia Thomas."

I clap my hands and cheer even though I'm so disappointed Samantha didn't win. Samantha's song was better, but I guess it's hard to compete with the theme song from the number one drama series this year. I glance over at Kate to see her reaction. She's clapping delicately like she doesn't mean it. Can't she be happy for someone else?

The rest of the categories fly by until we reach nearly the end. Time to see if Logan wins for "Best Supporting Actor in a Miniseries."

When they announce the nominees, I squeeze Logan's hand. It's unusually sweaty, but he seems calm.

"And the winner is…Logan Canfield!"

We stand and hug before he skips up the stairs and onto the stage. After thanking a gazillion people, he stops and looks right at me. *Don't do it, Logan. You didn't even know me when you did that miniseries.*

He holds up his little gold statue. "I'd also like to give a shout-out to Elle, my beautiful girlfriend. Having you by my side makes winning this even sweeter." He stares down at me like a lovesick puppy, but there's a certain gleam in his eye that probably goes unnoticed by everyone but me. He's teasing. I can't help but laugh out loud. Kate raises her eyebrows in a warning. I probably shouldn't laugh, but he's acting so ridiculous, it's hard not to.

Logan jogs down the stairs back to our seat. "Congratulations!" I say, hugging him. He tips me backward and kisses me on the mouth. I can't pull away on live TV when he's supposed to be my boyfriend, but I'm not laughing anymore. It doesn't feel right. It's one thing to hang out and be seen and let people imagine we're dating, but this is going too far.

I look over at Cam again, and he meets my gaze and holds it. He takes a giant breath and exhales, then purses his lips. The lips I wish were the ones kissing me. The ones that never will. I step back so Kate and Cam can congratulate Logan too. Cam shakes Logan's hand and says, "You won.

Take care of the prize." He's staring at me as he says it, and Logan punches him in the arm.

Then Cam hugs me, and it seems like he's using Logan's win as an excuse to do it. I didn't win anything, that's for sure. He holds me way too long, and I wish more than anything he didn't have to let go. I close my eyes and memorize how it feels. The soft, cool fabric of his tuxedo on my cheek. His chin touching my forehead. The smell of his hair. His hand on my back. Reluctantly, I peel myself away and sit down.

We go to a commercial break, and I feel like running away, but I have to stand my ground. I've made a terrible mistake, but I have to see it through now, no matter what.

AS SOON AS the ceremony's over, the truce I thought was genuine among the four of us falls apart. The studio insists that we attend a network gathering before we head off to the more casual after-parties all over town. It's another photo op, and since the song Samantha was nominated for was for a show on our network, she'll be there too. Kate planned our after-party outfits, but for the network party we were going to stay in our red-carpet gowns. *Were.* But because my dress is a *Who Wore It Best* nightmare, I have to change, ASAP.

"Bad news," Kate says to me as the four of us head upstairs. "Your after-party ensemble is MIA."

"What?" Logan asks.

"Missing in action, Einstein. Not here." Kate keeps walking. "I even called my mom to see if we left it, but it's not at my house either. It's so weird."

"It's not weird. It's diabolical," Logan says.

"*Diabolical?* I'm impressed. Logan used a big word!"

"Is yours here?" I ask, not even trying to hide the accusing tone in my voice.

"I had nothing to do with this. You know, the two of you should be grateful this happened. You're guaranteed to be the top story on every internet gossip site and entertainment show tomorrow. Besides, Elle looks way better in it. That's all that matters. Samantha will be the one who'll be criticized for not pulling it off the way Elle did."

I look down the hallway behind us and see Samantha walking in the crowd. I don't really care about the mix-up—it's only a dress—but she's had a bad couple of weeks. Not only has she had to deal with her breakup with Sam, she's had to do it while being relentlessly hounded by the paparazzi. The last thing she needs is to have any more pictures taken of her and me in the same dress.

Cam finally speaks. "It's okay with the shawl now, right?"

"Don't call it a *shawl*, please. It's a *wrap*. Shawls are for grandmas," Kate says.

"Great," Logan says sarcastically. "My date looks like a grandma."

Is this the same guy who just professed my beauty on national television?

"Thanks for reassuring Logan, Cam." Kate rolls her eyes. "Listen. Just deal with it. We have some publicity to take care of tonight."

"She's not dancing with me in that grandma shawl." Logan turns to me. "Just go home and change like I told you before, Elle. The network party sucks anyway. The real parties aren't until later. I'm calling Chris again. He's been hanging around the vicinity." Logan takes his phone out and dials Chris.

"She's not leaving," Kate says, reaching for Logan's phone. He holds it away from her and grabs her wrist with his other hand.

"Hey," Cam says. He pulls Logan's grip off of Kate's wrist and stands between them. "Don't touch her like that."

"Chris. Have the driver park down the block at our regular getaway," Logan yells into his phone, ignoring both Cam and Kate.

"No!" Kate shouts, but even if Chris hears her, it doesn't matter.

"I'm leaving," I say. I glance back at Samantha again. I'm doing this for her, no matter what anyone says.

Logan slips his phone into the pocket of his tux. "Go out that door over there." He points to an emergency exit. "Don't worry, the alarms are off. Then go right to the end of the block. Chris is waiting."

"She's not going anywhere," Kate says.

I don't care what she says anymore. I'm leaving. I move toward the door.

"Elle, wait. Remember what we talked about—about keeping up appearances. I'd hate to see you lose your job."

My hand rests on the door lever. I'm about to throw it all away. Why does Kate care if I lose my job?

"The alarm will go off," Kate adds. "Then you'll really draw attention to yourself. Go ahead."

What if she's right? I turn around. "Logan said it's not on."

"What if he's wrong?" Her voice is testing me. Pushing

and daring me yet still claiming she wants me to stay. Why—
to humiliate me further?

Cam comes over to where I'm standing. "Do you want to
leave, Elle?" He pushes the door open, obviously not caring
whether the alarm goes off or not. It doesn't make a sound. He
holds the door wide open, waiting for me to make my choice.

I stand frozen at the threshold looking at Kate. Her eyes
lock on mine, steely and demanding. I glance at Logan for
help, but he's already turned and walked away, like he's done
with all of it. Done with me. Then I look into Cam's eyes,
and there I see a reflection of my old self.

"Thanks," I say, and walk out the door.

I don't look back. I go to the right like Logan instructed
and walk about a block, chastising myself for feeling betrayed
by my not-real friends. Maybe Aunt Jess has a point. Maybe
it would be different with unfamous friends, if I had any. I
can't see myself fitting in, not here or there, no matter how
hard I try.

Chris is standing outside of a black sedan, and he opens
the back door for me. I slide in and fight the urge to bawl
my eyes out as Chris climbs in next to me and tells the driver
where to take us.

"I heard what happened, but you shouldn't have left."
Chris pulls the door closed. "It'll only make it worse."

"Logan didn't want to be seen with me."

"Logan's an idiot."

"I didn't know what to do. And now Kate will see to it that
I lose my part on the show."

"She's bluffing. Believe me, she needs you more than you
need her."

"I can't do this anymore. I'm so tired of following Kate's orders."

"Then don't."

"I have to. It's either that or a life of misery in Salinas."

"Would living in Salinas really be that bad?"

"It's not Salinas that bothers me. It's living with my dad's family. It sounds heartless, but I know, stronger than I know anything else, that it's a bad idea." My chest feels tight. It's not only where I'd be going, it's what I'd be losing. My job. My life. My *animals*. And worse—my dad, *as is*.

"Why does it have to be either or? Write your own script, Elle. It's your life. Don't let anyone else write it for you." Chris lays his head back against the seat and closes his eyes.

Write your own script...

I take a deep breath. He's right. Why does it have to be one or the other? I can't let Aunt Jess, or Grandpa, or Kate, or even Dad map out my life for me. For the first time in a long time, I feel hopeful. Aunt Jess wants us to eat her "crap sandwich," but maybe we won't have to.

WHEN WE GET to my house, I wake Chris up. "Thanks for everything." I kiss him on the cheek.

"Did I fall asleep?" Chris pushes his hair out of his eyes and sits up. "I'll wait here for you while you change for the after-party."

"I'm not going to the after-party. Good night!" I try to shut the door, but Chris stops me.

"Whoa. You have to. I promised the studio you'd have plenty of photo ops tonight."

"Sorry! I don't have to take orders anymore. I'm writing my own script!" I shut the door and jog to the entryway of my house. I turn and wave at Chris before going in.

I go straight to Dad's room, change out of my dress into one of his T-shirts, and pull the large cardboard box out from under his bed. I throw the top off and riffle through the papers until I find what I'm looking for, my favorite TV script that Dad wrote with Mom before she died. He and I used to work on episodes for it until a few years ago. After several rejections, Dad tried a few new ideas for shows before finally giving up on it.

I prop up the pillows on his bed and sit back, poring over the words. Now that I'm older and have worked on more shows, I might be able to make this salable. I work through the night on it, falling asleep in Dad's bed as the sun comes up.

eighteen

I WAKE UP to Coco licking my face. I never even heard our rooster crow this morning. I look over at the clock—it's almost noon. For a minute I panic, thinking I'm late to the studio, but then I remember we have the day off today to recover from the after-parties. I see the silver Georgi Ivanov dress draped across the chair in Dad's room and cringe. Today is doomsday. I wonder what time Deidra's red-carpet review show is on.

I make Dad's bed and put the cardboard box away, minus the manuscript I was working on. I glance down at it. It's no use. It was rejected by every production company in Hollywood. Why do I think my changes will be enough for it to get a second chance? I need to come up with something new. I take the box back out and shove the manuscript in and then grab the dress and take it to my room. I hang it up in my closet and shut the door so I don't have to look at it.

My cell phone battery is almost dead, so I plug it in and scroll through dozens of notifications. I see there's at least one message from Kate, a message from Dad, a few from Chris. Even Jimmy called this morning—that can't be good. I don't want to deal with all of this now, so I leave my phone on my desk in my room and take the dogs out to the barn with me to check on the animals.

Bill is leaving the barn as I walk toward it. Coco runs to him and sits in front of him, as if waiting for a command. He pats her on the head. "Heel," he says, and she follows him back to me.

"Morning," I say, even though it's close to noon.

"What's with all the paparazzi?"

"What?"

He points toward the road. "Good thing we fenced in the perimeter of the property last year. There's at least ten of them out there. They practically mugged my truck when I pulled in this morning. And it was five o'clock."

A paparazzo climbs to the top of the fence and points a telescopic lens at us. "Let's get in the barn," I say, panicked. I'm still wearing Dad's T-shirt and my pajama bottoms. This is such an invasion of privacy.

"Walk, don't run," Bill says. "Just move like it's nobody's business."

We go into the barn and shut the door. I try to explain the prior evening's events to Bill. I was wearing the same dress as a famous singer last night, but other than that, I see no reason for there to be paparazzi outside my house. Well, except for the picture in *Meteorite* of me being mauled by the one and only Logan Canfield…and for being in public with him last night…as his "official" girlfriend. On second thought, I guess there are plenty of reasons.

"Does your Dad know about it?"

"Not that I know of." *But I'm sure you're going to tell him as soon as you get the chance.* That's all Dad needs right now, to worry about me and Grandpa at the same time. I say a little prayer that Aunt Jess doesn't catch wind of this, but I know that's impossible. Annie texted me a dozen times last night saying she was taping the entire ceremony, from the red-carpet preshows to the news coverage afterward, so she could watch me on TV, over and over.

"I'll tell them to skedaddle," Bill says. "I'll be back to feed the animals this evening, but call me if you need me to come back sooner. You shouldn't be here alone." He looks concerned. "Do you have any friends that could come over and stay with you?"

Friends? Aunt Jess would pipe in with an *I-told-you-so* on that one. But how do you make friends when you don't go to school, don't have any neighbors close by, and get tutored on a movie set with child actors who won't give you the time of day? Kate is about the closest thing I have for a friend, and that isn't saying much. "I'll be fine. I've got the dogs."

"Well, you know how to reach me."

I nod and Bill goes out the door, locking it behind him. I have to grab Coco's collar so she doesn't follow him. "You're my dog," I tell her. "Remember?"

The animals and Dad have always been enough for me, but it's been weeks since I've helped in the barn or even visited the animals. I'm not even sure they'll remember me. I go from pen to pen, petting and talking to each of them.

When I get to Wilbur, I climb in and sit on the fresh straw in the corner of his stall. Guilt washes over me. He needs attention—daily attention—just like a dog. I used to walk him around the property when he was little and sneak him into my room whenever I got the chance. I remember how I used to read with him on my bed, him burrowing underneath my pillows, his tiny pink snout sticking out from under the ruffled pillow sham.

Wilbur lies down next me and puts his head on my knee. I rub his wiry-haired forehead, and suddenly an idea for a new show comes to me. A cop show. A comedy? A drama? Definitely a "dramedy." A police officer in Beverly Hills, but instead of a cop and his dog—it's a cop and his pig! *Beverly Hills Pig*. I can see it all. The play on words. The parody from the title of that old movie, *Beverly Hills Cop*.

Maybe this young guy becomes a police officer, and as a joke, his friends give him a baby potbellied pig as a present. He plans on getting rid of it, but in the few days it takes him to find a home for it, he falls in love with his new pet. He's lonely, and the pig gives him something to care for, someone to come home to. The pig gives him unconditional love.

Episodes flood into my mind—funny scenes where the pig makes all kind of messes in the cop's house. He invites a girl over and tries to hide the pig. He's kissing the girl, and suddenly you can hear pig snorts coming from somewhere. I laugh out loud, feeling giddy. I grab Wilbur's head and kiss the top of it. "You're going to be a big star! We'll have to find a baby pig that looks just like you for the first season, but then it's all you, big guy."

"Come on, dogs, we've got a pitch to prepare." I hop

over Wilbur's fence and skip out of the barn and back to the house. The paps are still out there, but I'm so happy, I actually wave at them before I close the door. This just might solve everything.

I WORK ON the new show proposal all afternoon, ignoring the constant texts I get from Kate. They go from apologetic—well, almost apologetic—to threatening. She keeps telling me to check TMZ and about twenty other gossip sites. She says "we're" blowing up the World Wide Web. She must be thrilled. At around six o'clock, I get one that says, in all caps, "TURN ON THE TV!!!!!! DEIDRA'S ON!!!"

I look down at my proposal for *Beverly Hills Pig*. I think it's perfect. I'll pitch it to Jimmy first thing tomorrow. I might as well watch Deidra so I know what to expect when I hit the lot in the morning. I turn on the TV and scan the guide. I don't even know what network she's on.

I finally find the right channel, and the first thing I see is a split screen with me on one side and Samantha on the other. The words *"Who Rocked It?"* are plastered across the screen. Deidra and her minions take turns giving their opinion. Kate was wrong: Samantha wins every time, hands down. No one on the show even says my name without venom in their voice.

Then they show clips of the evening, catching every awkward face I made, claiming I'm jealous of Kate because of her long-standing past with Logan. Someone took a few seconds of grainy cell phone video of the four-way "dress argument" we had in front of the emergency exit, and it plays on the screen. It doesn't show much, but Deidra's eyes widen and the cameras zoom in on her face. "Sources tell me Elle was so jealous of Kate that she stormed off through an emergency exit while her costars tried to calm her down."

"It's true," one of the minions echoes. "And she blew off her own network's gala after the awards. Talk about biting the hand that feeds you."

I can't believe this garbage. Someone calls me "an ingrate," and another laments that Logan had to go it alone all night after I disappeared. I shouldn't care. But I do. I really, really do. I have to talk myself off the ledge. It's all fake. It doesn't matter. It's all a part of show business. I take in a sharp breath, but tears prick my eyes anyway. No. I will not cry over this.

Another text from Kate pops up: "I told you so, didn't I?" She did, but I was sure it was because she wanted to further humiliate me. She was the one who set me up by giving me the dress to begin with. How was I supposed to trust her after that?

Next Deidra and her posse talk about the rumors surrounding our set. They blame me for breaking up Kate and Logan, and then Deidra says, "Up next, pictures of Logan and Elle kissing at a Hollywood party months ago," and she cuts to a commercial break. I guess *Meteorite News* sold the pictures to everyone now. I knew it was only a matter of time before they ended up on television, and what better timing.

Another text from Kate comes in: "R U WATCHING?!!" I ignore it and hit record on the remote in case I miss any part of the train-wreck-that-is-my-life unfolding on Deidra's show.

As soon as it's back on, the discussion resumes on the timing of when Logan and I supposedly got together as a couple. A "source close to the set" supposedly told Deidra "off the record" that Logan and I started dating before the pilot even began taping. I had never even *met* Logan until the day we went on location. *Source close to the set?* You mean Kate, or one of her flying monkeys? Do they even remotely care if any of this is accurate?

Next, they put up a photo of Cam and Kate on the red carpet. They hoot and whistle and say all kinds of inappropriate things about Cam. He's only seventeen, and Deidra, for one, is old enough to be his mother.

Then they discuss whether or not they think it's true that Kate broke up SAM. "With this hunk as her boyfriend?" Deidra says, referring to Cam. "No way, honey!" The rest of her crew murmurs in agreement.

And I thought the publicist's plan was flimsy and full of holes. Apparently, it worked like a charm. Suddenly, I'm public enemy number one, and Kate is off the hot seat. Now I understand how Kate felt last week, but at least she deserved it. I'm innocent of all charges. I was not angry about the dress mix-up, I'm not a diva, and I did not break up Kate and Logan. Finally, they move on to humiliate someone else whose outfit they hated last night, and I turn off the TV. I stare at the black screen and then down at the proposal for *Beverly Hills Pig* on the coffee table. It means more to me than ever. I'm glad I left last night. All I want is to be behind the scenes, working on scripts and story lines that use animals in movies and on TV, and handling those animals on set. I'm on the wrong side of the camera, and it's too late to rewind my life.

Chris has texted me almost as much as Kate has today, and even Cam sent one text that said, "Are you okay?" I sent them both back a smiley face, but that's all. Logan hasn't texted me once, not even when I didn't come back last night. Jerk.

What's wrong with me? This is what I signed up for. And Logan is not my real boyfriend anyway, so why do I feel so angry with him? My phone rings again. This time it's Dad. I answer, cringing, hoping he's been too busy with Grandpa to watch TV.

"Hi!" I say in my chirpiest voice. "How's Grandpa?"

"Not too good. We almost brought him back to the hospital last night. The nurse is here now." Dad pauses, and I hold my breath. "Rough time last night?" he finally asks.

"Aw, you know. Showbiz stuff."

"That's not what your Aunt Jess said. I haven't had a chance to see any of it, but Annie has recorded about three hours' worth of stuff she says is about you on TV. We're going to sit down and watch it after dinner. Anything you need to prepare me for?"

"It's all fabrication, Dad. You know this town."

"It's different when it's your little girl. Jess has seen enough to be on the warpath. She said it proves her argument that you need to move here and start a normal life, as soon as possible. I'll bet there are paparazzi hiding outside the gate right now, just waiting for you."

I guess Bill didn't call him. He probably didn't want to bother Dad while he's away and there's nothing he can do about it.

"Everything's fine here, Dad. I don't want you to worry." I think about changing the subject and telling him about *Beverly Hills Pig*, but I want it to be a surprise.

"Sorry, honey, but the nurse just finished with Grandpa.

I need to speak with her before she goes. We'll talk later. Love you."

"Love you too." I hang up and go to the front window to see if there are still cars parked out front, but it's too dark to see anything. My phone keeps buzzing with notifications. Two missed calls and five texts in the short time I was speaking to Dad, mostly from unknown numbers. I ignore all of them and turn the TV back on. I know Deidra's isn't the only show covering the Globes, and I might as well know what other people are saying about me.

A pet food commercial comes on, and I get wrapped up in watching a kitten act. Anyone who trains animals knows that the domestic cat may be the hardest animal to wrangle on the planet. The next commercial is selling laundry detergent and stars a dog. We haven't worked on any advertisements for a long time, but using animals seems to be a trend. If *Beverly Hills Pig* bombs, I'll move on to Plan C. If companies aren't calling us, I'll start calling them.

nineteen

I HAVE NO idea what to expect as I walk into the conference room the next morning. The networks protect the images of their biggest stars—like Kate—to keep them happy, but I could easily be sacrificed as collateral damage. I'm nothing but a prop. The room is empty, so I pick a seat and lay my head in my arms on the table. I brought the spec with me, and as soon as this meeting's over, I'll pitch it to Jimmy to see if he'll bring it to the network execs. And then if they buy it, nothing else will matter. Not my image, and not this pilot. For the first time, I actually hope it doesn't get picked up.

As members of the team file in, I feel guilty for wishing the show will fail. Almost everyone pats me on the shoulder or hugs me or fist-bumps me as they come in. Logan, Kate, and Cam all come in at the last minute and sit down. I wave at them in one quick gesture.

The network publicist, Wendy, is jubilant. "Great news. After your segment on *Inside Hollywood*, I nabbed you an interview slot with *Los Angeles Mix*. Kendra Parker is doing a press junket at the Four Seasons, and she has to bail on the last reporter of the day. I happen to know him and smoothed things over by offering the *Mix* an interview with the four of you. Because of what happened at the Golden Globes, he was stoked."

We go over what we're supposed to say during both interviews. They've been warned: *No questions about our personal lives. We are there only to promote our show.* "Good," Logan says, "because I don't like this setup anymore. Elle's bad publicity for me."

What?

"Nonsense," Kate's publicist says. "You haven't had this much coverage in months."

"Don't give me the 'any publicity is good publicity' line. That's bull and you know it. They're making fun of all of us. Except for *Cam*." He says Cam's name like a pouting kindergartner.

The publicist sighs but doesn't answer. She knows she's improved her client's image, but at what cost to the rest of us?

Wendy jumps in. "Last night wasn't good, we can all admit that. But at least we've closed the door on the 'Kate breaking up SAM' fiasco, and that could have been a fatal blow to the show. I know we said rumors of an on-set rivalry between Kate and Elle would help ratings, but that's all it should be. *Rumors.* Keep them guessing. We'll plant and deny. I want the four of you to come across today as the four best friends the world has ever seen."

"What should we do if they ask us a personal question?" Cam asks.

"They won't. They know we're their bread and butter." Wendy smiles. "Exclusive interviews like this are too valuable for them to burn any bridges. Any more questions?"

Logan blurts, "Can we drop the Logan/Elle romance thing? I need to be single again." He looks at me. "No offense."

No offense? Is this the same guy who followed me around like a puppy last week calling me *babe*? Even if none of it was true, I feel truly rejected. I swallow hard.

Wendy practically throws her hands up in the air. "Stick with the program."

The meeting adjourns, and I wait until everybody's left the room except for Jimmy and his personal assistant. Jimmy excuses her and then looks at me. "Everything okay, Elle? How's your dad holding up?"

The sad truth: I don't really know. My life has spiraled so far out of the ordinary that I haven't even paid attention. "He's fine." A good guess. "In fact, I have a spec here he's been working on. He wants your opinion before he pitches it to anyone else." I hold out the paper, watching it shake. Before I opened my mouth, I hadn't planned on lying. But who would look at a spec written by a sixteen-year-old girl who babysits pets for a living? I wish I could pull the lie back in, but it's too late. I hand him *Beverly Hills Pig* and hold my breath.

Jimmy looks it over slowly and bursts out laughing. "Tom wrote this?"

Is he laughing because it's funny, or because it's a joke? "Well...he will write the pilot. We work together." My heartbeat accelerates. "I wrote the spec. But he writes with me. He's just busy right now. I wanted to give him credit too, even though he's not here." I hope I've undone the lie as much as possible.

Jimmy takes a deep breath and looks at the spec again. He doesn't say anything for what seems like forever. Finally, he looks up at me. "I'm not sure if it has legs, Ellie. It'd be cute for a couple of shows, but as a series..."

I've made the novice mistake of not mapping out a couple dozen episodes, at least in my mind. Maybe he's right. After the pig messes up the house a few times and scares away a couple of love interests, what would we do next?

Jimmy sets the papers on the table. "I suppose I could propose it to the studio, if you and your dad could bring more depth to it."

"That's all right. It was a dumb idea."

"No. It's not. It's good." Jimmy pats me on the shoulder and gets up to leave. "Keep it up, Ellie. Maybe not this one, but try again."

I nod my head and will myself not to cry.

Time is running out.

twenty

THE FOUR OF us sit waiting for our interview in the *Inside Hollywood* greenroom. Logan and Kate keep fighting like a couple of preschoolers.

"If you would just stop dating other people's boyfriends, things like this wouldn't happen," Logan snaps.

Kate stands up and gets a glass of water. "I wouldn't have, if you hadn't decided to do that stupid single guy, made-for-TV movie."

"It was a career move. You of all people should understand that."

"Oh, I do. And the best move I ever made was away from *you*."

I smile at Cam and roll my eyes, hoping we can bond over how silly they sound, but he raises his eyebrows at me, like he's saying I'm not any better than they are. If that's what he's thinking, it's not fair. I'm sacrificing my image to keep this show going, not making a "career move."

Logan leans back on the leather sofa and puts his feet up on the glass coffee table. "You better all have a career move ready in your back pocket. Rumor has it we're on the bubble."

"I was practically given a guarantee before I even agreed to do this show. I don't believe you," Kate says.

"Do you have it in writing?"

"I don't need it in writing. They all but begged me."

"You'll be the one begging in a couple of days." Logan narrows his eyes at Kate. "Has anyone made plans for you to go to New York for the Upfronts?"

I ignore them and shuffle through the reading material on the table. *Newsweek*, the *Wall Street Journal*, then *Teen Celebrity News* and *Hollywood Splash*. I put the non-tabloid stuff on top of the others and push the whole pile away. All four of us are in every issue of every tabloid. I can't look at it anymore. If I don't even have friends, how are they finding so many "insiders" to give them the scoop?

A handler from the show opens the door to the greenroom and escorts us out. I'm trying to be the last one out the door, but Cam waits for me to go through before he will. Of course he does. He's a ladies-first kind of guy. Logan followed Kate out the door right away without even looking back at me.

The assistant arranges us on four stools. Logan first, then me, then Cam, and finally Kate. At least the two toddlers are separated by as much distance as possible. There's a stool angled away from us for Sofia Alvarez, the main host for *Inside Hollywood*. She strides in, glowing from the makeup that has been airbrushed all over her. She doesn't even look like a real person.

Sofia gushes over us like we're her best friends. "Elle, you look great!" she chirps at me.

"You too!" I chirp back.

I watch Cam as she moves on to him, grabbing his hand. "Camilo!" she says. "So nice to finally meet you!" He responds with only a polite smile, and I wonder if he'll ever loosen up. Then she hugs Kate like she's her long-lost sister.

"I love your shoes!" Kate squeals.

I look at Sofia's heels. They're at least five inches high, but she floats on them as if they were flats. She reminds me of an Afghan hound, her shiny hair swishing along with her stride.

"Aren't they fabulous?" Sofia says, glancing from me to Kate and back.

Someone from the crew shouts that we're going on the air. I sit up straight and take a deep breath. I get my smile set so that I'm not caught off guard. With all the ups and downs, I'm not sure how to act. I remember our instructions: *behave like the four of you are the best of friends.* It will take a lot of imagination, but I've got plenty of that.

After all the greetings and small talk, Sofia focuses on Kate. It's her show after all. Kate is lively and cheerful, and suddenly I remember why everyone loved her when she was a child actress, before fame swallowed her whole and spit out an entirely new person.

"Now, tell us about the show!" Sofia says to Kate.

Kate gives her the spiel we've all memorized from the studio, highlighting the fun and glamour of *Born in Beverly Hills.*

"There seems to be a lot of overlap with your real life," Sofia says.

"Yes and no. I'm nowhere near as spoiled as my character on the show!" Kate pushes a shiny blonde curl behind her ear and laughs.

We all laugh with her, and I hope my laugh sounds real. My chest feels heavy, and I try to draw in deeper breaths without looking nervous.

"The four of you must have a lot of fun on the set," Sofia says to Logan.

"We have a blast." Logan gives me a playful punch on the arm. Gulp. I know it's a cue for me to chime in. So far, Cam and I have been completely silent, except for the laughing. I open my mouth to speak, but everything goes blank. The moment freezes in time.

"Logan and Elle are our comedians on the set," Cam says for me. "And don't believe anything you hear about this girl—unless it's good." Cam reaches over and touches my arm. "She's all heart. Super sweet. She wouldn't do anything to hurt anyone."

My heart pounds, and I spread my fingers out, pressing them into my jeans so they stop shaking. I look at Sofia. Her face changes, but only for a second. I hope there isn't some unspoken rule that if the interviewees bring up a taboo topic themselves, it becomes fair game, no matter what was agreed upon beforehand.

I regain my composure, but I don't want to say anything fake after Cam broke the rules to defend me. I search my mind for the right response, but before I can get any words out, Logan says, "As you can see, Cam is our ladies' man."

Everyone chuckles again. Sofia says, "That's funny coming from you, Logan." Then she goes back to talking about the show. "Cam, tell us about your character."

"I play the son of the gardener."

"What would you say to people who might find that stereotypical?"

I catch my breath. Our producers will definitely resent Sofia for asking that. But she's right, and I admire her for bringing it up.

Kate immediately interjects, "It's not like that, Sofia. My gardener in real life is Spanish!" She beams at Cam.

I can't take it anymore. I finally find my voice. "From Spain?" I ask Kate.

"No, from Mexico!"

Sofia chuckles and gives me a knowing smile. There's no need to drive the point home, but I do anyway. "Cam's parents came here from Mexico. Spanish people are from Spain."

Kate's eyes squint, and I can see the wheels turning. She looks embarrassed, and my heart sinks. In my attempt to stick up for Cam, I've made things worse. Cam reaches over and holds Kate's hand.

Sofia changes the subject, and I keep my mouth shut while Logan and Cam rib each other a few more times, and then suddenly it's over. We're whisked back into the greenroom to get our stuff. Kate won't even look at me.

When we get to the limo, I wait for everyone else to climb in and then get in last, sitting as far away from Kate as I can. Finally, she looks at me.

"I'm sorry," I mouth to her.

"Why did you embarrass me? On national TV?" she says out loud.

"You're the one who *misspoke*."

"You didn't have to draw attention to it." Kate puts her arm through Cam's.

"It's just..." I try to think of an explanation. "It's wrong to say."

"Hey, it's okay, Elle. I know what you meant, but there's a reason we speak Spanish in Mexico." Cam laughs.

"I'm sorry, Kate," I say again. "I didn't mean to embarrass you." *Like you did to me with the dress.*

"You're really bad at this," Logan says to me. "I mean you can act, but they need to keep you locked up afterward. I thought Chris was coaching you."

"He is." I feel terrible.

"This isn't easy," Cam says.

"It's not hard," Logan says.

I thought I was a nicer person than Kate, but maybe I'm not. I can't seem to do anything right.

twenty-one

THE LIMO DROPS us off at the Four Seasons, and Wendy ushers us through the lobby. Kate grabs her by the arm and says, "I need to tell you what happened with Sofia Alvarez."

I wish I could disappear into the wallpaper.

Wendy looks at her watch. "We'll have to talk later."

A guard standing by the interview suite motions for us to stop. The door swings open, and A-list celeb Kendra Parker storms out of the room with her entourage. I glance at Cam. He looks like a pound puppy who doesn't know where the dog snatchers are taking him.

They herd us to four chairs in front of a black backdrop and pin microphones on us. Someone stands off to the side with a stopwatch. A woman shouts, "Don't let the reporter in yet." Someone else yells, "We're already off schedule by twenty minutes."

Wendy crouches in front of us. "Stick to the topics we discussed. They sent us this dimwit named Richard that I went to school with." She looks at us, one by one. "If some-thing's brought up that's off-limits, steer the conversation back to the pilot."

Cam and I both nod. Logan flashes his million-dollar smile and winks. Kate rolls her eyes and says, "Wendy, I've been through like a thousand press junkets." Like Wendy doesn't know that.

Logan looks around the room. "Do I need my makeup touched up?"

"Remember, this one's print media," Wendy says. "And we're sending pictures, so don't worry."

Cam exhales. "Good. No on-air mistakes."

Logan shakes his head. "This is worse. Trust me. Magazine writers spin things any way they want to—that is if they don't care if they ever interview you again."

"How can it be worse?"

"For example, you walk in all friendly and shake their hand, but they write in their story, 'Logan Canfield strode into the room with a smug look on his face and greeted me with a sneer and a wimpy handshake.'"

I glance at Cam's face, expecting to see fear, but he looks like he's ready to burst out laughing.

"Media present!" Someone shouts as a nervous-looking reporter enters the room. He shakes each of our hands and says, "Richard, *Los Angeles Mix*," before sitting in his chair. He sets a recorder on the table between us.

While Richard asks us the usual questions about the pilot, I search my brain for something nice to say about Kate to smooth things over.

Richard leans in. "Elle, what's it like to work with Kate?"

Of course he's fishing for dirt, but it gives me the perfect opportunity to compliment her. "Kate and I have become great friends. I'm so lucky to learn from such a talented actress."

"It's true. We've grown really close," Kate chimes in. "Elle always supports me. Even when she goes too far—like purposely wearing the same dress as Samantha Rey to the Golden Globes because she'd started those false rumors about me."

I can't believe she said that!

Logan and Cam both stare at me. I shake my head with my mouth open, but nothing comes out.

Logan blurts, "Ha! These two are always joking around!"

"True!" Kate laughs. "Elle was just giving me a hard time in an earlier interview today because she misunderstood what I meant when I said my gardener is Spanish!"

So this is how it's going to be. I can play this game too. "I was merely trying to be sensitive to—"

"Richard, you have to understand, Elle's family owns a lettuce farm. She's understandably embarrassed about how migrant workers are treated there." Kate reaches over and pats my arm.

I feel like slapping her hand off me. I hate the lettuce farm, but at least Grandpa's always prided himself on doing everything legally and paying more than minimum wage. I guess Cam did tell her why I need this pilot to work, and now she's using it against me. I smile at her. "Says the girl who eats lettuce for *every* meal! I've never heard you voice concern before over *who* picked it or under *what* conditions."

"But I *am* concerned. Similar to how you are about dogs.

I mean, I care about the welfare of animals, of course, but I especially care about *people*."

I choke. "That's true." I address Richard. "Kate cares so much for her fans that she's decided to donate her own Chihuahua—that she doesn't want anymore, only because she thinks he's *too* big—to a sick child in the hospital." I turn to Kate. "You can't trust those puppy mills. Is that why you named him Hairy Winston *the Third*? Because you dumped two other dogs before him?"

"Stop the tape!" Kate rips off her microphone and lunges, but Cam grabs her before she reaches me.

"Is this thing off?" Logan waves at the recorder.

Richard grabs his recording device and holds onto it like a bulldog biting down on a chew toy. "This tape is my legal property!"

Logan gets in Richard's face. "But when we say it's over—"

"Don't worry. It's off!" Richard starts pushing buttons. "It's off? *No*." He frantically turns it on and off, rewinds, plays. There are only three sentences on the entire recording. Richard glances at his notebook on the table. "I'll use my notes. I remember everything. I'll describe in detail how you treated me."

Wendy grabs Richard's notes and glances through them. "Chicken scratch. You don't have a single direct quote—"

"I don't need them. I have my memory—and witnesses."

Wendy rolls her eyes at him. "The girls were doing a parody for you…to draw attention to the charities they support. We'll give you an exclusive."

"I'm not an idiot."

Wendy hands him his notes and gestures at the recorder. "I think you might be. Now if you'll excuse us." She smiles at Richard and leads him to the door. "I guess you no longer need those pictures." She hands him her business card. "Call me, and we'll set up a new interview!"

As soon as the door shuts behind Richard and his assistant, Wendy turns and glowers at us. "Now we'll have the Farm Workers Association *and* PETA after us! I'll try my best to take care of Richard. What happened with Sofia Alvarez?"

My heart sinks. I am no better than Kate. Maybe Aunt Jess is right—it's inevitable. You step onstage and even if you don't drink the Kool-Aid, they inject you with it. I look at Cam, and our eyes lock. He's turned out to be a good actor, so good I can't read his eyes. If I had to guess what he thinks of me, it'd fall somewhere between disappointment and disgust.

Because that's exactly how I feel about myself.

When I get home, Dad's truck is in the driveway for the first time in weeks. I run into the house, but he's not there, so I quickly change and go to the barn. He's sitting in the office with Bill. Coco is sleeping at Bill's feet. Her tail moves up and down a few times when she sees me, but she doesn't get up.

Dad gets out of his chair and comes around the desk to hug me. He cups my cheek, his fingers moving back and forth on my heavily powdered face. I should have taken the time to wash my mask off, but I couldn't wait to see him. "I just got back from an interview," I explain, pulling back. "How's Grandpa?"

"You'll see for yourself in a couple of days." Dad sits back down in his chair and puts his elbows on the desk. My heart beats faster. A couple of days? We don't even know for sure if the pilot will get picked up yet. Dad must notice the look on my face. "He's coming here to see a specialist in LA."

I barely remember the last time Grandpa visited, but I know he hasn't been here since Grandma died. "Is he coming alone?"

Dad looks sheepish. "No, the whole lot is coming of course. The kids can't wait to see the animals again, and Jess says she'll help us clean up the place. You know, get rid of stuff in case we move. If we get word the pilot's canceled in time, you can go back with her to register for school."

My breath leaves me, and I struggle to find air. His voice sounds so defeated. I look away so Dad can't see my face.

"A specialist? I thought he was out of the woods," Bill says.

"He is for now, but it never lasts for long. Jess heard about some doctor with cutting-edge treatments for heart failure." Dad leans back in his chair. "Believe me, he's coming against his will."

It seems like everything is against Grandpa's will, and even if he sees a thousand specialists, it won't stop him from being angry. I don't see how uprooting our lives will do any good.

Finally, Bill changes the subject. "We're going to start advanced training with the wolf cub tomorrow," he tells me. "It's going to be tough. We chose Lobo because he seemed to be the most intelligent in the litter, but he's turning out to be the most stubborn."

"I have a few tricks up my sleeve," Dad says. "He can't be any harder to train than a domestic cat."

All three of us laugh, and it reminds me of the pet food commercial I was watching the other day, with the kitten. Dad's eyes light up when he talks about training Lobo, and seeing him back in his element gives me a glimmer of hope. If I could just land a good advertising deal for one of the animals, something ongoing, maybe he'd change his mind about giving up.

twenty-two

THE NEXT DAY, I sleep in, glad for the time off so I can clear my head. There's nothing left to do now but wait for the news about the pilot and try to come up with an advertising campaign for one of our animals. I head to the barn to see if any of our actors will trigger an idea.

Dad and Bill are training Lobo. I watch through the glass observation window, waiting for a break in the session to approach so I don't disrupt the cub's lesson. Lobo is doing great, and Dad looks happier than I've seen him in weeks. This is where he belongs, what he needs to be doing with his life. We need this show to get greenlit. As soon as they give Lobo a break, I go inside the training room. "Can I work with him a little?" I ask.

Dad looks at Bill, then frowns. "I'm sorry, honey. I was showing Bill a technique I used with a bobcat years ago, but we really need to let Lobo bond with Bill. The cable network is making a decision on whether or not to make this show tomorrow. If they do, they're going to move quickly."

"But they'll probably need all three of us. If so many of the scenes will be out in the wilderness, they'll need more animals. A ton of them, probably."

"They're using us for only the wolf." Dad runs his fingers through his hair. The smile I saw only minutes ago has vanished.

"Why?" My voice cracks.

"Because you're right. They need birds and a beaver and a whole slew of other wildlife for this show. And we don't have that big of a selection anymore. They're using another company for everything but Lobo."

I turn around and squeeze my eyelids together. "I'll go exercise Scarlet," I say. She's the only chore I can think of that might still need to be done this late in the morning. The memory of the day a trailer came to pick up our other horses—four of them at once—stabs at me. One of them was Scarlet's foal. I can still see them forcing her up the ramp as she struggled, Scarlet whinnying for her from inside the barn. I almost lose it remembering.

"I already rode her a couple of miles this morning," Bill says quietly. I can tell by his voice that it hurts him to say it. "But you could brush her down some more. I rushed it so we could start training Lobo. I'm sure she could use it."

"Sure!" I say with fake cheer, not turning back to face them. I leave the training room, gather the horse brushes, and go into Scarlet's stall. Her coat is shiny and perfectly smooth, with no sign of the sweat she was undoubtedly covered in after Bill's ride. But I already knew it would be. Bill would never do a half-baked job cooling her down. I brush her a few times for good measure and comb through her mane and tail, even though there isn't a single knot in either. I put my head down on her neck and fight the urge to cry.

A while later, I take Wilbur for a walk, even though I know he hates it. As soon as we enter a shady spot next to the driveway, he lies down. I give up and sit under the tree, letting him rest. Thankfully, the paparazzi are nowhere to be seen. They seem to have lost interest in stalking me. I guess it's all about Kate and Cam now.

"What are we going to do, Wilbur?" I scratch behind his ears. We should have heard by now if Kate's show is a go. The network heads are going to New York for the Upfronts next week, and usually we'd know the name of every pilot picked up by now. I've been around long enough to know that no news can be bad news...and usually is.

I could check some industry gossip sites that sometimes scoop the story before there's official word from the network, but I'm afraid to see what the fallout is from our appearance on Sofia's show yesterday or what that Richard guy might have written about us. Kate hasn't sent any threatening messages, so I hope her "Spanish" comment was ignored. Chris hasn't called to reprimand me either. The silence from all parties could mean one of two things: all is well—or impending doom.

I don't have to wait long to find out which. As soon as I see Dad walking toward us, I know. A pit forms in my stomach. He sits on the ground next to me.

Before he can open his mouth, I say, "They called. It's been canceled, right?"

Dad looks me straight in the eye. "More or less. Technically, it's been 'canceled with possible future redevelopment.'"

"That's great. We can live off the wolf movie, and then they'll pay us again when they redevelop Kate's pilot," I say halfheartedly, already knowing the chances of that happening are slimmer than the chances of Cam ever talking to me again.

"Ellie, we weren't given any guarantees. They didn't mention anything about contracting you as an actress to play a part in it, or even Coco. Some Richard guy is spreading rumors that we mistreat our animals on the set. But the biggest reason they're holding off is some backlash over Cam's part. They're receiving a lot of bad press."

My heart feels like it has stopped beating, if that were possible. "What do you mean?" *What have I done?*

"Sofia Alvarez is making a meal out of it, claiming Cam is being stereotyped because he's playing a gardener, and it's catching on." Technically, he's playing the son of a gardener, but I know that's a moot point. Dad reaches over and squeezes my forearm. "I'm sorry, Ellie, but maybe it's for the best. We can help Grandpa figure out what to do with the farm. I think he should sell it, but it's not something I can convince him to do overnight. And you can experience going to a real school, having a bigger family..."

I told Dad that day in the hospital chapel that I'd move to Salinas, but in this moment, I want to take it all back. I nod my head, even though all I want to do is run away.

"I talked to Aunt Jess. She thinks you should start school next Monday, so you don't get any further behind. She said they can spend the weekend, and she'll help you pack. Then you can go back with them and not miss any more school."

I feel like I can't breathe. A huge lump forms in my throat. "What about you?"

"I'll wrap things up with Bill, make sure everything's going well with the wolf cub. I'll come soon."

It doesn't seem like he's in any hurry. So not only do I have to move to the lettuce farm with the Dysfunctionals and go to a real school, I have to start without Dad. I open my mouth to say I can't do it, but I can't get any words out.

"I'm going into the studio this afternoon to pick up some stuff now that we've been canceled. Come with me?" Dad gives me a weak smile.

"Sure." As much as it will break my heart, I don't know when, or if, I'll ever get back on the lot, and I need to say goodbye. Not to any person in particular, but to my life.

WE'RE ALMOST TO the studio when I get a text from Logan that merely says, "The deed is done," with a link to a press statement. He sure didn't waste any time "breaking up" with me. I click on it and read his sappy, regret-laden diatribe. At least he changed his mind about making it all my fault and added that we're still "the best of friends." Yippee yay. I don't say a word about it to Dad. What we are about to do is hard enough.

We pull up to the VIP entrance, and the guard waves us in without even asking for our passes. Is this the last time I'll go through these gates? Dad parks in our regular spot, and I get out of the truck. I walk around to his side, shielding my eyes from the sun with my hand. "I'll meet you back here when you're ready to go."

"Where're you headed?" Dad puts his arm around me, and we walk toward the offices.

"Around."

I stop and watch Dad enter one of the buildings before I hunt down a golf cart. It's the only way I'll see every place I want to visit before we leave. I go slowly toward Main Street, passing the commissary where I've eaten meals for as long as I can remember. I pass the picnic tables where I ate with Cam and Logan, and where I used to sit and have ice cream with Dad when I was little.

A tram full of guests on a VIP studio tour passes me, and most of the people on it stare at me, trying to figure out if I'm somebody worth taking a picture of. But no one seems to recognize me without makeup, with my hair pulled back in a ponytail, and wearing shorts and a T-shirt. A small girl with pigtails waves at me, and I wave back.

I avoid Carson Street, where a big production is being filmed. The area is filled with extras milling around, cranes, a helicopter circling. I see smoke in the distance and marvel at the craziness around me. A world where things explode and nobody is alarmed. Where a room can be filled with water and made to look like an ocean. Where people act like they're in love when really they can't stand the sight of each other the minute someone yells cut.

I pass every soundstage I've ever worked in and then go to the farthest part of the back lot, where junk goes to rust until someone needs it. A tractor, pieces of airplanes, a few smashed-up cars. I silently say goodbye to all of it.

Finally, I make my way to my beloved street. I park the golf cart in front of my make-believe house and walk up the front stoop. I touch the sunshiny-yellow clapboard, run my hand across the white trim of the doorway. Whenever I felt down as a kid, I'd sit on these steps and pretend it was my home, even though it's empty inside. I'd imagine my mom was in the kitchen baking something—cookies, cupcakes, a casserole. Waiting for me.

I put my head against the door and lean my shoulder on it, closing my eyes, wishing that all I had to do was knock and my mom would answer, take me in her arms, and make everything all right. I squeeze my eyelids shut and purse my lips, but a sob comes out all the same. Somehow, leaving my life here feels like I'm leaving her.

Finally, I cry like a baby, like someone who has just lost her mom in this very moment, instead of somewhere in a past she can't remember.

twenty-three

THE SUN BEGINS to set as I take the golf cart back to Jimmy's office to look for Dad. Even walking through the building makes my breath come in starts and stops. I pass the giant, bigger-than-life-size poster of Kate, Logan, Cam, Coco, and me on the wall in the hallway outside of the conference room. I'm surprised no one has taken it down. Will I ever see Cam again? I swallow hard.

I find Dad and Jimmy sitting in the matching leather chairs in the lounge area of his office, laughing about old times. I smile, hoping neither one of them can tell that I've been crying. I hope Jimmy doesn't blame me for what happened. I may have made things worse, but it was obvious Sofia Alvarez had an agenda before I made the Spain comment. Nonetheless, guilt floods me when I see him. My stomach tightens, and I look down.

"Hi." I stick my hands in my pockets.

Jimmy motions to the sofa in front of them. "Have a seat, Ellie."

I sit down, averting my eyes. There's an open laptop on the coffee table, but the screen is black.

"You should see this. It's pretty funny." Jimmy refreshes the laptop, and I see that it's been paused on a video of Kate. He hits play. It's a spoof someone made out of our *Inside Hollywood* interview. The majority of it is Kate in a replay loop, with a fake sombrero cartoon drawn on her head, saying over and over, "No, from Mexico! No, from Mexico!" She probably wants to kill me.

My throat tightens, and my ears start to burn, but the two of them burst out laughing. Jimmy hits play again. "No, from Mexico! No, from Mexico!" The entire thing is so ridiculous. I laugh too, then cry, and then laugh harder. "I'm sorry," I say, finally getting control of myself. "I ruined everything."

Jimmy shuts the laptop and sits back. "This is bigger than a silly comment you evoked from Kate. Numerous factors went into the network's decision. But it isn't over by any means. Kate and Cam have great chemistry, and the suits all recognize his star potential."

Dad nods in agreement. "Have you talked to Cam about his role? He might agree with Sofia Alvarez."

"We'll find out. He's going on her talk show tomorrow— with Kate." Jimmy leans forward. "The publicists from both the network and the studio gave him talking points, but you know Cam. The kid's great, but he doesn't take direction when it comes to his personal life."

"Nor should he," Dad says.

Nor should you, Dad. Why does he let Grandpa and Aunt Jess decide his life for him? Decide *my* life for me?

"Should be interesting." Jimmy gets up from the couch,

a signal that we should be going. I stand up too, and so does Dad.

"Don't look so blue, Ellie. It was fun while it lasted, wasn't it?" Jimmy puts his arm around me.

"I feel like I blew it for everyone—especially Cam."

"Don't worry about him. I saw him over at Epic yesterday on a callback. He auditioned for a minor part in a movie, and they gave it to him, on the spot, right after his second audition. He'll be filming in Canada in two weeks."

It's been a hard day, but that news makes me happy. I'm nervous about how this town might change him, but I'm glad if he's getting to do what he wants to do. "That's great!" I say, and I mean it. I hope Kate finds something right away too.

Jimmy walks us to the door. "Keep working on your writing. I see real talent there." He pats Dad on the back. "By the way, sorry I couldn't do anything with *Beverly Hills Pig*, Tom. But the idea was great. Keep them coming."

"*Beverly Hills Pig*?" Dad scrunches up his forehead. "Never heard of it."

I gulp. Jimmy looks at me, and Dad raises his eyebrows.

"I wanted to surprise you. I was going through some of the old shows you and Mom dreamed up, and then the next day a new show occurred to me."

When I mention Mom, Dad's pupils get bigger, like they always do, and he gets that look on his face that I've worked my entire life to prevent as much as possible.

Jimmy winks at me and doesn't tell Dad that I'd tried to pass the spec off as his work. Maybe Jimmy knew all along.

"I can't wait to hear all about it." Dad puts his arm around my shoulders. "We better get going."

They shake hands one more time, making it seem so final. I wave and walk toward the door so Jimmy doesn't turn this into a major goodbye scene, like a bad ending in a B movie.

When we drive off the lot, I wave to the guard on duty and take a deep breath. As hard as I try not to, I look into the side mirror and watch my life as I know it grow smaller and smaller.

twenty-four

AUNT JESS HELPS Grandpa to the couch in the den while I follow behind with a throw blanket. He leans his cane against the side of the sofa and sits instead of lying down. Not daring to baby him, I set the blanket on the arm of the sofa, pick up the TV remote, and hold it out to him.

Grandpa waves my hand away. "Doesn't do anybody any good to turn that idiot box on as long as the sun is still shining."

"Oh shush, Dad. What else do you have to do?" Aunt Jess takes the remote from me and turns on the weather channel. "There. Be a good farmer and worry about your crops."

"If I didn't trust my foremen, I wouldn't have let you drag me here." Grandpa reaches out and touches his cane, like he's making sure he can get up and leave whenever he wants to. "And I trust my own doctors too. I didn't need that fancy physician to tell me I should start meditating. What a bunch of hooey."

"I was kidding. That's the whole point. There's no reason to worry about your crops or anything else."

"If I don't worry, who the heck will?"

"See what I deal with, Ellie?" Aunt Jess plops down in the recliner next to the sofa and clicks through the guide while the weather channel continues to show on the screen. She goes right by Sofia Alvarez's talk show on the menu, and I feel relieved. I decided this morning that I wasn't going to watch Cam and Kate make googly eyes at each other while Kate tries to make amends with Mexico. But suddenly Aunt Jess goes backward and clicks on the show just as Dad and the kids come in.

Dad looks at the screen. "Don't change the channel. That's Cam."

"There's Kate!" Annie squeals, plopping herself on the floor. I brace myself and sit next to her. This might be like watching a train wreck, but once my eyes land on Cam, I can't look away.

"Alvarez is right, you know," Jess says. "That role was demeaning."

How is everyone so sure when no one outside of the focus group even saw the pilot? I guess I don't know. I mean, maybe it was, and maybe so was my part—and Kate's too. I really don't know what to think anymore.

Aunt Jess keeps talking to me over the interview. "I know you're disappointed, but things happen for a reason. Everything works out for the best."

I wish people would stop saying that. It's such a lie. Was it for the best that my mother died? That my dad is giving up his life's passion to grow lettuce because his sister tells him it's the right thing to do?

"Let me hear this," Dad says to Aunt Jess. She glares at him but turns up the volume on the TV.

"But you're so young, Camilo." Sofia's perfectly made-up face is the only thing on the screen for a few seconds before the camera pans wide. "When a Latina actress who's been in the business a long time, like Fabiana Herrera, is on record saying she regrets playing a maid and would never do it again, isn't there a danger in ignoring her counsel?"

"Actually, I think there's a danger when we ignore the truth. Some people want to portray minority characters only as successful people at the top, to combat stereotyping. I can understand. But maybe that gives the illusion that every-thing's okay. That there is no disparity." Cam leans forward, and the camera zooms in. "The truth is, there are a lot of Latinos doing landscaping. And go into any hotel in any state with a high Latino population, and you'll see that a lot of the cleaning personnel *are* Hispanic."

"So you're saying it's okay to show Latinos predominantly in these types of roles?"

"No, but there are undocumented workers picking straw-berries in the heat until they can't stand up straight anymore. They shouldn't be invisible. In my neighborhood, some-times two families share a one-bedroom home, and another entire family lives in the garage. There are successful Latino doctors, lawyers, politicians, and business people. Latinos that *own* strawberry farms. It's not one or the other. But there is a gap. Isn't it worse to pretend it doesn't exist?"

Sofia leans back and momentarily seems without some-thing to say. The show's producers must sense it too, because suddenly Sofia breaks for a commercial, even though they just came back from one.

Aunt Jess looks pensively toward the screen and then back at me. "Your friend is pretty smart."

"Yes, he is." I take a deep breath. All the anxiety I felt about Cam going on Sofia's show is gone.

After the commercial, Sofia appears much more light-hearted and jokes a little with Kate before introducing another guest. It's Dean Callahan, the teen celeb who will be costarring with Logan in his upcoming made-for-TV movie—the one he ruined my chance of having a real first kiss to get on. I've seen enough. Just watching the way Kate looks at Cam makes me want to leave the room. They clearly can't be pretending anymore.

Apparently, Jess has seen enough too. "I'm going to make dinner. Ellie, how about a cooking lesson?"

What is she going to teach me to make? Crap sandwiches? I look at Dad for help. Normally, we would order a pizza in a situation like this, but I sense that Aunt Jess sees another opportunity to show me what "real life" is like.

"We could order in," Dad says.

"Don't stop me from cooking with my niece. We've got this. Right, Ellie?"

I give her what I am sure is the lamest smile ever seen on a girl's face and follow her into the kitchen. As she goes into our pantry, I imagine a different kind of reality will hit her. There's nothing to make. Zip. Nada.

I hear her rummaging, and then she comes out and grabs a garbage bag from under the kitchen sink. "I can't believe you two live like this." She begins tossing things into the bag. "This pancake mix expired *two years* ago."

It's not like we would have eaten it, but I don't say anything and instead help her check expiration dates. She sets aside a box of pasta and a jar of spaghetti sauce. "Do you have any hamburger meat?"

"I'm not sure." I leave Aunt Jess in the pantry and open the freezer. For people who rarely eat at home, it's packed. I think of all the times Dad and I have gone to the grocery store intent on making a home-cooked meal and then found ourselves caught up in something else. Days later we'd decide we had better freeze the ingredients or throw them away. We have a year's supply of frozen ground beef. I throw a couple of freezer-burned packs away without telling Jess and put the best-looking one on the counter. "We do."

"Any frozen vegetables?"

"Yep. Green beans or broccoli?"

"Beans. Broccoli doesn't go with spaghetti."

Neither do green beans, in my opinion, but what do I know? I set the bag next to the hamburger meat and wait for my next instructions. Aunt Jess shows me how to brown the meat, scraping the cooked parts off the frozen mass as it slowly thaws.

At the same time, we boil the pasta. Aunt Jess takes a piece out of the boiling water with a fork. "Do you know how to tell when it's done?"

"When it's soft?"

She throws it against a kitchen cabinet. As it falls, Coco catches it and eats it, and we both start laughing. "It's not done. If it sticks to something when you throw it, it's ready."

I look at Aunt Jess, surprised that she'd throw spaghetti noodles, and even more so that she's laughing about it. She takes another piece out of the water and hands me the fork.

"It can take only a minute to overcook. Take it off and fling it!"

I whip the noodle as hard as I can, and it sticks to the refrigerator door. We laugh harder.

"Perfect!" Jess takes the pot to the sink and dumps the noodles into the strainer. "*Al dente*, which in Italian means that it's not too soft. You can still sink your teeth into it."

Coco positions herself in front of me and does a sit-stay without me asking her to. Then she gets into her begging position. I pull the pasta string off the fridge and toss is to her. Frozen meat and vegetables, boxed pasta, and sauce from a jar. Not exactly a gourmet Italian dinner, but knowing the pasta is "al dente" somehow makes it seem better. I feel a lightness I haven't felt in a while.

Then I remember why Aunt Jess is here. Not just to get Grandpa checked by a specialist. Not to teach me how to cook. She's here to help me pack up my life—or more like throw it away. My dream has expired like the food in the pantry.

After dinner, Dad and I leave Aunt Jess with Grandpa and take Annie and Brett into town to buy some groceries. We pass by the large Mexican grocery store that's a few blocks away from the store we normally go to. All of the usual Día de los Muertos decorations are out in full force. Intensely colorful flowers and skulls are everywhere. All of my life the Mexican culture has surrounded me, but I never noticed it in the way I do now after getting to know Cam.

"Dad, can we stop at the Mexican grocery store?"

"Sure." Dad makes a U-turn. It's one of the things I love most about him. He's always ready for a detour.

"What do you want to go there for?" Brett complains. "It's only for Mexicans."

"I want to go," Annie blurts. I think if I asked her to clean horse poop from the stalls with me she'd say, "Yay!"

We get out and walk inside. The aisles are packed, and everything seems brighter and more intense, as if even the food has more feeling. I walk up to the section that has all the stuff for Día de los Muertos, the Day of the Dead. I remember when I took the customary lessons that all California kids get on Mexican culture from my tutor at the studio. At first I couldn't understand celebrating with skeletons—celebrating death. But my teacher told me I had it wrong, that they were celebrating their loved ones who had died. The dead weren't forced to the back of people's minds. They were celebrated with joy. They remained real.

I reach out and touch a beautiful, brightly painted plaster skull. It's definitely a woman, with yellow and orange marigolds for hair and bright pink eyelashes. There's a smile painted on, and it occurs to me that skeletons can't look like they're smiling without help because the teeth are the only part of a smile they have left, and those always look the same.

"It's kind of creepy." Annie picks up a small, complete skeleton, a boy who is wearing a sombrero and holding a guitar.

"Maybe it's not. Maybe thinking that death is only darkness and mourning is creepier."

Dad and Brett walk up, and Brett seems to be fascinated with a row of bright, edible coffins with little skeleton treats inside. "Uncle Tom, can I have one?"

"Sure. Annie?"

"No, thanks."

Dad puts his arm around me. "What was it you wanted in here, sweetheart?" He stares at the beautiful display of the dead, and I wonder if he's thinking of Mom too. I consider buying the flowered-hair skull, but I don't need to. It makes me happy just thinking about her.

I look at Dad. "I guess I just wanted to see." I think about what Cam said in his interview—about people who are invisible, even when they're right in front of you.

Maybe my mother has been with me all along.

twenty-five

THE NEXT DAY I begin working on my room. I have to decide what from my old life to bring to the farm. Coco lies on the ground watching me, her head on her paws, and I can't bear to think that she isn't one of the things I can bring. Dad says she can stay with us whenever she's not working, but it's not the same. I get down on the floor next to her and curl my body around hers, resting my cheek on the fuzzy poof of hair on the top of her head. My door is open, and I hear Aunt Jess arguing with Brett and Annie downstairs. Finally, she shoos them outside. The sounds of my future.

I stretch out on my back and look around the only bedroom I've ever had. The room that started out as my nursery. It resembles a time capsule, and it comforts me. I've kept all my books for as long as I can remember, and all my stuffed animals. And they aren't white-and-pink unicorns or purple teddy bears, either. When I was little and wanted to help Dad train dangerous animals, he always placated me with a lifelike imitation, like the black stuffed panther with realistic green eyes that seems to be looking down on me from my bookshelf. He's one of my favorites.

Aunt Jess comes barging into my room with an industrial-sized garbage bag. I'm not sure what she intends to do with it, pack or purge. She looks overwhelmed. "What's the plan here?" she asks.

I scramble up. There is no plan.

Thankfully, Dad appears in the doorway. He's holding the box of scripts, and it looks even more worn and torn on the edges than ever. Something worth so little, yet priceless to him and me. He comes in and sits on my bed, the box open on his lap, the top upside down cupping the bottom. On the top of the pile are all the new ideas that I've added to Mom and Dad's old and forgotten projects, and below that, *Beverly Hills Pig*. I stored it there with the others, a cardboard container bursting with unfulfilled dreams.

Dad takes *Beverly Hills Pig* out of the pile. "Trying to get Wilbur a job?"

"He's an out-of-work actor. We have a barn full of them."

"It's cute." Dad sets the script back in the box. "Jess, can I have a moment alone with Ellie?"

She leaves the bag on the bed. "Sure. I'll go check on Dad. But we need to leave first thing in the morning, and there's a lot to do here."

Dad waits, probably to make sure Aunt Jess has made it all the way down the stairs. He takes a deep breath. "Jimmy just called. The studio wants to reshoot the pilot in a few weeks, not during pilot season next year. They want to cut Kate out completely." He pauses. "And they want you to star in it."

My heart catches. *Me?* It's a first-class ticket out of this mess, but somehow, I don't feel the slightest bit elated. Kate must be so upset. I think back to the comments we overheard outside Jimmy's office, when he called her a monster. In show business, if they don't want you, they don't want you—even Kate knows that—but I still feel guilty knowing I played a part in this.

"I don't get it. The publicity I got after the Globes was terrible. Why me?"

"Jimmy said it was all in the tapes and the results from the focus group. The network sees potential in you. Sure, it will change—it won't be a spin-off of Kate's old show, naturally—but they want to give you a chance." Dad gives me his best attempt at a poker face, but he doesn't seem thrilled.

"And Coco?" I ask.

"Her too. I told him we'd come in on Monday and give him an answer. I've thought about it, and I'm leaving the decision up to you."

"What about Aunt Jess?" I realize that this is mostly about her. Not Grandpa. Not the farm. We sit in silence. The weight of losing everything pushes down on my chest, making it difficult to take in a decent breath. I stare at the box of scripts. Maybe they weren't a waste. Like Dad used to say when we'd work on them, from each one, you'd learn more.

"Remember that script-writing book we used to read that encouraged the use of double binds?" Dad looks at me, and it seems like he has a dozen new wrinkles at the corner of his eyes. Or more likely, I just hadn't noticed them before. "That's what this is, Ellie. We're in a double bind. I don't feel it's right for me to give you the answer. Just remember when you make your decision that sometimes what people want isn't what's best for them. Like Aunt Jess says."

I know where this is going. How the "normal life" I don't want is probably the best thing for me. For all of us.

Dad sighs. "I thought giving you a couple of years of real school and a bigger family while we convince Grandpa to give up the farm would be a good compromise. But you're not a kid anymore. When I left Salinas to follow my dream, I didn't care what my father said. As the eldest, and his only son, I knew it was his dream for me to take over the business. But I left anyway. I'll never forget the freedom I felt living my own life. You're not eighteen yet, but when I read some of the things you've written in this box..." Dad's voice cracks, and his eyes water.

I know with everything in my heart that he's crying over Mom. It's contagious. My eyes fill as I picture her listening to us now. I feel like I know her, too, from reading the things she wrote.

"Don't answer right now." Dad tightens his grip on the box and sighs. "Go for a walk. Really think about it."

I look at the alarm clock on my nightstand. It's already ten o'clock. I'm supposed to be packed and ready to go by tomorrow morning.

I pass Aunt Jess in the kitchen on my way outside with Coco. I need to get away from everyone, sit in the barn alone, and think. This could be the answer to everything. We could stay in Los Angeles. Work in the industry. I could be a star like Kate and never be a "below the line" grub in Hollywood again.

"Where're you going?" Aunt Jess calls out as the door

closes behind me. I stop on the top step, tempted to pretend I didn't hear her, but then decide to go back in. I put Coco in a sit-stay and swing the door open just as Dad comes down from upstairs.

"You can go, Ellie. I'll tell her." Dad nods at me, so I turn and leave.

I hear Aunt Jess say, "Tell me what?" But this time I don't look back. I close the door, jump over the last step, and break for the barn.

The kids are playing in the yard and instantly follow me. "Where are you going?" Annie asks.

"I'm just going to check on the animals." I know there's no way they'll let me go in alone. "You can come, but just look, don't touch."

"We know." Brett kicks a chunk of dirt at the side of the barn. "We already helped Uncle Tom feed them."

After I open the door, Annie grabs my arm and looks up at me. Her eyes are probing and concerned, almost sad. "Can we do a show with the animals? For Grandpa? We need to cheer him up."

Poor child. She doesn't realize yet that there is no cheering up Grandpa. It's not possible. Never has been. How old was I when *I* finally gave up?

"Yay!" Brett squeals and dances around. "Let's make a show!"

Annie's eyes are so hopeful, I can't say no. "I have a lot of work to do, but I suppose we could. A very short one."

They both jump up and down, and Brett does his signature jig, which is to flail around like a crazy person. I laugh. Usually it's annoying, but at least he has enthusiasm.

"What animals should we use?" Annie asks.

"The snake!" Brett flails around again.

Annie and I both say no at the same time. I unlock the barn, and we go in. I'm going to make this easy. Wilbur, Scarlet, and Coco only.

"Brett, I'm going to teach you how to handle a pig. Annie, you'll handle Coco." I get Wilbur's leash and walk toward his pen.

"Only two animals?" Brett grabs the leash out of my hand.

I take the leash back. "And the horse, Scarlet. That's more than enough." I put my hand on his shoulder. "Listen to me. Wilbur weighs twice as much as you do. You need to follow my instructions exactly. Do you understand?" Brett nods, and I hand him back the leash.

"Coco doesn't need a leash, but let's dress her up a bit, shall we?" I smile at Annie and open the door to our costume closet. "Pick something you like." I pull out a box of dog outfits and open it. "Brett, some of these will fit Wilbur too. Come take a look."

We end up dressing Wilbur like a bandit, with a black mask around his eyes. Annie dresses Coco in a purple tutu with a matching bow on her head. I grab a horse bonnet for Scarlet and a wreath of fake roses to go around her neck.

"What about us?" Brett picks up a superhero cape and wraps it around his shoulders. It was something we used on a cow once, so it's way too big for Brett. I tie it for him so it doesn't fall off.

Annie puts on a giant pair of white sunglasses and wraps a pink feather boa around her shoulders. "Do I remind you of Kate?"

"Well, she doesn't usually wear feather boas, but yeah, you do."

Annie beams like she's just received the biggest compliment of her life. I don't think Aunt Jess would approve of Annie impersonating Kate, so I'm glad when Annie takes the sunglasses off and digs deeper in the box. She decides to stick with the boa and adds a tiara. "I'm going to be a princess." She looks at me. "What about you?"

"I'll be the narrator."

"What's that?" Brett spins around, making his cape fly out behind him.

"I'll tell the story to the audience, so you won't have to remember too many lines." I tell the kids to sit on the ground near Wilbur's pen while I go into the barn office to get some paper and a pencil. Now for the hard part—to think of a skit using a bandit pig, a ballerina poodle, a granny horse, a miniature superboy, and a princess. I sit down with Annie and Brett and teach them how to brainstorm, like this is our own little writers' room in our own little studio.

I explain to them what tricks the animals already know how to do, and we try to come up with a story that works. When we finish planning our little show, I'm actually excited. It's not Shakespeare, but it's not bad.

We bring the animals to the outdoor corral to practice. I can't believe Aunt Jess hasn't hunted me down by now and demanded an answer. I glance toward the house, feeling uneasy. She's watching us from the living room window. Quickly, I look away and focus on making the best show possible, but not really for Grandpa. If anyone needs cheering up, it's her.

"Okay, Annie, you go get the grown-ups. Brett, come with me to the garage to get some folding chairs for our audience."

Brett groans but follows me to the garage. I hand him one chair and take the other two.

"Thanks for doing the show, Ellie!" He can barely walk and carry the chair at the same time. It's a miracle. He's helping, and he said thank you. I feel like the Grinch—like my so-called nonexistent heart has grown a size or two.

Dad meets us halfway back to the corral and helps Brett with the chair. We set the seats just inside the fence where we have Wilbur tied up. Annie runs to help us, followed by Aunt Jess, who comes in tentatively, then shrieks and scurries outside the fence when Wilbur roots her in the thigh with his nose.

We all laugh, except for Aunt Jess. She presses her lips together. "Grandpa's not coming. I'm sorry, kids."

"Why?" Brett jumps up and down in tantrum mode.

I can see Aunt Jess thinking before she answers, and I can guess why. She's obviously trying to think up a legitimate excuse, other than the fact that he's just plain mean. She frowns. "You know he's not feeling well."

That's such an excuse.

"But this is to make him feel better!" Annie's eyes fill with tears.

I hear Dad say he'll talk to him, but I'm already in motion. Before I can stop myself, I'm marching toward the house.

twenty-six

I STEP INSIDE the front door and pause. Do I really think I can convince the most stubborn old goat in the universe? The man who thinks that what he wants is the law, no matter what? The only person in the history of mankind who is never, ever wrong? If he really was a stubborn old goat—a real goat—what would I do? With animals, I use only positive training. I guess it's the least I can do for a person too.

From where I'm standing, I see him lying on the couch in the family room with his eyes closed. I almost lose my nerve, but I finally go stand near the couch, hoping he'll open his eyes without me saying anything. He doesn't.

"Grandpa?"

He doesn't move, even though I know he must've heard me. I say it louder. "Grandpa?"

He opens one eye and glares at me. "Can't you see I'm taking a nap?"

"I'm sorry. But could you please come outside and watch a show the kids are putting on for you? It would mean a lot to them."

He sits up slowly, looking pale. I guess I wasn't thinking about his physical condition.

"Are you feeling well enough to come out? It will only take a few minutes."

"My heart is slowly failing, Ellie. How do you think I'm feeling?"

I feel like telling him it failed a long time ago, but instead I sit on the sofa next to him and force myself to touch his hand. I remember Grandma telling Dad once, when he was upset with Grandpa, that he shouldn't expect little doves to hatch from a hawk's eggs. Later, when I asked her what she meant, she told me that everyone is different, that we get in trouble when we assume another person will think or act the same way we do—or worse, expect them to. In his own way, Grandpa's probably doing the best he can. And I guess the same could be said about Kate. She's annoying, no doubt, but considering her upbringing…or lack thereof…

Grandpa wraps his fingers around mine and squeezes. His hands resemble the skeleton ones in the Mexican grocery store, only with thin, brown-spotted skin covering them. Again, I feel my heart stir, and I squeeze his hand back. I muster up all the good feelings I can for him.

"I'm sorry, Grandpa. Maybe later, if you're feeling better and want a little fresh air."

"Come on," Grandpa mutters. "Help me up, and let's get this over with."

He leans on me and gets to his feet. I hand him his cane, and we walk arm in arm through the house, out the back door, and across the driveway to the corral. I don't let go all the way to his chair, and neither does he.

Both kids jump up and down and clap when they see us coming. Dad looks at me and smiles. I glance at Aunt Jess, but her expression is the same—tired and scrunched.

When everyone is situated, I signal Coco to take her mark and then give the kids a thumbs-up.

"Once upon a time," I shout, "there was a young princess who was very lonely." Everyone claps as Annie strolls onto the field. "One day, when she was walking in the forest, she came upon a dog who appeared to be lost." Coco puts her head on her front paws and whimpers.

"No matter what the princess said to the dog, the poor creature continued to cry." I ask Coco to howl, and she lets out a deep wail. We all laugh, and Coco hams it up, yowling louder.

"So the princess took off her royal sash and wrapped it around the shivering animal."

Annie takes off the pink feather boa and winds it around Coco's neck. I direct Coco to stand on her hind legs and turn in circles.

"As if it were magic, the dog began to dance, and so did the princess!"

Annie twirls around in time with Coco. Our audience cheers.

"They danced and they laughed, all the way back to the castle. And so it was that the princess and her new companion were filled with joy, until one day when they returned to the forest for a picnic." I wave Annie and Coco over and hand Annie a blanket. They go back to our make-believe center stage, and Annie spreads it on the ground.

"A mean and cruel pig bandit came into the forest and

stole the royal sash!" I nod to Brett, who has been patiently holding on to Wilbur with all his strength. As Brett leads Wilbur onto the field, I follow a few feet behind. When Wilbur gets close enough to Coco, I direct him to bite onto the sash. Then Brett runs back to the fence with Wilbur, who's trailing the sash from his mouth. Brett ties him up and unhooks Scarlet.

Aunt Jess looks panicked when she sees Brett holding on to a horse, but Dad reassures her. I continue. "The pig disappeared into the woods, and immediately, neither dog nor girl could dance. They were both very sad. So they stayed in the forest waiting, wishing the pig would return with the magic sash. Darkness fell, but the princess did not leave the forest. As the night grew cold, the dog began to howl, and the princess felt fear enter her heart."

Annie and Coco huddle together on the blanket, and I instruct Coco to cry once again. She whimpers and howls, and Annie pretends to weep.

"Then they heard a twig snap! Someone was coming! Was it the pig bandit, coming back to steal the princess's crown?" I nod to Brett, and he leads Scarlet in. I instruct her to paw at the ground, and when she does, I hear Aunt Jess gasp and then laugh. I say, "A hero in a cape approached the pair with his mighty steed."

"Why are you crying?" Brett bellows in the deepest voice he can muster. There's a long pause. Annie must have forgotten her lines. I'm about to cue her, but Brett whispers them to her.

Annie shushes him and says, "A wild boar has stolen my magic sash and, with it, our joy!"

"I will hunt him down and find it!" Brett exits with Scarlet in my direction, and I give him a small piece of the pink feather boa that I'd cut off earlier. He leads Scarlet back to Annie.

"When morning came, the hero returned and handed the princess a tattered rag." I keep Coco in a down, stay position, with her paws covering her eyes.

I nod at Brett, and he says, "Here is your sash, Your Highness." Both Brett and Scarlet bow, and our audience claps and cheers. I glance at Grandpa, a little worried that this might be too much for him, but he looks better than he did when he was in the house resting. Aunt Jess is fixated on the kids and has a huge grin on her face.

Annie takes the piece of feather boa from Brett and cries, "It's ruined! We shall never dance again!"

"But the dog lifted her head and took the tattered sash and danced." I signal Coco, and she grabs the mangled chunk of feathers in her mouth and dances in a circle. "Seeing that it was possible, the princess also began to dance." I pause while Annie twirls around and then whispers, "Leave it," to Coco.

I laugh as Coco tries to let go of the boa, but it sticks to her mouth. Brett pulls it out and drops it on the ground. I signal for Coco to keep doing circles. "And even when the battered sash fell to the ground, the dog and the princess continued to dance. And dance! And dance! The princess looked all around her. She looked at the flowers, the trees, and the sunshine."

Annie floats her arms up and down and looks from side to side, as if she's really in an enchanted forest, noticing all the beauty that surrounds her. I pause and let her dance longer than we'd planned, until I notice Brett getting impatient.

"And the princess grew wise, and she knew, deep in her heart, that magic was everywhere, and that she had always been able to dance."

"The end!" Brett screeches. He hands Scarlet's reins to Annie and runs to get Wilbur. They all bow in the center of the field. Well, all of them except Wilbur. I was never able to teach him that.

"Come on, Ellie!" Annie waves at me to join them.

I stand in front of Wilbur and get his attention. I move my head up and down, and he copies me. Then I clap for the kids and turn toward our audience. It's a standing ovation— even Grandpa is out of his chair, leaning on his cane. I look at Aunt Jess, and she smiles at me. I hope she picked up on the theme of our little play. Maybe her life didn't turn out the way she thought it would—but she could still dance, if she wanted to. Her smile fades as fast as it appeared, and I guess she could be thinking the same thing about me, that even if we move to the lettuce farm, I could still be happy.

After I get everything put away and the animals taken care of, I hang out in the barn alone for a while. It's decision time, and I still don't want to face Aunt Jess. It's either let her down or let Jimmy and the network down. Lose my life to the lettuce farm or lose it to celebrity and all that comes with it. Nothing will be my version of normal either way. I sit in Wilbur's pen and lean against him. Coco curls up next to me, her head on my lap.

The barn door creaks open, and I take a deep breath. I know I can't hide out here forever.

Dad comes around the corner and leans against one of the support beams. "I knew I'd find you here." He smiles at me as if there's nothing wrong. "That was nice—what you did for Grandpa."

"It was nothing," I say, thinking of Cam and the phrase *de nada*. "It was the kids' idea."

"I just wanted to let you know, you don't need to pack your room today. I asked Jess to give you a couple of days. If you decide to move to the farm, I'll drive you up myself next week. You've already missed ten years of school—what's another few days?" Dad laughs.

"Not funny." I search his eyes but see only confusion. I want to make him choose for me. He's the parent after all. He should know what's best.

I scratch Wilbur's head and get up. "Come on, Coco."

Dad waits for me as I close the gate and walk toward him. He puts his arm around my shoulders and squeezes the top of my arm.

I know he would probably rescue me from this decision if I asked him to, but I don't.

BEFORE I GO to sleep, I text Cam. "Hi. It's Ellie," I type, in case he deleted my number.

"Hi." He answers within seconds, so maybe he doesn't hate me.

"I just wanted to tell you—" I write all kinds of apologies, backspace, write more, backspace again. He can probably see that I'm typing and is wondering when I'm going to hit send. "Congratulations on the movie." Add smiley face. Delete smiley face. Send.

"Thanks. Congratulations to you too. You got what you wanted."

Really? I feel like typing, "Why don't you add 'I hope the

end justified the means,' while you're at it?" Instead I write, "I didn't mean for Kate to lose the part."

"You didn't mean a lot of things."

My heart clenches. He doesn't understand, but why should he? He was right from the beginning. I shouldn't have gone along with the publicity stunt. And even when Kate pushed my buttons, I didn't need to strike back. I try again to type an apology, but every explanation I come up with sounds hollow. I write, delete, write, delete, so many times that Cam probably thinks I'm writing him a novel. I stop trying and sit staring at my phone screen. I'm about to give it one more attempt when I see he's typing.

"See you around, Elle."

When cows fly? "Yeah, see you around," I type back. I add a smiley face, and this time I send it.

A smile. With the touch of a screen.

And you don't even have to mean it.

twenty-seven

AUNT JESS AVOIDS my eyes at the breakfast table the next morning, and I can feel the guilt she's telepathing hanging in the air like the Day of the Dead banners at the Mexican grocery store, only not as light and bright. I give an excuse about having to exercise Scarlet before it gets too hot and say goodbye early. Everyone's bags are piled in the entryway, so I maneuver around them and open the door.

"See you in two days!" Annie calls to me happily.

I nod my head and give her half a smile. I can't think with everyone staring at me, waiting, watching my every move.

Outside I walk past Aunt Jess's car. Even looking at it makes me tense up. I just narrowly escaped being trapped in the back seat with Annie and Brett for hours, driving toward my doom. At least if Dad drives me to the lettuce farm, Coco can ride along to comfort me. I head for the barn to saddle up Scarlet, but she's already gone. Bill beat me to it again.

There's no way I'm returning to the house, so I sneak out the back door of the barn and hide in front of the jacaranda tree, sliding my back down the bark until I'm sitting on the ground next to Belle's grave. I close my eyes and talk to Belle in my mind, then to Mom. *How am I going to do this, Mom? No matter which way I go, I'm letting people down, letting myself down.* I keep my eyes closed and stay perfectly still, listening to voices and car doors slamming. A motor running. Aunt Jess's car tires on the gravel road. They're gone, but my problem is not. I still have to decide.

Aunt Jess says I'm like you, Mom. I've always known I wasn't as soft as Dad, and I've tried hard not to be like Grandpa or Kate, who go after what they want, not seeming to care about who or what gets in their way. Even though you're not here, I've always wanted you to be proud of me, as if you were.

I open my eyes and see Bill riding Scarlet in the distance, about halfway up the sunlit hills behind our home. How can Dad even think about leaving? I can see him, hear him telling me the story of how he and Mom got this place. It's one of my favorite stories about Mom, because Dad always smiles with his eyes when he tells it. How they didn't have enough money for a down payment, so she convinced the owner to let them rent to own. How a few years later, when they were ready to buy, the landlord found some legal loophole to raise the price. Dad was ready to move on, but Mom wouldn't give up. They ended up bringing Bill in as a partner to make it work, and Dad was so proud that Mom had found a way.

I watch as Bill slowly maneuvers Scarlet down one of the rocky paths that lead up into the hills from our property. One path shoots straight up the hill and is too steep for Scarlet.

One winds around the bottom of the hill—Dad's favorite. And then there's the curling, twisting path that wanders up the hill eventually. *Three paths.*

I smile. *Thank you, Mom.* I get up and move over next to Belle's grave and put my hand on her headstone. *Don't give up,* I hear inside my head. It's my own voice that speaks to me in the quiet. Don't give up. Why did I believe there were only two options, Hollywood's or Aunt Jess's? There was always my own.

I go back to the house and find Dad doing the breakfast dishes, and then I do the one thing I've never been able to do before—talk to him about Mom. I mean really talk to him about her, not just in passing. We cry our eyes out, and Dad finally sees what we both should have seen all along, that we can't live Grandpa's life for him—or fix Aunt Jess's. That even if there's only the slightest chance we can still make it, we can't give up.

AS DAD AND I pull into the studio lot, I laugh at how only a week ago I dramatically said goodbye to it. I definitely prefer writing drama than actually living it. It's amazing how you can plot to make things turn out the way you want them to, but then life does a rewrite anyway.

Dad parks a gazillion miles away from Jimmy's office in a visitor's spot, and we pass by a large group of extras dressed in extravagant period garb, chatting away. Rachel whizzes by on a golf cart carrying Celeste Vander, who played Kate's mom on the show—an improvement over her real one, if you ask me—and her two pugs. She's dressed like a member of the French royal court in the 1600s. They do a U-turn when they see us.

"Oh, Ellie!" Rachel is breathing heavy, as usual. "I'm so glad you're back. Won and Ton were barking in Ms. Vander's trailer, and it was disturbing Jake Taylor's dog, Fitz, who's in the trailer next to hers. Jake's trying to sleep a bit until his call time, so we had to remove them—even though Jake was super nice about it and said they were fine. He's such a doll. And now we don't know what to do with them! Are you available, like, right now, to take them?"

Won and Ton pull against their leashes to get to me, so I move closer and scratch their heads. They're so sweet. I pick up Ton, and he licks my face.

Dad speaks up right away. "Ellie isn't—"

I put my hand on his arm. I don't need him to answer for me. "I wish I could," I say to Ms. Vander. And I almost mean it. I put Ton back down. "But I'm on my way to a meeting." I'm about to add that I won't be pet sitting anymore, but I'm not sure I won't want to, once in a while. No matter, Rachel steps on the gas and peels away while Ms. Vander shouts, "Thanks anyway, dear!"

Dad and I laugh as we watch Ms. Vander hold on to her pugs for dear life while Rachel jerks the golf cart around. Some things never change.

When we enter Jimmy's office, his secretary sends us to the conference room. He's sitting at the table with the show-runner. I'm relieved there aren't any suits from the studio. No lawyers, no publicists, no one from the network. No Cam. No Kate. No Logan. Even when every seat in this room was filled, I should have been myself. Realizing that now makes my heart heavy.

"Congratulations, Elle!" The showrunner stands and embraces me. I hug her back, hoping she won't be too disappointed by my decision. And then I remind myself it's okay. We are going to disappoint people, and I need to learn to live with that.

I don't want her to spend even a minute of this meeting believing I'll do it, so before Jimmy finishes shaking Dad's hand, I blurt out my answer. "I'm not going to star in *Born in Beverly Hills.*"

"Sit first, Ellie," Jimmy chides me. "Let us down easy."

I pull out a chair and slide in, determined to stand my ground. No matter what carrot they dangle in front of me, I won't cave. "I don't want the role—but thank you for the offer."

Jimmy looks at Dad and then me. "Moving to Salinas?"

"No," I say. "We're animal trainers...and maybe writers." I smile at Dad. "But neither one of us wants to grow lettuce. Not that there's anything wrong with that."

Jimmy moves his thumb across his goatee and shakes his head. He exchanges glances with the showrunner, and they both frown. "Are you sure?"

I nod. I've never been more sure in my life. "Please give Kate another shot at it." I pull a folded square of notebook paper from my pocket. It's a list of ways Kate can counter the bad press she's received by promoting the welfare of animals, such as becoming a spokesperson for local shelters and explaining how the dogs she's worked with, like Coco, were originally rescue dogs that we adopted and trained. Cam seems to have already helped her with the people angle. "You can give this to Wendy. It's some ideas to help Kate's image."

Jimmy passes my publicity notes to the showrunner and winks at me. "Don't feel too sorry for Kate. She landed a gig this week as a guest star on *Times of Our Lives*—as a cheating girlfriend. Whatever life throws at her, she throws it back. She stopped in here a few minutes ago on her way to the greenroom to say hello, even though she's aware we're writing her out of her own spin-off."

The showrunner laughs quietly to herself and looks up from reading my notes. "Not really my forte, but these are a definite improvement over Wendy's 'duplicate-dresses-on-the-red-carpet' idea. You were a good sport to go through with that one."

What? "I didn't—" I almost choke. "Everyone was in on it?"

Jimmy jumps in instantly. "Ellie, I didn't know until after. And by then it was too late. We had to let it play out. If it makes you feel any better, Wendy claims she had to go rogue because she couldn't take the chance someone would give you the heads-up. She said she was especially worried about Kate telling you because she thought Kate had gone soft and wouldn't go through with it."

"I can't believe it." But really, I can. I take a deep breath and get a grip. This changes nothing. I always suspected—knew—it wasn't a coincidence. But I always thought it was Kate—or at least Isa.

"I'm sorry, Ellie, but you know how things are."

I *do* know how things are, but I'm no longer going to just accept it.

Jimmy takes the list back from the showrunner. He skims it and chuckles. "Not bad. Thinking of becoming a publicist too?"

"Nah." I take in another deep breath and look at the show-runner. "But if you ever need an extra helper in the writer's room, even if you just need someone to get coffee..."

"You wrote that spec about the potbellied pig, right? Jimmy told me about it. Hilarious!" She laughs. "If we do try and rework this pilot—again—and Jimmy hires Animal Stars Inc., I suppose you can sit in the writer's room and listen once in a while. But we can't violate any child labor laws by you working two jobs. Be a kid, Elle. You only go around once."

I think of Mom, how she didn't get very far on her round. Maybe that's one of the gifts she left me—the realization that none of us knows how long we have, so we have to do it right. I look up at the *Born in Beverly Hills* poster on the wall in the hallway across from the conference room, clutch Mom's silver heart, and whisper my apologies to everyone in the picture, including myself.

"I guess we're done here." Jimmy stands up, signaling the end of our meeting. "I'll let the network know about your decision, and we'll go from there."

Dad rises, too, and shakes hands with Jimmy and the showrunner. I say a general goodbye to all—for now—and almost skip out of the conference room. I feel light, like I'm flying from the rigging above the stage—free.

As we walk toward the exit, I tell Dad I'll meet him at the car. I have one last stop to make. I head over to the green-room of the soap Kate's guest starring in. I'm not sure what I'm doing here, but it feels like the right thing to do. There's a security guard hanging around the hallway, and he stops me from going in.

"I need to speak with Kate Montgomery," I plead

with him, holding up my temp badge. "Don't worry. We're...uh...we're friends."

"Oh yeah, I know who you are," the guard says after giving me a good stare. "Go on in."

I quietly open the door and peek inside. I have no idea who else might be in the room. There's a guy in green scrubs sitting on a couch reading over a script, but no Kate. I close the door and turn to go. The security guard stops me. "Change your mind?"

"She's not in there."

"Listen, there's no other way out of that room, and I saw her go in myself. She's there." He looks at me like I'm a little off.

I open the door again and go all the way in. The scrubs guy looks up, and I nod at him.

"Do you need me?" he asks.

"Sorry to bother you. I'm looking for Kate Montgomery."

"You dare disturb my pregame?" Kate pops up from where she's slouched in a chaise that faces away from the door, opposite a window that looks out onto the lot.

I stand there feeling uncomfortable. "I didn't see you there."

"That's the point." She gets up. "Come on. They told me a few minutes ago there's another thirty-minute delay. Let's get out of here."

"Are you sure you don't need to prepare?"

"Hello? I was born prepared."

The guy on the couch gives us a look, and Kate makes a face at him, something between a smile and a buzz-off smirk. She grabs my arm and drags me into the hallway.

"Sorry, Doc," I blurt as the door closes, and Kate cracks up.

We stop in the middle of the corridor, and Kate gets all serious again. "Yes?" She puts her hands on her hips.

"My dad's waiting for me. I just wanted to apologize. Jimmy told me Wendy orchestrated the dress fiasco."

"As *Elle* would say, *whatever!*" She looks bored. "Is that it?"

"Yeah, that's it." I turn and start walking.

"Ellie, wait."

I stop and face her without getting any closer.

"I knew about the dress. Not until the day *of*, but Isa let it slip. She was in on it too. I could have warned you." Kate's voice is soft, her eyes apologetic.

I nod and exhale. We stand looking at one another. "I turned down your part."

Kate nods too. "So does this mean you have to move to your grandpa's farm?"

"No. It means we're not giving up." *And not giving in, either.* I smile at her, and I can see she's happy about it. After what seems like forever, I give Kate a little wave instead of saying goodbye.

She waves back, and we go our separate ways.

IT TAKES ME three entire days to call Cam to properly apologize. I can't go through trying to text it again, even though actually choking out what I want to say is going to be harder. I thought I was Grandpa's and Aunt Jess's opposite in every way possible, but it's obvious that admitting I'm wrong isn't one of my strong points, either.

"Eleanor." Cam answers in one ring, and my heart jumps.

"Yes, that's me," I squeak.

"I'm about to hop on a plane. We start filming tomorrow."

"Oh, sorry! I'll call you some other time. Have a great flight!"

"No, I've got a couple of seconds. Is everything okay?"

"Great, um…" Silence.

"Ellie, are you still there?"

"I…I just wanted to tell you, you were right, and I'm sorry. And don't go saying 'de nada' again, because it was something. You were something to me." Everything. "So I just wanted to say that." I hear girls laughing in the background and someone calling Cam's name. He doesn't respond right away, and I hope I don't have to repeat myself. "Cam?"

"Sorry. I've got to hang up. But I heard you, Ellie. And I always hear the real you, even when what you say and what you do don't match. You know what I mean?"

"Yeah." And I do. And those might be the nicest words anyone has ever said to me. "Have a nice flight. And good lu—break a leg!"

We hang up, and I imagine Cam on his flight and hope he never gets tired of flying through the clouds.

twenty-eight

WILBUR ROOTS HIS nose into the dry patch of grass on the side of the driveway. I know summer is officially over, but that doesn't mean much in Southern Cali.

"Not the best climate for a pig, huh, Wilbur?" I think about making him a mud puddle with the hose, but I just gave Coco a bath, and I know she'd get in it too. And probably Brett when they get here. Funny how just when you think you're getting away from something, it follows you. Or rather, *they* follow you.

Another text from Annie: "FIFTEEN MORE MINUTES!!!!" She's learned how to use the GPS on her phone and has been giving me updates for the last three hours.

"Time to go back inside," I tell Wilbur. I leave him in his pen with some fresh water and a treat and then go in the office to give Dad the latest estimated time of arrival.

"They should be here any minute, Dad. Are you ready for this?"

He laughs. "If this doesn't go well, we can blame you. That animal skit you did with the kids for Grandpa was more like a magic show."

"Why? He said he's selling the farm because he's not getting better."

Dad looks at me. "I'm talking about Aunt Jess wanting to move here. I know she still seems unhappy for the most part, but I saw a light in her eyes that I haven't seen for a long time."

I nod. I saw it, too, when she was clapping after the show and when she taught me how to make spaghetti. Annie texts me again. "TWO MINUTES!"

"They're almost here." I stick my phone in my pocket and take a deep breath.

"Well, let's get out there, then," Dad says, closing the notebook he was writing in. He stands up and puts his arm around my shoulders. "I'm proud of you, Ellie. For not letting go of your dreams—or mine."

We walk outside and close the barn door just as Aunt Jess's car pulls into the driveway. Dad goes to the passenger side to help Grandpa, and Annie jumps out of the back seat and runs to put her arms around me. Even though it'll be for only a couple of weeks, I'm actually looking forward to having a little sister to share my room with. I give her a big hug and spin her around.

Aunt Jess gets out and opens the trunk, which is stuffed like a jack-in-the-box.

"The closing's in two weeks, not a year. What do you have in there?" Dad says to Jess. "Did the deal fall through and you're not telling me?"

"Just some things I didn't trust the movers with."

"And you say I'm the worrywart," Grandpa says under his breath. He has no idea, but he's been giving me a lot of material for a sitcom I've been working on. All four of them have. Grandpa bangs his cane against Brett's window. "Wake up, Sleeping Beauty!"

If someone would have told me a month ago that Grandpa, Jess, and the kids were going to move a mile away from us, I might have run away. But I think things will be a lot better this way. I'm sure it's not going to be easy, but it's like most of the bad memories will be left in Salinas. And I'll always have my own place to escape to.

I grab as much as I can that's pink and purple out of the trunk. "Come on, Annie, let's go set up our space."

"Have you heard from Cam?" She holds out her arms for me to load her up.

"Nah, he's busy finishing up a movie in Canada." I give her a few of the lightest things to carry.

"With Kate?"

Aunt Jess gives me a sympathetic look and says to Annie, "Don't be so nosy!"

"It's okay. I don't know if Kate's with him or not."

"You should tell her you're sorry," Annie says, adjusting the pile in her arms.

"Annie." Aunt Jess moves her along toward the house. "Are you going to wear Ellie out our first day here?"

"For your information, missy, I already did." I grab a few more things and follow behind them. But Annie's right. I apologized at the studio for doubting Kate about the dress, but that's not what Annie's referring to. So much more happened, and my apology wasn't enough.

When we get to my room, I put Annie's stuff on my bed, and she throws everything in her arms on top of the pile. Aunt Jess sets more on the floor. "Annie, please don't make a mess out of Ellie's room. This is only temporary. You don't need to unpack everything."

"It's okay. I don't mind."

Aunt Jess digs through one of the boxes and pulls out a gift bag. She hands it to Annie. "Want to give Ellie her present?"

Annie holds it out to me shyly. "Here."

"I saw this at the bookstore, and it reminded me of you," Aunt Jess says, her eyes bright.

I pull the tissue paper out of the bag and find a beautiful leather journal. The cover is a deep midnight blue, with pretty silver stars and a quote on it.

To be a star, you must shine your own light,
follow your own path, and not worry about the darkness,
for that is when the stars shine brightest.
~Author Unknown

"I love it." I hug Annie first and then Aunt Jess. She squeezes me tight, and I know that in her own way, she's given me her blessing.

LATER THAT NIGHT, after everyone's settled in and Annie's fast asleep in my bed next to me, I text Kate. "Forgive me?"

"Old news," she texts back. I text her a smiley face and an xo and then lay my head on my pillow with a strange sense of peace. I'm almost asleep when she texts me again about an hour later, proof that she really has forgiven me. "Are you free Friday night?"

"Um... let me see... I have three party invites, a couple of premiers, and a backstage pass to a SAM concert, but I guess I could squeeze you in," I reply.

"Right. And I'll be missing my Nobel Peace Prize ceremony to pick you up at six. I'll send a driver. Wear the Georgi Ivanov dress, because I have something special planned."

"Really? I'm supposed to trust you again and wear that dress?"

"Need I bring up 'No, from Mexico'? Even if my plan is to embarrass you in front of Sofia Alvarez, I think you owe me."

"You win," I text back. I actually miss her—in a strange sort of way. Kind of like how I don't mind having the whole family here, for a couple of weeks, anyway. I guess going it alone wasn't as great as I thought it was.

"You also owe me because I got a call from Wendy telling me I have to do one of those horrible, sad, rescue dog commercials. For free! Thanks to you."

Leave it to Kate to turn a favor into a cruel deed. "That's terrible."

"It is. See you Friday night at six. Now leave me alone and get some beauty sleep. Some of us need more than others."

Very funny. I put my phone on my nightstand and look over at Annie. Miss Annoying looks downright angelic when she's sleeping. I brush her bangs from her eyes and kiss the top of her comatose head.

A few minutes later I get one more text from Kate.

"That means you. Not me!"

twenty-nine

"KATE'S HERE!" ANNIE shrieks from downstairs.

From my bedroom window, I watch the limo driver park in front of our house and get out. "I'll be out in a minute," I text Kate, and she sends back a thumbs-up. I grab the shawl I wore at the Globes, both as a joke for Kate and as an insurance policy against the chance this really is a revenge plot after all. On second thought, I'd better grab a change of clothes too, just in case. I go back and throw some jeans, a T-shirt, and sneakers into a duffel bag. Finally, I come around the corner to the top of the stairs and laugh at Annie as she comes into view, dancing up and down in the foyer at the sight of me.

"She's coming down!" Annie cries.

"So what?" Brett says, shooting a foam ball at her from a plastic gun. He turns the gun toward me and aims. I've been shot by his foam bullets before, and they don't hurt, but there's a part of me that wants to take the gun away and break it over my knee.

"Don't shoot, buddy. That's my date!"

I freeze. That was Cam's voice. *Why is he here?* I stop on the first stair, immobile, as he comes into view wearing a dark-gray suit and tie. My breath catches. He looks so adorably handsome. He grabs Brett from behind and gently takes the gun away. I take in a deep breath and grip the railing.

Cam sets the toy gun on the table in the entryway, picks up a white rose corsage, and holds it in my direction. "Can we start over?"

"Where's Kate?"

"She's not here. She helped me surprise you." He walks to the bottom of the stairs. "Will you go to my homecoming dance with me tonight?"

Homecoming? Tonight? I nod my head and manage to blurt out a "Yes."

Annie squeals and grabs Brett's hands, dancing him around. He pulls away from her and bounces around the room like a Tasmanian devil.

I go the rest of the way down, taking Cam's outstretched hand on the last step.

"You're beautiful."

"Sorry you've seen this dress before."

"I requested it."

"So I can relive the most embarrassing night of my life?"

"No. Because I remembered how stunning you looked in it." Cam laughs. "And because I didn't know if you had any other formal attire."

I hug him and reach up to kiss his cheek. "Is this for me?" I touch the corsage. He nods and slips it on my wrist.

I'm glad that Grandpa and Aunt Jess are at their new house getting some work done. These child witnesses are bad enough. I look over toward the family room and see Dad leaning against the arched passageway, smiling. I have no idea how long he's been standing there.

"What time will you bring my little girl home?" Dad walks over to Cam and offers his hand.

"Good evening, sir." Cam and Dad do the handshake with a hug routine. "The dance is over at eleven thirty. Is midnight all right?"

I feel like Cinderella in more ways than one.

"That'll do." Dad smiles.

Cam leads me outside to the limo, and the driver helps us in. Annie, Brett, and Dad follow us and stand in the driveway, waving as we pull away. I roll down the window and wave back. "Are we really going to a homecoming dance?" I ask. "At your school?"

"Yep. But it's customary to go out to dinner first."

"You sound like a pro."

"It's my first dance too, but I did some research."

I'm hoping he picked a restaurant where there won't be any paparazzi. All I need is to hit the tabloids again in this dress. The limo winds up Lake Hollywood Drive to Canyon, and then the driver pulls the limo into the parking area at the dog park.

"Pit stop?" I ask.

"Nope. This is it." Cam opens the door of the limo, climbs out, and holds his hand out to me. "I also heard you're supposed to make a big deal out of asking a girl to a dance, but since this was a hijacking"—he helps me out the door—"I wanted to surprise you at dinner."

We walk along the gravel path that leads to the same table where we broke up our "almost relationship." I can't stop laughing when I see Kate there with her personal chef and a small army of assistants, standing guard over our table, which is covered with a white tablecloth and at least a dozen white votive candles. There's a vase of cream-colored roses in the center and rose petals strewn around two perfectly arranged place settings. Tiny white lights twinkle from the tree above us.

"Finally," Kate says. She motions for us to sit down and then barks orders to her crew as they lay cloth napkins on our laps, pour sparkling water into our champagne glasses, and set silver-dome-covered plates in front of us in a matter of seconds. When everything's in place, she says, "You're welcome."

We both start to thank her, but she throws her palm up like a stop sign. "I'm out of here. Charles will clean up. Ciao!" She winks at me before strutting off toward the parking lot with her assistants following behind her.

Charles removes the silver domes from our plates and genuflects. "Miss Montgomery instructed me to tell you that she did not approve of the menu." He bows and then disappears.

I look at the food on my plate. *Carnitas*. We both laugh. "Everything is perfect. Thank you."

"Thank you for giving me a second chance." Cam looks at the horizon, and I follow his eyes up the steep hills to the Hollywood sign. He looks back at me and then reaches over and takes my hand. "I'm sorry for not trying harder to understand."

"No, Cam, you were right." I can't go back and change how things went down, but I'll do whatever it takes to be true to myself in the future. "I'm sorry too."

Cams leans in like he's going to kiss me, but it's obvious the table is too wide to reach me. "I think we need to rearrange our table settings." He stands and picks up his plate, but before he can get to my side of the table, a posse of three dogs runs to our table with their owners yelling behind them. The biggest, a fawn-colored Great Dane, almost grabs a tortilla off my plate. Cam grabs the dog's collar just in time.

"Samson! Sit!" A young guy in a plaid shirt arrives breathless at our table. "I'm so sorry!" He clasps a leash on the dog's collar while a woman grabs the two smaller dogs and puts leads on them. They both apologize profusely. The woman stops in midsentence and cocks her head. "You're Cam Rodriguez..." She looks at me. "And you're Kate's..." She points back and forth between us. "Are you two... ?"

I look and smile at Cam. I'm ready to shout, "Yes! Cam Rodriguez is my boyfriend, and I don't care who knows!" The only thing that stops me is not knowing what we are. This is technically our first real date. I can't be presumptuous.

Cam seems to read my mind. "I'm working on it." He smiles at the couple.

"Can we get a picture with you?" the woman asks.

"Honey, let's go. Don't interrupt their dinner." The guy is holding on to the Great Dane as hard as he can, and drool is dripping from the dog's mouth. The two little ones alternate between whining and barking.

Charles comes out from where he was hiding. "I'm not a bodyguard, but can I be of assistance?" He addresses Cam and me, but then he turns and glares at the couple.

"Thank you, Charles. Would you mind taking a picture of the four of us?" I look down at the dogs and correct myself. "The seven of us." Cam and I get up from the table, and I motion for the woman to stand next to me. She comes over, and I put my arm around her back as the guy hands Charles his cell phone. The littlest dog jumps on my dress, so I reach down and pick her up for the picture. Cam stands next to me, and the man positions himself on the other side of Cam with the giant pooch still tugging his head toward our food.

Charles takes a couple of photos and then sends the couple off. As they walk away, Cam whispers in my ear, "Thanks for not denying me in public," and we both laugh. Our romantic dinner hasn't lived up to its fairy-tale beginning, but it's been perfect.

Cam looks at his watch. "We'd better eat fast. The principal said anyone who arrives more than an hour after the dance starts won't get in."

I feel a strange thrill when he says the word "principal," like I actually have one and I might get in trouble. Who would have thought that would sound like fun?

We eat quickly, thank Charles, and go back to the limo. "One more stop," Cam says. "My house. According to my research, the final customary duty is taking pictures."

When we arrive at Cam's, his family comes outside and acts like the paparazzi, but there's such a big difference between fans who adore the famous you and the people who love the real you. His mom wants pictures of us everywhere and with everyone. In front of the limo, in front of the house, with me holding baby Alma, with Santos in between us. Even one with Paco.

We kiss everybody on the cheek and say our goodbyes two or three times. Cam picks up Paco and hands him to his mom so he won't follow us, and then he kisses her cheek again. "We have to go, Mami, or we'll miss the dance."

He slips his hand in mine and walks me toward the limo. The driver is standing there with the door open waiting for us to get in, but Cam stops halfway there. He takes a deep breath and holds both of my hands in his. "I'm sorry, Ellie, but do you mind if we go in my car? I don't want to show up at my school in a limousine."

I look in his eyes, and they've got that dark, intense stare again.

I smile. "I wouldn't have it any other way."

WE PULL INTO the parking lot of Cam's high school and drive around the building. One entire side has a giant mural depicting traditional Mexican dancers, doctors, and businessmen, firefighters and fieldworkers. There's a drawing of Earth held up by a collection of hands in every shade of skin color from light peach, to olive, to black, and every tint of brown.

My mind whirls a million miles a minute. It's like the reverse of how the visitors must feel when they tour the studio lot and see an entirely made-up universe for the first time. It's not like I haven't *seen* a real high school before, but I've never paid much attention to one—never actually entered one.

We park and walk to a side door that goes straight to the gym. Cam takes two tickets out of his suit pocket, and we check in. I can't help but laugh as I look around. It looks just like I thought it would, like a scene right out of a movie. Streamers drape from the ceiling, and there's even a disco ball hanging in the center of the room, like props from the warehouse on the lot.

My eyes land on the one thing I didn't expect, a giant Día de los Muertos altar against one of the walls, covered in beautiful flowers and colorful skulls. I think of Mom and how happy she must be watching over me right now. Because I'm happy, and when you love someone as much as my mom loved me, all you want is their happiness.

A few guys fist-bump Cam as we make our way to the middle of the dance floor. Some people stare and whisper, but for the most part, we're not treated any differently than anybody else. I cling to Cam's arm, wobbling in my heels after almost bumping into another couple. "Sorry! I'm so clumsy."

We stop under the disco ball, and Cam turns to face me. "You know you have to take that back." He laughs. "You're beautiful...and graceful..." I'm afraid he's going to make me repeat it, but instead, he reaches over and pushes a strand of hair away from my eyes. "*Quieres bailar?*"

I know that *bailar* means dance, but I'm going to use this moment to my advantage and pretend it means something else.

"Yes, you may." I get closer to him and turn my head up toward his.

He breaks into a huge smile and then leans down and kisses me.

My first real kiss...

And it's picture perfect.

thirty

COCO LOOKS ADORABLE sitting between Kate and Logan as they sign paw print–stamped autographs. She lifts her paw to shake every kid's hand that comes by.

It turns out Dad didn't make a mistake by taking a chance on us. We still haven't heard anything from the studio about a remake of *Born in Beverly Hills*, but I did land Coco a pretty lucrative job selling Bellucci Brothers' Pasta.

Today she's helping both Kate and Logan improve their images at an animal adoption fair on Hollywood Boulevard. Fans can come down and adopt a shelter pet and meet some stars—both two-legged and four—at the same time. Cam and I are working directly across from them, helping make matches between people and pets.

It's hotter than a dog in a bun in this parking lot despite the canopies overhead, so I bring a bowl of cool water over and let Coco have as much as she wants. Logan sticks his tongue out and says, "What about me?"

Kate rolls her eyes. "Give it to me when she's done, and I'll dump it over his head."

I shake my head at them and go back to help Cam. A girl about Annie's age, wearing a T-shirt with a picture of Kate on it, is debating with him about which dog she should choose. She's got it narrowed down between a terrier-pug mix we temporarily named Wrinkles and a Pekingese. While I ask the girl's parents questions about the environment they'll be bringing the dog home to, Cam tells her, "I think you're leaning toward Wrinkles."

"I'm just not sure," the girl says, looking around in the other pens. "What about that one?" She points over to where Kate and Logan are signing autographs. I follow her as she walks over, leans down, and picks up Hairy—who Kate had the bad judgment to haul over here in this heat—from his makeshift bed under the table.

Logan swings his hair out of his eyes and nudges Kate. "Your evil planned worked. Somebody wants to adopt Hairy."

Kate gasps. "No!"

I put my hand up and nod at Kate so she'll know I've got this. She has a new reputation to maintain, after all. I hold my arms out toward the girl. "Careful! That dog has a peeing problem. You should probably pass him over to me right now."

acknowledgments

MY FIRST ATTEMPT at these acknowledgments went way too far, so in fitting with the theme of this book, I'm going to pretend this is a TV award's speech with a timer ticking in front of me. And so the countdown begins...

To my agent, Tess Callero: even if I get pulled off the stage with the microphone still in my hand, I need to tell the world how fabulous you are. If I wrote a detailed description of the ideal agent, you would still surpass it. You've amazed me every step of the way with your editorial insights, your professionalism, your kindness, and your superb competence. I can't believe so many skills and qualities exist in one human form. I've thanked my lucky stars for you more times than I can count. Thank you, Tess—a million times over!

I'd also like to thank everyone at Curtis Brown, Ltd., especially Ginger Clark, who saw something in my manuscript and gave it to Tess. Ginger, I will always be grateful!

To everyone at Turner Publishing: you've given me a glimpse into the hard work it takes to transform a manuscript into a novel. Thank you Stephanie Beard, Heather Howell, Madeline Cothren, Lindsey Johnson, Kathleen Timberlake, Kenny Holcomb, President and Publisher, Todd Bottorff, and everyone else behind the scenes. Thank you for believing in this story. I am so glad this book and I found a home at Turner.

I might not have reached this milestone if not for the Society of Children's Book Writers and Illustrators, especially the Florida region. Huge thanks to my friend, author Kerry O'Malley Cerra, who introduced me to this writing community. Kerry, there is so much I need to thank you for. Thank you for generously sharing all your knowledge and talents with me all these years (and your room at conferences—and your shoes!) Above all, thank you for your friendship. I could write pages and pages about you and it would never be enough.

I am also indebted to my friend, author Dorian Cirrone, Co-RA for SCBWI Florida, who took me under her wing and mentored me, expecting nothing in return. Dorian, you give above and beyond in everything you do. Thank you for reading for me more times than I can count, for sharing your expertise, and especially for your friendship. You always root for my success and go out of your way to foster it.

To all my friends in SCBWI, I wish I had the space to name each and every one of you. You know who you are, and you are all stars to me! Linda Bernfeld, your long-time leadership at the helm has provided so many opportunities for learning and advancement in the industry, and along with your ever-present encouragement, have been invaluable to me. Thank you for your years of dedication and support.

Alex Flinn and Aimee Friedman, I hold your work in the highest regard! Thank you both for being willing to read an ARC of this book despite your beyond-busy schedules.

I wish I could make a whole second speech just for my critique partners! Kerry O'Malley Cerra, Michelle Delisle, Jill MacKenzie, Meredith McCardle, Ty Shiver, Nicole Cabrera, how it pains me to give you a group thank-you when you really each deserve your own page. Each of you have contributed to this book and my life in innumerable ways. You have read, and reread, and given support, ideas, and insight. You have been on this journey with me from Day One. We've shared laughter and tears, heartbreaks and breakthroughs. We are a sisterhood that has stood the test of time, and I know we are forever. You all mean the world to me.

To all my non-writing friends and family: your support makes all the difference. Thank you for understanding when I disappear for long periods of time and not holding it against me. I wish I could mention you all by name! Amy Kuebler, thank you for always reading my first drafts and saying nice things about them. Kelly Pulido and Cheryl Bivins, thank you for listening and offering ideas. Thank you to my parents and siblings (especially my sister Cyndie, my essential writing wing-woman) and my entire extended family. Darwin Espinal, my "unofficial" son, you make me laugh and give me lots of material. You stick to the truth even when it's not in your best interest better than anyone I know.

My son, Alex Miranda: you are living proof that good guys exist in real life and not just in YA novels. You inspire me every day by who you are as a person. Thank you for always encouraging me to go for my dreams.

My daughter, Gaby Miranda: you are my muse and the coolest girl I know. You make everything better by just your presence. Thank you for always reading for me and being my biggest fan.

Fernando Miranda, my leading man: thank you for believing in me and supporting me during this production, and in life, no matter how many takes I go through. You are the most patient person I know. Of all the stars in this show, yours shines brightest.